chris

She was Drowning in the Sweet Fire of His Kiss

Their hands touched again, and heat flowed from his flesh into her's. His eyes had never left her, and they seemed to grow larger, and she was drowning in them. A feeling of faintness crept over her, and she leaned against him for support. A groan came from deep in his throat. His hand closed around her's almost painfully, and then she was in his arms. His mouth was hard, and then soft, incredibly soft, and she was drowning in the sweet fire of his kiss.

The
DISINHERITED

Clayton Matthews

BANTAM BOOKS
Toronto • New York • London • Sydney

THE DISINHERITED
A Bantam Book / January 1983

ISBN 0-553-22846-3

Published simultaneously in the United States and Canada

Bantam Books are published by Bantam Books, Inc. Its trademark, consisting of the words "Bantam Books" and the por-
trayal of a rooster, is Registered in U.S. Patent and Trademark
Office and in other countries. Marca Registrada. Bantam
Books, Inc., 666 Fifth Avenue, New York, New York 10103.

PRINTED IN THE UNITED STATES OF AMERICA

H   0 9 8 7 6 5 4 3 2 1

This book is dedicated, with much affection and considerable alliteration, to a lovely and literate lady, my excellent editor, Linda Price.

One

Debra Moraghan stood on the veranda—packed earth for a floor, a thatched roof, a pole for a railing—and waited for her mother to come out of the adobe house behind her. Her father had just returned from his weekly trip into town for the mail pouch. In the pouch was a letter from her grandmother, Nora Moraghan, residing on the family plantation outside of Nacogdoches, in East Texas. Her mother had gone inside to read it.

Hands clenched around the railing until the knuckles shone white, Debra stared unseeingly into the distance.

Not that there was much to see in Brownsville, Texas—flat, arid land, dotted with mesquites, cactuses, and palms. The first time Debra had seen a palm tree she had thought of a shy girl standing on one leg, desperately trying to pull her skirt down to hide her nakedness. It was an image that had caused her to laugh then, and still brought a smile to her lips when she thought of it.

That had been nine years ago. Now, eight months short of her twenty-first birthday, Debra had more than fulfilled the promise of great beauty that Grandmother Nora had glimpsed in her long ago. Even in the long, faded gingham dress, the fullness of her figure was evident in the fine, full thrust of her breasts. She had

1

brown eyes that could blaze with quick anger or sparkle with unexpected humor, and long auburn hair flowing to the sweet curve of hip. Her complexion was the color of bone china. She never browned, but instead burned a fiery red when too long exposed to the sun, and she had an infuriating tendency to freckle after the burn faded.

Debra had been afflicted by twin curses at approximately the same time—the female curse and the propensity to burn under the sun's blaze. She blamed the second on the semitropic sun in Brownsville. Back home—she always thought of East Texas as home, always would—she could play in the sun and not burn. It was only after coming here that her skin became so sensitive. One more black mark against this cursed country.

A warm wind had come up as Debra stood on the veranda, and it picked up fine sand from the ground, which became a brown cloud. The minute particles stung her exposed skin like a thousand insects.

Dear God, was there ever such a dry, godforsaken place! she thought. Water, her father said; water was the answer. With water the thirsty earth would turn rich and fertile. But the only sources of water were the rare rains, the Rio Grande—a brown trickle just out of sight to the south—and artesian wells. Deep, deep down in the bowels of the earth was an inexhaustible reservoir of sweet, sparkling water, but it was too expensive, too laborious a process, to bring to the surface in a quantity large enough to provide life to plants.

Her poor father! He had planted cotton but had yet to raise a decent crop—the rainfall was not sufficient. He had tried growing fruits and vegetables and had raised a profitable crop about one year in four. Their meager existence was due primarily to the sale of dates and figs—trees that could produce fruit with little water.

Poor father indeed! It was his fault that they were here, in this place of heat and drought and hungry bellies. True, he worked, worked harder than it seemed possible, from dawn until dusk, and then often, after a meager supper, he labored long hours by lantern light, endlessly scheming ways to bring water to the thirsty land.

But none of this was necessary, Debra reflected. But for his stupid pride, he could still be in East Texas, directing that prodigious energy and sharp mind—she did not deny his intelligence—toward attaining what was their rightful heritage. Grandmother Nora had offered them the use of her house, the only thing left to her in Sean Moraghan's will. Not only had she offered, she had begged her youngest son to stay.

Kevin Moraghan would have none of it, and here they were!

Debra gave an exasperated sigh, then turned her head and called, "Mother! You must have read that letter through a half-dozen times by now!"

"Coming, dear," her mother said in an unruffled voice.

In a moment Kate came out onto the veranda, the letter folded in her hand. Kate was still a great beauty; age had yet to mark her. The climate had not parched her skin, wrinkling it like a dried date, as it did most Anglo women. Her skin was without a blemish, her figure still firm, her eyes clear and usually laughing, despite the hardships of their life the past nine years.

Maybe, Debra thought with a flash of ribald humor, that's how come she had a third child some years back; she still heats Daddy's blood on occasion!

Kate said mildly, "The letter, Debra Lee, *was* addressed to your father, I do believe."

"Mother! How many times do I have to tell you that it's Debra, not Debra Lee!"

"Heavens above! May the good Lord forgive me that I should ever forget that my daughter reserves the privilege of choosing her own name."

"You know I hate two first names. Half the simpering girls in the South have two names. Betty Sue. Mary Louise. Boys, too, for that matter. It's disgusting."

"Disgusting it may be to you, young lady, but it's your birth name, and as long as you're in my household, it's what you'll answer to. Now, as to this letter"—Kate snapped it against the railing—"you wrote to Nora, didn't you?"

"Of course I did. Is that a crime? She *is* my grandmother."

"Writing to her isn't, no. But you asked her if you'd be welcome to visit."

"What's wrong with that? Every time she writes to us, she inquires as to when we're coming."

"Several things are wrong with that, my darling daughter. It's bad manners to ask. We can't afford the money for the fare. You're too young, and most important of all, you know how your father feels. So long as—"

"So long as Uncle Brian's on Moraghan, not one of us will ever set foot there. I should know, I've heard it often enough. What does Grandmother say in the letter?" She reached out a hand. "Let me see."

"Oh, no, young lady!" Kate stepped quickly to one side. "This letter is to your father."

"Then why did you read it, Mother?"

"You would make a good attorney, that you would." Kate's smile was edged with grudging admiration. "I read it, Debra Lee, because your father gave it to me to read."

Debra half-turned away, then said casually, "Speaking of attorneys, did Grandmother mention Stony . . . Mr. Lieberman, in the letter?"

Kate stared. "Stonewall Lieberman? No reason she should, is there? You didn't ask about him in your letter, did you?"

Silence.

Kate sighed in exasperation. "Honest to God, Debra Lee, you can be a trial . . . no, worse. A pain in the ass."

Debra said stiffly, "I see no reason to be vulgar, Mother."

"Well, I do! Are you still mooning over that man? It's been nine years, and you saw him . . . what? Twice? At Sean's funeral and at the reading of the will. A total of an hour at the most." She laughed. "You may think you're mature enough to pick and choose your own name, but you've got a lot to learn about men, young lady. He's probably married, with a passel of kids by now. If someone mentioned your name to him, it likely wouldn't even register. Do you *really* think that he remembers you?"

Debra gave a toss of her head. "I don't see why you're carrying on so, Mother. I was just curious, is all."

"Sure, you were just curious. But to satisfy your curiosity . . . no, Nora didn't mention Stonewall Lieberman."

"But how about my visit to Moraghan? You said she—"

"Of course you're welcome, more than welcome! Nora has been after us, all of us, to come back since the day we left. But you're not going, Debra Lee. I've already gone into some of the reasons. If that's not good enough for you, I'll talk of this to Kevin tonight, and I'm sure he'll have a word or two to say on the subject."

Kevin Moraghan had more than a word or two to say, and they were said forcibly. "You are not going to East Texas, Debra Lee, and that's final! From your willful ways, I know that what I say usually has little effect on you. But you are still under my roof, and you're not yet twenty-one. So long as both of these things hold true, you will do as *I* say."

Less than a year short of twenty-one, Debra thought, and that won't stop me anyway. For once, probably for the first time in her young life, she chose caution and didn't voice her thoughts.

Kevin was going on, "Furthermore, I forbid you to write to your grandmother again. It can only upset her."

"Yes, Daddy," she said submissively.

He peered at her suspiciously. "Headstrong as you are, I imagine my words are like hailstones bouncing off a tin roof, but one thing will stop you. It costs a great deal of money to get to East Texas from here, and I'm not giving you a cent toward it!"

Debra hugged a secret to herself—over the past few years she had been squirreling money away, a few coins at a time, and she had a respectable amount, at least enough to pay stagecoach fare to Corpus Christi. From there she would walk to Nacogdoches, if need be.

She said softly, "Yes, Daddy."

Her surprising meekness blunted the edge of Kevin's anger, and he had to grope for something to say. "Very well, just so you understand," he finally said lamely, and

5

glanced at Kate, to find her staring at their daughter thoughtfully.

"If you will excuse me now, I think I'll go to my room," Debra said. As if nothing untoward had happened, she sailed across the room to Kevin and embraced him. "Good night, Daddy." She turned to kiss Kate. "Good night, Mother."

"Good night, dear," Kate said to her already retreating back.

There was a lengthy silence after she left the room.

Finally Kevin sighed and said, "What do you think, Kate? Did I get through to her at all? I've never seen her so . . . so agreeable. Do you think she's finally beginning to grow up?"

"Oh, she's grown up, right enough. She's a woman, is our Debra Lee." A pensive smile played about Kate's mouth. "Or hadn't you noticed?"

"Damnit, Kate, that's not what I meant!" Kevin said, exasperated. "You know she usually goes her own way, no matter what we say. I'm surprised she hasn't gotten into trouble long before this."

"Stubborn, willful, opinionated . . . all those things she is, but she's also bright as a new coin. She can handle herself well. In most situations, anyway."

"But she *is* headstrong, and liable to take it into her mind to do as she goddamn well pleases. Do you agree?"

"I agree, Kevin, and that troubles me, too." Without thinking she added, "She comes by it naturally, I suppose. . . ." Oh, dear God, of all the things to say, Kate thought. She was afraid to look at her husband.

"Speaking of that—do you think she knows? Or even suspects?"

Kate forced herself to look at him. His worn face was calm, and she was uncertain as to his feelings.

Mentally she squared off, then said, "You mean, of course, does she know about Brian?"

His gaze didn't waver. "That's what I mean, yes."

"I'm sure not. There's no way she could know."

"We may have made a mistake in not telling her. If she ever finds out, it could destroy her, you realize that."

A walk across his few cultivated acres was an almost nightly ritual for Kevin Moraghan. Even this evening, when he was more upset than usual following the scene with Debra Lee.

It seemed that he was always upset nowadays. Limping along, he kicked angrily at a clod of dirt and winced as a sharp pain shot up his leg. Nine years since Sonny Danker had lodged a bullet in that leg, and it still bothered him. Always would, to a degree, the doctors informed him.

In the pale fall of moonlight, he looked down at the dry soil. So frustrating! The soil was rich and fertile. With the addition of that extra element, water, a man could grow wealthy off this soil. The farmers nearer the Rio Grande had devised a crude means of piping water from the river and were intermittently prosperous. Kevin's neighbors talked of pooling money and manpower to extend the pipes to their places. They had tried to enlist Kevin's support and leadership—it baffled Kevin why men should look to him for leadership. What else could men be but failures when they looked to another failure for leadership?

Anyway, he was not too enthusiastic about the project. It would be costly, and the Rio Grande dried up to a trickle during the drought years, which came along all too often. Even in a year of normal rainfall, the river, capricious as a female, was apt to fail them right when water was the most needed.

Artesian wells, that was the answer, he knew it deep in his soul. He had seen one farther north, on the King Ranch. Sweet water coming up in a never-ending supply from deep in the earth.

Returning from that visit, he had been in a lyrical fever about it, talking to everyone. No one would listen. How would they water their crops, *if* the water could be brought up? By the pail full, one at a time? A pump powered by steam, Kevin replied, like the river steamers. Impractical, his neighbors had said; he was a visionary, a dreamer. And when he'd spent money of his own, money he could ill-afford, and had produced not a drop of water, he had been battered with laughter.

7

And yet, they all still looked to him for leadership. Inexplicable!

Kate had said, "Not so strange. People look askance at a visionary, yet history has proven visionaries and dreamers often right. All men have dreams, my darling, but are bashful about voicing them, fearful of being laughed at. So, they look to other dreamers from time to time, when they are not too obviously mad."

Wise, patient Kate! What would he have done, how would he have survived, without her?

Unfortunately Debra Lee had not inherited her mother's tolerance and patience. But then, Debra Lee's father was not known for his tolerance and understanding.

Even after all these years Kevin's heart gave a wrench in his breast at the thought that Brian, his own brother, was the father of Debra Lee. Not that Kate had ever once tried to deceive him about that, and she could have, easily.

His thoughts jumped back to that long-ago day, on the riverbank up from the big house on Moraghan Acres, the day he had asked Kate to marry him.

He had been on the verge of proposing, which Kate, with that perceptive mind of hers, apparently had guessed. Before he could blurt the words out, she had told him that she was pregnant by Brian. Brian knew, she had told Kevin; that was the reason he had gone off to join the Texas Rangers. Kevin had been shocked, yet his love for her had been such that he still asked her to be his wife.

Kate had said, "You still wish to marry me after what I just told you?"

"Of course," he had replied. "If you love someone, you accept them for what they are."

"You won't feel like you're taking Brian's leavings?" At his wince she had taken his hand and squeezed it. "I'm sorry, Kevin, but it must be spoken of."

"If you mean, I'd rather it hadn't come about this way, yes. I would have been happier if I had been the first man in your life. But it didn't happen that way, and ... well, Brian is Brian."

8

"And you still want to marry me?"

"I do, yes. Even if you don't love me, I'll accept you on those terms."

"But I do love you. You are the dearest, sweetest man in the whole, wide world, and I love you. . . ."

Although Brian had known that Debra Lee was the product of his loins, he had never revealed it to another soul—at least not to Kevin's knowledge. Kevin had always had the feeling that Sean Moraghan had known, or suspected, but if he had, he had taken the secret with him to his grave, shot to death by Sonny Danker on the same day Kevin had been wounded.

But Momma didn't know, Kevin was positive. At the thought of Nora Moraghan, still alive and feisty, that is, if her numerous letters were any yardstick, a wave of great longing swept over him. Nine years it had been since he had turned his back on Nora Moraghan, and all that the name Moraghan represented, and brought his family down here to poverty, hardship, and fruitless labor.

Kate, bless her, had never once uttered a word of censure or complaint over the sad state that his stiff-necked pride had brought them to. But not so Debra Lee.

To be fair, she had a right to feel disinherited, more of a right than she suspected. Since she was Brian's daughter, she should share in the Moraghan wealth. For Brian was a wealthy man. Enough news had trickled down to Brownsville to tell them that Brian had prospered mightily during the past few years. He was a big man around Nacogdoches. If Debra Lee ever found out who her real father was, Kevin was sure that the knowledge would alienate her from Kate and him forever.

That was one reason he refused to grant her permission to visit her grandmother. Once there, the likelihood of her finding out would be ever-present. It was not beyond Brian to tell her himself!

Brian hated him, blaming him for their father's death. It was unfair, yet often, in the black hours of a sleepless night, Kevin suffered a worm of doubt. Maybe he *could* have saved Daddy. The Danker-Moraghan feud went

9

far back, back to 1836 when Sean and Nora Moraghan came to Texas from Tennessee to take possession of a land grant outside of Nacogdoches and found the Dankers squatting on the property. Sean had chased them off, and later, while Sean was off fighting in the Battle of San Jacinto, the Dankers had sneaked back and abused Nora. The details of that were vague, but what happened next was a legend in East Texas. When Sean returned home and learned of it, he tracked the Dankers down and killed the older brothers, Lem and Jed. Sonny was just a boy then, but Ma Danker, vindictive soul that she was, had sworn revenge; an oath that held even beyond the grave. Sonny Danker had grown up to become an infamous gunfighter and had finally gotten Danker revenge on that day nine years back, slaying Sean and sorely wounding Kevin. Kevin had killed Sonny, but it had been too late to save his father.

Kevin sighed, shaking off the thoughts of ancient history and old guilts, and turned back toward the house. He knew that Kate would be waiting; she always waited up for him.

They would have to keep a close watch on Debra Lee. She was a determined girl, and once an idea lodged in her mind, she followed it up, come hell or high water. Of course they couldn't keep a rein on her forever; she would soon reach her majority. And if she wanted to visit her grandmother, there was little they could do to stop her. It had been their hope that she would fall in love with some local boy and marry. But she had shown absolutely no interest in any local boys, and in truth Kevin had to admit that the pickings were poor. All she could hope for if she wed a local youth would be a life of childbearing and drudgery.

His step quickened as he saw the light in the adobe, and he did his best to shake off the doldrums.

Debra sat at the window in her nightgown, the bedroom behind her dark. She saw the figure of her father approach the house, and she shrank back into the shadows. She held her breath until she heard the kitchen door slam after him, then leaned forward again, slender

10

fingers once more counting the small hoard of coins in her lap, doing it quietly so as not to awaken light-year-old Lena on their bed behind her. The total came to the exact amount as the other two times she had counted.

She had hoped to wait until she had at least enough to book passage by steamboat up the Gulf Coast and to either Corpus Christi or Galveston, but she had just enough for a trip by stagecoach to Corpus Christi. Stagecoach travel was much more uncomfortable than transport by water, but she didn't have a choice.

It seemed to Debra that if she didn't leave within the next day or two, she would never make the journey to East Texas. She knew from the look on her mother's face that evening that Kate suspected she had it in mind to sneak away.

And that was another reason she was taking the stagecoach. Checking, she had found out that one left Brownsville at noon the next day, while a steam packet was not scheduled for three days. Her parents were to attend the wedding of a neighbor's son and would be gone most of the day; Debra was supposed to stay home and watch after Michael and Lena. Not that Michael needed watching after, he was almost seventeen—a quiet, introspective lad who seldom got into trouble. But since Debra had no desire to attend the wedding, she had been happy for an excuse to stay home. Now that she had finally decided to put her plan into action, she was doubly glad.

While her parents were gone, she would pack up her few things and be on the stage, well away from Brownsville before anyone was the wiser. All she had to do was wait for the proper moment, wait until Michael had wandered off, in his usual brown study, then ride their mule into town, leaving it somewhere easy to find.

The wedding of the oldest Carson boy was a rollicking, foot-stomping, joyous affair. Tip Carson was a tall, rawboned lad of twenty-two, not particularly handsome, but affable, a good worker, and well-liked. At one time Kate had hoped that he and Debra Lee would hit it off, but they mixed like oil and water. Debra Lee thought

11

him a bore, and Tip was baffled by Debra Lee. In her heart Kate knew that it was just as well; married, they both would have been miserable.

Still, Debra Lee had to marry soon; in this country a woman unmarried after eighteen was considered an old maid, and to be pitied. And, Kate thought guiltily, it would be such a relief to have the girl married!

Betsy, Tip's new bride, was a homely little thing, but she was bright, lively as a cricket, and she adored her gangling husband.

Planks on trestles groaned with food, lemonade, and punch. In the shade of a nearby tree a fiddler sawed away, and a banjo player plucked. Boots thumped the dust as the dancers spun and whirled in the boiling sun.

At Kate's shoulder Kevin said, "Would you like to dance, love?" His breath smelled of bourbon.

She smiled around at him. "Since when have you become a dancer?"

He held up a tin cup. "Since I've been slurping up Jess Carson's skullbuster." He frowned. "Have I had too much, do you think? I wouldn't want to disgrace you, Kate."

"You'd never disgrace me, darling." She placed a hand on his arm, this sober, hardworking, devoted man, who knew so little relaxation. If he fell flat on his face, she'd pick him up bodily if necessary, glare at anyone who dared to sneer, and lug him home in the buggy. She might criticize him on occasion, but she loved him, limp, stubborn pride, and all. "But I don't feel like dancing right now, it's too hot. A person is liable to get sunstroke."

He brooded as he watched the whirling dancers, then said abruptly, "I'm worried about Debra Lee."

"I know, Kevin," she said soberly. "So am I. But I don't know what we can do about it, short of chaining her to a post in the yard, like an idiot child."

"Sometimes she *is* an idiot child!"

The sudden stiffening of her fingertips on his arm telegraphed her reaction, and he looked at her contritely. "I didn't mean that, not really. She's a bright child, probably brighter than either of us. Certainly"—his smile was rueful—"brighter than me."

"But willful, stubborn, arrogant."

"All of that. In that respect, she reminds me of—" He broke off.

"Of her father? Of Brian?"

He nodded mutely.

"It's true. I well remember when Brian ran off to join the Texas Rangers. Then, against all our arguments, even that of his father's, he marched off to fight with the Confederacy."

"And was captured, imprisoned, and came within a breath of dying. Yes, in that, she's certainly Brian's daughter."

"But only in that, darling. She has your moral strength, your warmth, and capacity to love."

"And your beauty."

They smiled pridefully at one another. Then Kate said, "Nora said to me once, in what context I don't recall, that bad blood will out is an old wives' tale used to scare unruly children. She said that how a child was raised was more important than blood, that love and respect for others were the answer, and God knows we've tried to give Debra Lee that."

"I sure as hell hope so," he said glumly.

Kate touched his cheek. "Shall we go home, Kevin? I'm ready if you are."

"You don't think the Carsons will mind?"

"The wedding's over. We'll tell them you have work to do, they'll accept that."

A half hour later, their farewells said, they were in the buggy, heading home at a fast clip. It was over an hour's drive home, and it was mid-afternoon when the house came in sight. The ride had been made mostly in silence, and both were plagued with a sense of urgency.

And when Kate saw Michael waiting in the yard for them, jumping up and down and waving, her apprehension mounted. He was at the buggy before it slowed to a stop, gripping the seat on Kate's side. His face was grim and white. "Momma . . . Daddy!"

"What is it, boy?" Kevin demanded. "What's wrong?"

13

"It's Debra Lee. She's gone! She saddled that old mule and left for town with her things, before you were hardly out of sight! I'd've come after you, but I had no way, with the mule gone."

Kate's breath caught in her throat. "You say she took her things? Did she say where she was going?"

"I didn't have a chance to ask. I had wandered out back with Lena, to show her a bird's nest I'd found. When I saw Debra Lee, she was already riding away. I ran hard and yelled at her, but she just whipped up that old mule and rode on!"

Two

Debra clutched her reticule in her lap as the stagecoach bounced and swayed along the strip of rough road. Already three hours out of Brownsville, her tailbone was numb, and she was sure that tomorrow she would be black and blue all over. There was only one other passenger in the coach, an oily dry-goods salesman out of San Antonio. She didn't know if this was a blessing or not. If other people had been packed into the coach, it would be smelly and hot, much hotter, but at least she wouldn't be thrown about every time the couch bounced in and out of a pothole or swung too sharply around a curve in the road.

And the salesman was a problem, not a problem she couldn't handle, but a problem nonetheless. He had introduced himself at once—Ned Bronson—and had kept up a running, if mostly one-sided, conversation for the first hour. He had given her a history of his travels and his marital problems—his wife had deserted him because he was on the road so much. Oh, it was a lonely life for a man, and female companionship was much to be desired.

Finally Debra, having had more than enough, said through gritted teeth, "Mr. Bronson, your conversation bores me. I have no interest in your marital problems, and if you're hoping that I might relieve your loneliness, think again! I'd sooner bed down with a rattlesnake!"

"Well! There's no need to be nasty, young lady. I was just passing the time of the day."

"So now you know that I don't wish to pass the time of the day with you."

Ned Bronson angrily retired to his corner of the coach, and when their glances chanced again to cross, his held pure venom.

Debra cared very little for his feelings. She had enough on her mind without fending off advances from a randy salesman. Uppermost in her mind was the possibility that her father would come chasing after her. Their mule would never be able to catch the stagecoach, but he could hire a horse and catch up to the stage before it reached the first stage stop. To be dragged kicking and screaming off the coach and taken back home would be humiliating. Debra thought she knew Kevin Moraghan well; ordinarily, being basically a shy man, he would never do such a thing, yet if he became incensed enough, he just might.

As the distance increased between the coach and Brownsville, her fears lessened, and when they had reached what she judged to be the halfway point, she leaned out for a last glance back down the road. Naturally the land here was flat, the road inches deep in dust, and she could see for several miles beyond the trailing dust cloud. There was no sign of a pursuing horse.

Debra refused to give way to relief, but she was more at ease in her mind. There was one other possibility—he could wire ahead to the stage station and have the law there retain her until he could come for her. She was not yet of legal age. But that would mean involving total strangers in family problems, and she doubted very much that her father's pride would permit him to go that far.

And with that thought, for the first time, she felt a wrench of regret and sorrow. She loved her folks, Michael, and Lena, and she was leaving them behind. It was likely that the break was irreconcilable; the farther she traveled from Brownsville, the wider the breach. She would miss them. Later, she knew, there would be tears, yet it had been time to go. She was being stifled there, and the feeling had been growing in her that, if she remained much longer, she would never make the break.

The stagecoach lurched, a wheel bouncing over a rock. Debra, caught unaware, was catapulted across the coach and into the arms of the salesman. He caught her, as surprised as she. Before she could recover her balance, Bronson tightened his arms around her.

In flying across the intervening space, her long skirt had come up around her thighs. Bronson chuckled hoarsely, and one hand went under her skirt, fondling her flesh.

Debra stiffened in outrage. "Let me go!"

His hand clamped cruelly on her thigh. "What's the hurry, little lady? I like it this way. Gives us a chance to get better acquainted. You might even get to like me. I ain't a bad fella, everything considered."

Debra snarled, "You bastard! If you don't let me go, I'll—" A rank, sickening odor from his sweat-stiffened shirt and unwashed body clogged her nostrils.

"Now what can a tiny thing like you do?"

In his lap, she felt a stirring, a swelling, and disgust rose in her throat like bile. She began to struggle, hitting out with her arms and legs. His arm tightened around her like a steel band; he was far stronger than she would have imagined. Debra realized that struggling would only increase the indignity and fuel his lust. His member was swollen now, throbbing through his breeches. She wasn't afraid of being raped, not in the cramped quarters of this jostling stagecoach, but she knew that he likely could attain his pleasure by just stroking her thighs and buttocks under her clothes.

Debra ceased struggling and sat very still. The hand under her dress began to fondle again, inching upward.

"Ah, that's the girl. Be nice now, and I won't hurt you," he said, panting.

She waited until the hand had reached the crotch of her drawers and he began to move rhythmically against her. Then she moved just enough to attain some lever-

17

age and drove the point of her elbow viciously against his bulging organ.

He yowled and threw her from him, into the opposite corner of the coach. "You bitch, you goddamned bitch!"

He doubled up, hands cupped over his groin.

Debra hid her smile of triumph, not wishing to anger him further. Yet she was highly pleased. All along there had been a niggling doubt in her mind that she would be able to defend herself, out in the world on her own for the first time. She was not unworldly by any means—Kate had imparted the facts of life to her early on—but she had been sheltered to a certain extent. Brownsville was a quiet, sleepy town.

Yet Texas, in the 1870s, was still pretty much a frontier country. And the myth that women were sacrosanct was just that. In actuality, women, especially those alone, were fair game.

But now Debra was reasonably confident that she had the fortitude and ingenuity to handle herself in most situations.

There was nobody waiting to take her into custody when the stagecoach arrived at the way station. Another stagecoach was leaving for Corpus Christi shortly, and Debra purchased a ticket from her few remaining dollars. There was just time to gobble a quick meal—pinto beans and salt pork, accompanied by bread as tough as cowhide.

Debra was travel-weary from the long haul up from Brownsville, but she didn't want to spend precious money for a room for the night; so she got onto the stage going to Corpus Christi. Bronson was remaining behind, for which she was thankful. After their set-to in the coach, he had retired into sullen silence, groaning with pain whenever he shifted position, and he had bolted from the stage the moment it arrived.

The stage was crowded now, and Debra rode all scrunched up into one corner, pinned there by a matronly woman with bosoms like cannon snouts. The stagecoach left the stage station in the late afternoon, and before long it was dark; the stage had to travel slowly, running by the light of two coach lamps. Debra was grateful for the reduced speed and was able to doze in troubled snatches.

It was long after dark when they reached Corpus Christi, and Debra was so numb with exhaustion she could scarcely walk. The town was asleep, the only light coming from a saloon up the street from the stage stop.

Lugging her straw suitcase, she trudged up the dusty street. Off to her left she heard the grumbling roar of the surf and smelled the tang of the sea. It had a different smell here than in Brownsville. There, it had a more tropical odor, the air faintly permeated with the scent of rot.

She recalled hearing that her Uncle Brian had once been here, to enlist in the Texas Rangers. She had heard that Corpus Christi was showing signs of a boom, becoming a winter and summer resort of the wealthy of Texas.

From what she could see, there was little indication of this. The town had a sleepy look, and the two buildings she saw with hotel signs in front were dark and shuttered. Recalling how depleted her funds were, she hesitated to rouse anyone in search of a room. As late as it was, any hotelkeeper was bound to be grumpy at being hustled out of a warm sleep and probably would be inclined to hike the price.

Then, at an intersection, she saw a pinkish glow of light in the window of a two-story structure down a side street. Two saddle horses, and a horse and buckboard, were tied to the long hitching rail in front.

Debra walked down the street and stopped at a picket fence, freshly whitewashed. She looked at the building. It must be a boarding house, she thought. It was neat and clean-looking, recently painted a rather garish yellow. She saw that there definitely was a lamp burning in the window. Pushing open the gate, she followed the short brick walk up to the veranda. As she did, she thought she heard voices inside.

She knocked timidly on the door. There was no response. She knocked again, louder, and a voice called crossly, "I'm coming, I'm coming!"

The door opened to reveal a young-old woman in a long satin dress, her long, dark hair in disarray. Strangely, the sight of the woman brought Debra such a feeling of relief that she was swept by dizziness, and she realized that she was in a fog of weariness and had been moving her limbs with a conscious effort since stepping down from the stagecoach. She scarcely took note of the woman's exposed shoulders, white with a dusting of powder, and the daringly low-cut dress exposing the swell of bosom.

The woman's eyes went wide with astonishment. "What in heaven's name do *you* want here, honey?"

"A room?" Debra said hopefully. "A room for the night. I've been traveling for close to four days and haven't lain down in all that time."

"A *room?* You want a room here?"

"If you please. Anything will do, I'm so worn out I'll sleep on a pallet on the floor."

The woman started to laugh, then choked it off, but her brown eyes sparkled with what struck Debra as mischief. Debra was too weary to puzzle it out.

The woman said, "Well, now, why not? Gert is gone. You could use her room, I reckon. Course, you have to pay. Rose has a house rule. No free time."

"Oh, I have money, I'll pay." Debra fumbled her reticule open. "How much?"

"How much?" The woman seemed disconcerted. "Oh ... a dollar all right?"

Debra had never stayed in a hotel or rooming house, but she recalled hearing that fifty cents was the going rate. She was so exhausted that a dollar seemed cheap enough for a night of sweet sleep, yet she felt that she should at least bargain. All the while she was thinking this, she was fingering the silver dollar in her purse. "Does that include breakfast?"

"Breakfast? Aw-w, honey!" This time the woman let her laughter go. In a moment she got it under control. "About that you'll have to speak to Rose, honey."

"Rose? That's the landlady?"

"Landlady?" Again the woman seemed about to explode with mirth. "Yup, that she is, in a manner of speaking."

Debra had the dollar out now. "Here's the money, miss."

"So it is." The woman looked at the dollar in wonder. "Oh, they're going to love this!" She stepped back, motioning. "Come along, honey. I'll show you your . . . room."

"My name is Debra Moraghan."

"And I'm Belle." She performed a curtsy rather awkwardly. "Pleased to make your acquaintance, I'm sure."

As Debra followed the woman's rustling skirts up the stairway, she idly glanced to her right. The lighting was muted, but from the one glance she had into the parlor, she saw shadowy figures moving. She also heard tinkling laughter. At least there were other women staying here, she thought.

At the top of the stairs she followed Belle down the hallway, dimly lit by a single wall lamp. Belle opened the last door on the right. "Wait out here, honey, until I light a lamp. It's black as midnight in here."

Debra waited, eyes drifting closed, until a light bloomed in the room, then went in. It was a cramped room, with only a few items of furniture—a narrow bed, a chest of drawers, a clothes cupboard, a washstand with a marble basin, and a pitcher of water. On the wall above the bed hung a picture of plump angels fluttering above a fleecy cloud. The lamp had a pink globe, casting a faint glow.

"It ain't much, honey, in the way of luxury, but it—"

"But it has a bed, and that's what is important right now."

"Right," Belle said, her face sober but the corners of her full mouth twitching slightly. "So I'll leave you to make good use of it. Sweet dreams, honey." At the door she paused, looking back over her shoulder. "Oh—if it gets a mite noisy, don't let it bother you none, honey. Sometimes the—uh, guests get a touch rowdy. In fact, it might be a good idea to latch the door after me."

Then she was gone, and Debra stood in a daze of weariness. The woman's warning pinged a tiny bell of

21

alarm in her mind, but she was too tired to ponder on it. She did, however, follow Belle's advice and latched the door. She figured that any guest would have to raise an almighty ruckus indeed, to rouse her once she was asleep.

She removed only the outer layer of clothing, and her shoes and stockings, then sank down into the bed. Kate was a fanatic about bodily cleanliness and had instilled in her children a similar appreciation—they always bathed once a day, even if it was only in cold water or just a wash in a hand basin.

"Forgive me, Mother," Debra mumbled. "In the morning, first thing, I promise."

She knew that splashing cold water on her face and hands would shock her awake, and she ached toward the sweet oblivion of sleep with the longing of a moonstruck girl toward her lover.

Three

Debra slept like the dead and awoke to sunlight streaming through the room's one window—and to a bellow of pure outrage. Uttering a small cry, she sat bolt upright in bed. The bellow came again—in the hallway just outside the room, and this time the words were distinguishable. "You did *what*, you ninny?"

"I thought it would be a lark, Rose. And Gert's room *was* empty. You always say a dollar is a dollar. The girls and me, we've been laughing ourselves silly."

"You're already silly, to act so stupidly! I'll flay your hide right off, Belle, so help me Jesus, I will!"

"Aw-w, Rose, what's the harm?"

"I'll tell you what's the harm, you great nit! You know we're already in trouble with the decent element, so-called. So what happens if they learn we've rented a room to one of their own kind?"

"We don't know that she's a lady, not for sure."

"Belle, you've been in this business long enough to know one of your own kind when you see one."

The truth had burst on Debra like a great light when she had overheard the first few words—she had spent the night in a brothel! How could she have been so stupid! The signs had all been there. True, she had never seen one before—the only whorehouse in Brownsville was in the Mexican section of town, and she had been mind-numbing tired the evening before, yet she should have realized. Like a halfwit she had bumbled into a situation laughable in the extreme—to someone else. There went her conviction that she could handle herself out in the cold, cruel world.

The icy shock of the revelation had rendered her temporarily frozen, but now another spat of words in that bellow of a voice— "Well, hell, let's go in and wise up Miss Goody Two-Shoes"—galvanized her into action.

She leaped out of bed and began scrambling into her clothes, glad that she had removed very little the night before.

She was far too late, however. A hearty thump on the door sent it flying open. So much for the protection provided by the latches in this place.

She looked up from drawing on her stockings as two women sailed into the room. Belle trailed a diminutive female with long, flaming red hair and shrewd blue eyes. It struck Debra as incredible that that bellow should belong to such a small woman.

The woman stalked up to Debra and stopped, feet wide apart, hands on hips. "Well, young lady! Do you know what kind of a place you picked to stay the night?"

"Not until a few minutes ago," Debra admitted sheepishly. "But I was tired, half-asleep last night—"

"She did look dead on her feet, Rose," Belle said virtuously. "That's why I took pity on her and—"

The other woman cut her off with a curt gesture. "Shut up, Belle. Don't make it worse by lying." Her gaze had never left Debra, and now her countenance assumed a softer expression. "Lord, you ain't but a bit of a girl. Reckon it's me who should be asking pardon. Belle here thought she'd have a little sport with you." She motioned again. "Say you're sorry, Belle."

Belle took two steps forward, grinning embarrassedly. "I *am* sorry, honey. Honest, I didn't mean any real harm."

Rose grunted. "That's what Sherman said when he marched through Georgia."

24

"Rose, that's hardly fair!"

"What's fair around here is what me and the Lord say is fair. Don't you be forgetting that. I'm Rose Sharon, girl. Naturally it's not my real name"—her sudden grin was bawdy—"but I've gone by it so long now, that I've come to think of it as such." She held out her hand.

Debra jumped up to take it. "I'm Debra Moraghan."

"From where?"

"Brownsville."

"Running away from home, are you?"

"I'm leaving home, yes. But it's not what you probably think. I'm on my way to Nacogdoches, to visit my grandmother."

"At least you're honest," Rose said wryly. "And I'm not one to talk. I ran away from home at fifteen. Course, some folks would say"—that rowdy grin again—"look what happened to her. Came to a no-good end. By the way, Debra—" She delved into her pocket, took out a silver dollar, and held it out. "Here's your money."

"Oh, no! I paid for a night's lodging, it's yours."

"I'm not running a boardinghouse here, girl. Take your dollar back and don't argue with me. Besides, I'd wager you're skinny in the purse."

Debra took the dollar and said ruefully, "You're right there. I don't have enough money left for coach fare to East Texas." She added hopefully, "You wouldn't know where I could get a job for a week or so, would you?"

Rose studied her appraisingly. "What can you do?"

Debra flushed. "Not a great deal, I'm afraid. But I'm not afraid of hard work."

"Rose," Belle said, "Gert's gone. How about—?"

"Hush up, Belle! I haven't slipped so far down that I stoop to turning decent girls into whores. Ida May Jones, she runs the eating place at the hotel over yonder. Her daughter, who usually waits tables, is about to give birth. Might be you could fill in for her for a spell. Ever wait tables?"

Debra shook her head. "Only at home for my folks."

"Same thing, except on a bigger scale."

"Speaking of eating . . ." Debra's gaze went to Belle,

and she was surprised at her own daring. "Belle here promised that breakfast was included for my dollar."

Belle gasped. "I never! Rose, I swear! I said she'd have to talk to you about that."

Rose's blue eyes narrowed, and for a moment Debra feared that she had gone too far.

"That dollar I just returned, if you recall," Rose said tightly. "You've got gall, girl, I'll hand you that. It should take you far." Then she laughed, a rolling bellow, throwing her head back. She spread her hands wide. "But why not? Lupe should have it on the table about now." She stared coldly. "Unless you object to eating with my girls?"

"If it doesn't bother them, it won't bother me." In truth, Debra was inordinately curious about the "girls" and was anxious to see them.

"Well, you'd better get dressed. I have a house rule: everybody gets dressed for meals in my house. No slopping around. The dining room you will find downstairs, in the back. Come along, Belle."

Nodding her head curtly, Rose swept out of the room, Belle in her wake. There certainly was something commanding about the small woman, Debra thought.

As she hurriedly finished dressing, Debra thought about her parents. How shocked they would be to know that their wayward daughter had spent the night in a brothel! At least her father would be. She had a feeling that her mother would be secretly amused.

She hastened downstairs and to the dining room in the rear. The others were already there—eight in all, including Rose. Despite Rose's warning that everyone dressed for meals in her house, Debra was surprised at what she saw. In her mind had been a vision of painted and bedizened doxies slouching about in grimy wrappers, the very picture of debauchery. Such was not the case. All the women were dressed decorously, and all faces were scrubbed and shining. It could, she thought in wonder, be a social gathering of church ladies.

Rose patted the empty chair beside her. "Sit here, dear."

Debra slid into the vacant seat, and then something

happened that further astounded her. Rose folded her hands beside her plate, lowered her head, and closed her eyes.

"Dear Lord, who art in Heaven, we thank thee for thy bounty. We thank thee for our good health and welfare. We thank thee for the good food you have seen fit to grace our table. . . ."

The girl next to Debra muttered, "The horny men of Corpus should come in for some thanks."

With barely a pause Rose reached across Debra and whacked the girl across the mouth with the back of her hand. The girl flinched and cried out.

Rose continued, "Dear Lord, we are most grateful for your blessing on us. Amen." After a small pause, she added, "This is my last word on it, Sally. One more such remark out of you, and you're out on your irreverent butt." She raised her voice. "You may serve now, Lupe."

A middle-aged Mexican woman came out of the kitchen carrying a steaming platter of eggs, ham, and fried potatoes. Muttering to herself, she set the platter down into the center of the table, and Rose began serving, filling Debra's plate first. The girls waited patiently, as Rose served all around the table, from left to right.

Debra found that she was starved, yet she had time to notice that all the women ate with hearty appetites but also with good manners.

As though reading her thoughts, Rose chuckled. "I know what you're thinking, girl. People tend to think of 'soiled doves' as frail creatures, dying from some horrible disease. Not Rose's girls. They're all healthy, examined regularly by Doc Price, the old sot. The joke around Corpus is that Doc takes his fee out in trade. They don't know him like I do. He hasn't been able to service a female in a coon's age. It all went down the bottle. But my girls now. . . . The Lord and me"—she raised her eyes heavenward—"see to it that they stay in good health."

Debra ducked her head, hiding a smile, and busied herself with the food. The combination of piety and bawdiness in Rose Sharon was humorous in the extreme.

"I provide a service, girl, as much needed as a dry

27

goods store or a livery stable." Again, the woman seemed to read Debra's mind. "Those against us are hypocrites, every one. The Lord knows that the needs of the flesh must be served. It says right there in the good book that he laid healing hands on a whore, instead of scorning her. Those church-goers"—her mouth curled in disgust—"think only *they* know the blessing of our Lord, that he smiles only on them and scorns the rest of us."

Down the table a woman murmured, "I'm finished, Rose. May I be excused?"

"Of course, dear," Rose said benignly. "I would suggest a lie-down, and that goes for all of you. We must look our best tonight." To Debra, she explained, "This is Saturday night, our busiest night of the week." She glanced at Debra's plate. "Are you finished?"

"Yes. And thank you, it was a fine meal."

"Then I'll take you to Ida May now," Rose said briskly, pushing back her chair. She swept the table with a stern glance. "Now, girls, behave yourselves. I won't be gone long."

A chorus of "yes, Rose," went around the table.

Rose and Debra strolled together toward the business section of Corpus Christi. Rose looked the very essence of a lady. In one hand she twirled a pink parasol over her head, and with the other she held her long skirts dutifully up out of the dirt.

The sun scorched, but a cooling breeze swept in off the gulf. All the front yards were a riot of blooming flowers and trees, and stately palms stood like sentinels on guard along the gulf-front streets two blocks down.

"Corpus, you know, is becoming a summering as well as wintering place for the rich of Texas," Rose said conversationally. "Those that can afford it come here in summer for the cool breezes and sea bathing. Politicians come here from Austin when the legislature is not in session. Wealthy sheep owners and cattle ranchers flock here in summer. Several have summer homes here. For one, Captain Richard King of Rancho Santa Gertudis has a house here. And up there, on the heights"—Rose motioned to her left—"are the fine houses of the 'quality' people."

Debra glanced that way and saw a bluff rising above the lowlands where the commercial part of Corpus Christi was situated. The houses she could see were fine indeed, with green lawns and giant trees throwing cooling shade.

They turned left again and were on Chaparral Street, the artery of the commercial district. It teemed with carts, wagons, and buggies. Some of the vehicles had as many as six yoke of oxen, and the animals were lying in a tangle, stretching from broadwalk to broadwalk, placidly chewing their cuds. The street was also crowded with people, predominantly male, and the language Debra heard seemed to be chiefly Spanish.

Again divining Debra's thoughts, Rose said, "Yes, all these carts and wagons you see are here to load up with goods for the long haul down into Mexico. At the present, that's the main source of income for those Corpus Christians in the mercantile trade, selling goods for transport down below the border."

They were passing storefronts now, and out in front and through grimy windows, Debra could see all manner of goods on sale—clothes, oil lamps, clocks, sewing machines, hides, tallow, dried meat, wool, any and everything. The mingled odors were rancid and varied.

Then they entered a district a little more substantial— at least the buildings were larger, several two stories and more, and most were constructed of brick.

Rose motioned with her parasol to a three-story brick building, with a hotel sign in front. "Ida May's café is in there. You get the job, Debra, you should earn a bit in gratuities. Ida May doesn't pay much, but her clientele is first class, even better than mine"—that bawdy laugh—"so to speak. But one thing now. . . ." She put her hand on Debra's arm, stopping her. "When she asks if you've had experience waiting tables, tell her yes. I'm a great believer in the Lord's commandments, but there're times a person has to dodge around the truth a mite. You're a smart girl, I can tell, and you'll catch on in no time."

The hotel lobby they went into thronged with well-dressed men and women; each wore a prosperous air like a royal cloak. Rose led the way to a door off the lobby and into a spacious restaurant, with tables covered with snowy linen, fine silverware, and excellent china. Since it was past the breakfast hour and yet short of noon, only a few tables were occupied.

Two women were busy waiting on the few customers. Rose caught the eye of one, a middle-aged, rawboned woman, and beckoned her over. She had a harried air, and a few strands of graying hair escaped her cap.

"Rose, how you? I swan, with that girl of mine laid up, I'm working my tailbone off here."

"I have the solution to your problem, Ida May. Right here." Rose waved Debra forward. "Debra Moraghan, from Brownsville. She's looking for work."

"Is that so?" Ida May's faded blue eyes studied Debra critically. "Purty enough, I have to say that for her." The woman's gaze swung back to Rose Sharon. "She ain't one of your girls, is she? You know me'n you are good friends, but if word got out that I had a whore in here waiting tables, I'd lose most of my customers."

"Not one of mine, Ida May." Rose spread her hands, palms out. "I swear."

"Then how come you got to know her? Explain that, if you will."

"You're not going to believe how it came about. . . ."

To Debra's acute embarrassment, Rose explained how it was that she had spent the night in a brothel.

Ida May Jones whooped with laughter. "I swan! That's a story and a half!" Her glance moved back to Debra. "Ain't too bright, is she? But then you don't have to be, to wait tables. One thing, girl . . . I need someone for a month. That's how long it'll be afore that daughter of mine can be back to work. You promise to stay that long?"

"I promise," Debra said. "I'll stay the month."

"Then the job's yours. You start to work at supper time tonight. A dollar a day and two meals thrown in."

30

Four

Except that it was in need of a coat of paint, Moraghan looked pretty much as Debra remembered it.

She had rented a rig and driver in Nacogdoches that morning, and it had taken half of the day to reach the plantation. She could recall Grandfather Sean relating that it had taken nearly two days by wagon to reach Nacogdoches.

The familiar old house sat on the south side of the hill, built on that site by her grandfather so that the hill would offer some protection from the winter northers. To the south, the river wound like a ribbon. It had been a dry summer, and the river was very low, but she could vividly remember the marvelous times she and Michael had had splashing in that river, and the not so marvelous times when Uncle Brian's pair had gone swimming with them. . . .

"Missus?"

Her head came around. "Yes?"

The black driver motioned. "This it? This where you all wanted to go?"

"Yes, this is it. This is Moraghan. But hold just a minute before I get down, I want to look. You know, it's been nine years, and I was born on Moraghan."

The driver shrugged. "Time, it do pass. Yes, ma'am, it purely do."

"Of course, I wasn't born here, not in this house, I mean. My father's old house is about a mile up, you can't see it from here. . . ." She interrupted herself. "Godalmighty, I'm talking away like an idiot, aren't I? You couldn't be at all interested in this!"

The black man laughed suddenly, a rich outpouring of mirth. "It's all right, miss. Don't bother me none. I figure you're just a mite skittish, coming back to your birth-place after all this time."

"That's exactly right! The thing is, you see," she babbled, "I'm not sure how welcome I am."

"Debra Lee, is that you? Child, you going to sit in that buggy out there all night?"

The voice, as familiar as if the nine years had only been a day, jolted Debra, and then she was out of the buggy and running toward the erect, white-haired figure on the porch steps. As she ran headlong, Debra's mind raced. How old was Nora Moraghan now? Sixty-five? She seemed to recall that her grandmother had been born around 1810.

Then she skidded to a halt and embraced the woman on the steps. "Grandmother Nora!" she choked out. "It seems like forever!"

"All that and more, child, all that and more." Nora Moraghan stepped back and held Debra at arm's length. "Let me get a good look at you." With misty eyes she looked Debra over from head to toe. "My, my, you've turned into a real beauty!"

Debra wiped tears from her eyes. "Thank you, Grandmother."

"Of course, you had the promise at eleven," Nora mused. "I well remember thinking that at Sean's funeral, when you played the coquette with Stonewall Lieberman. Flummoxed him no end, as I recall."

Debra went tense at the mention of Stonewall Lieberman, but caution stilled her tongue—this was not the time to inquire about him.

Nora said briskly, "No need for that buggy to wait around." She raised her voice. "You there in the buggy!

Bring my granddaughter's baggage into the house, and you can go on your way."

"I didn't bring very much," Debra murmured, taking advantage of Nora's brief inattention to observe her grandmother more closely. In Debra's early years here, Nora had always seemed formidable, ageless, indomitable. She still had those qualities, but age had shrunk her once firm figure, lined her face, whitened her hair. And yet, Debra mused, why should that be so surprising? Nora Moraghan had lost a husband to violence, had seen a son permanently lamed by that same violent act; and she had seen hostility grow apace between her two sons to the point where one had left Moraghan, and Nora had not seen him since.

The driver came with Debra's one straw suitcase, and Nora led the way into the house. Once, Debra recalled, there had been several servants. Now, the house seemed strangely quiet, and there was a musty, closed-off odor. Moreover, as they followed the driver down the hall, passing the open door to the parlor, Debra saw dustcovers on the furniture.

Nora said, "Just put the suitcase in the sunroom off to the right yonder. We can take care of it from there."

They went into what was essentially a screened porch, an addition to the big house, added by Sean Moraghan shortly before Debra was born, Debra had been told. She recalled that her grandparents had used it as a sitting room, breakfast room, sometimes even as a parlor when company came. This was because the room faced the river and had three walls of windows, which could be opened out in summer, catching whatever breeze there was.

"Cost Daddy a fortune," Kevin had once commented, "buying all that glass and having it hauled in from Nacogdoches."

After the driver had been sent on his way, Debra said, "Where's all the household help, Grandmother?"

"Maria's the only one left," Nora said. She gave a soft snort. "And she's in worse shape than I am. About the best I can expect from her is cooking a meal once a day, supper usually. Fact is, I'd've let her go long since, except where would she go? What would she do?"

"But how can you care for this big house all by yourself, Grandmother?" Debra asked in dismay.

"I manage," Nora said tartly. "I managed years before I had any house help. Oh, I know what you're thinking, Debra Lee." Her grin was wry. "I'm getting on. I realize that every morning when I get out of bed. But enough of that. I was just about to pour myself some lemonade when I heard the buggy drive up. We'll have a glass and talk."

Debra sat down and watched as her grandmother busied herself pouring two glasses of lemonade. "How is Uncle Brian and his family?"

"Fine, far as I know. Don't see much of them nowadays," Nora said irritably. "Brian's become a big man these days, busy as all get-out. He's operating two sawmills now. If he has his way, all the timber in East Texas will soon be gone." She handed Debra a glass of lemonade and sat down. "I don't approve of what he's doing. Some men in the lumber business plant new trees behind them, but not Brian. He's too busy making money for that. All of Moraghan is stripped bare of timber, except here and along the river. He'd cut those acres, too, if I'd let him. Well I remember Sean saying that a man should replenish the earth always, and it'll always be good to him. But enough of Brian and his ways!" She made a motion as though swatting at a fly. "You know, child, I was getting almighty worried about you. Where've you been this last month, since you left Brownsville?"

"I reckon Daddy wrote you then? About my leaving?"

"Of course. Well, actually, the letter was from Kate. Kevin isn't much of a letter writer. Do you know I've had one letter from him in all the years he's been away? Thank God for your mother!" Nora's glance sharpened. "But I was getting worried, Debra Lee. You left Brownsville a month ago. What did you do, walk here? Where've you been all this time?"

"Waiting tables in Corpus Christi, Grandmother. My money ran out, and I had to work until I had stagecoach

34

fare here. Grandmother,—" Debra leaned forward tensely. "I *can* stay? You're not going to send me away? I warn you, I will not go back home, no matter what!"

"Of course you can stay, child," Nora said gently. "You're more than welcome. In my reply to your mother's letter, I told her that. Not that I wholly approve of your running off like that. The young, they never think that what they do will hurt their folks."

"I know, Grandmother, and I am sorry about that." Debra took a deep breath. "But I hate Brownsville! It's dry, dreary, and hot. You know what they say down there? Everything sticks, stinks, or stings. Oh, how true! I was stifling there."

Nora's stern look faded as she mused, "I know, child. I felt that way, back in Tennessee when I met your grandfather. There was one difference, however. I had no folks, only my sister, and she had a husband and family of her own. It might have been different if my folks had still been living."

"Would it, Grandmother? Tell the truth now. You fell in love, and nothing would have stopped you from going off with the man you loved. Am I right?"

Nora looked startled for an instant, then she gave a snort of laughter. "Bless you, child, of course you're right! Nothing could have stopped me from running off with Sean, nothing. And him a priest, too! I doubt that tongues have stopped wagging yet, back in Tennessee."

"Was he *really* a priest, Grandmother? I've heard that, but I've never known for sure."

Nora nodded. "Oh, yes, Sean was a Catholic priest, Father Sean Moraghan. No, that's not right." She paused, frowning. "He changed his name when we came to Texas. You know, I'd almost forgotten that. But good Lord, how I loved that man! I even defied God. You know something, Debra Lee? I know Sean loved me, but I've never been sure that he didn't regret leaving the church, in the end. I never dared ask him right out. Now, I'll never know, I reckon—unless there's some truth about meeting those who have passed on to another life. I never used to think much about such things, but of late—" She broke off, her lined face shadowed by melancholy.

Debra respected her silence for a little, but the question she'd been aching to ask, the real reason she was here, drove her to speak. "Grandmother, you mentioned Stony—Mr. Lieberman, a bit ago. Is he still living in Nacogdoches?"

Nora started. "What? What was that, child?"

"Stonewall Lieberman, is he still around?"

"Of course. Stonewall is still practicing law in Nacogdoches. He's quite successful. There's even been some talk of running him for public office."

"Is he—" Debra cleared her throat. "Is he married, with a family?"

Nora smiled faintly. "No. Stonewall's a confirmed bachelor, I do believe. I josh him about it. He was out here to supper just last—" She paused, eyeing Debra closely. "Why are you asking about Stonewall? Now I remember! Kate mentioned something in her letter. You still stuck on him, after all these years? Is that it, child?"

Debra felt herself flushing. "No, no. It's just that I remember him. He impressed me, when he was here reading Grandfather's will."

Nora nodded, her gaze still speculative. "He's impressive, right enough. But I suspect it's more than that with you. I reckon maybe I should warn him." Her eyes suddenly sparkled with mischief.

"No, please, Grandmother Nora. Don't do that. You'll embarrass me."

"I have my doubts about that," Nora said dryly. "I remember thinking that day, at Sean's burying, that you would probably get anything you wanted when you grew up. Well, you've grown up, and I doubt you've changed all that much. Anyway . . ." Nora stirred, getting to her feet. "I expect you're tired, after all that traveling. I've had a room fixed up for you, Debra Lee, since I got word from your mother that you were probably heading this way."

Debra stood up, stretching. "I am tired, yes."

Hiding her jubilation at the news about Stonewall Lieberman, Debra followed Nora down the hall to a back bedroom. Of course, it was fanciful thinking to believe that he had not married because he was waiting for her. But the fact remained—he was *not* married!

After Nora had said good night and Debra had gotten into bed, she lay awake for a time, tired as she was.

Her mind was occupied figuring out her strategy. It would never do to be too direct. She had to sneak up on him, contrive to let him know her a little better, and give him time to realize that he loved her.

She had no doubt whatsoever that it would all work out.

She awakened late the next morning to the odor of bacon frying and the sun coming in through the window. She raised her head, nose twitching like a rabbit's at the appetizing odor of the bacon. Scrambling out of bed, she washed hastily in the tepid water in the basin on the washstand, and got dressed.

As she started toward the sun porch, she heard the sound of voices—Nora's and the deeper voice of a man. The male voice had a familiar ring, and before she stepped out onto the sun porch, she recognized it as belonging to her uncle, Brian.

Her grandmother and uncle were at the table, and Maria was putting food before them. Nora turned at the sound of Debra's footsteps, and her face broke into a fond smile. "Debra Lee! You're up and about. I was about to send Maria to roust you out of bed."

"I smelled bacon cooking and discovered that I was starved."

She advanced toward the table, her gaze on Brian Moraghan, who was getting to his feet. Nine years had wrought considerable change in her uncle. She had expected the prosperous look. He wore a white linen suit, black string tie, and hand-tooled cowboy boots, and a fine planter's hat rested on the chair beside him. But he had also grown plump. Always a big man, he had added twenty pounds or more, and his face was florid and rounded. Broken capillaries in his rather large nose gave it a purple hue and attested to a generous intake of bourbon.

How old was he now? Close to forty, she knew. Kevin, younger by almost two years, looked older, worn, and stooped by hard labor. This aroused a spurt of loyal resentment in Debra. Nine years her father had grubbed in the earth like a mole, while his brother remained here, growing rich and fat. Her father was rightly entitled to half of Moraghan.

In the early years she had looked upon her uncle with admiration—he had been dashing, charming, volatile, an adventurer always kiting off to distant places. She knew that henceforth her attitude toward him would be colored by the resentment of the disinherited.

Brian was speaking, and smiling in welcome, yet there was a secretive, measuring look in his eyes. "Debra Lee, how you? It's been a long time. Seems to me that your daddy could pay us a visit now and then. Nine years is a long time not to see family."

"Daddy says he'll never set foot on Moraghan again."

"Aw, hell!" Brian threw his hands out. "Surely he don't still hold that old grudge, not after all this time."

Debra kept a rein on her temper with difficulty. "I happen to think he has reason, since he was done out of his rightful heritage!"

"That wasn't my doing," Brian said, giving her a condescending smile. "It was all proper and legal. It was all spelled out in Daddy's will, and I *am* the eldest son."

Nora rapped the table with her knuckles. "Sean was going to change his will, you know he was!"

"I don't know any such a damned thing, Momma. Anyway, he didn't, that's the main thing." Brian's face had reddened. "Besides, it was Kevin's fault that Daddy was killed. He was right there, when it happened. If he'd been a better man, he'd've blown Sonny Danker's head off before the sonofabitch had a chance to kill Daddy."

"Kevin did as much as any man could have," Nora said. "And he'll limp for the rest of his life because of it."

"That's my fault, I suppose?"

"I didn't say that, Brian."

"No, but you seem to think it. Why is it that you're always taking up for Kevin, Momma? I'm your son, too. Your firstborn."

Nora closed her .eyes, and took a deep breath. "Brian, I think you'd better go now. The first we've seen of Debra Lee in all this time, and we're quarreling. What will she think of us?"

"I hardly think I'll spend the day worrying about what Debra Lee thinks of me! But I'm going, Momma, I'm going!" He surged to his feet, his chair falling to the floor with a crash, and snatched up his hat.

"Why the hell is it, Momma, that every time I come visit you, we wind up fussing?"

"That is odd, isn't it, son?" Nora said in a dry voice. "But then I could ask you the same thing."

Brian jammed the hat on his head and stalked out of the room without sparing Debra another glance.

She sank down into the chair next to Nora, who had her eyes closed. Timidly Debra said, "I'm sorry, Grandmother. Maybe I shouldn't stay around. . . ."

"Why should you be sorry, child?" Nora's eyes snapped open. "If you think it's your doing, disabuse yourself of the notion. We get into it over something, without fail, every time Brian comes by. I can depend on it happening, so I've come to dread his visits. Brian, too, I reckon. As for your staying around, Debra Lee"—she reached for Debra's hand—"not only are you welcome, you're to stay for as long as you like. I felt happier this morning since I don't know when, waking up knowing one of my own was in this old house with me."

Impulsively Debra leaned across to embrace her. "Thank you, Grandmother. I've missed you, I hadn't realized just how much."

"I missed you, too, child, as well as your folks. The new girl I haven't even seen, you realize?" She became brisk. "Eat, Debra Lee. If you don't eat hearty, Maria won't speak to me all day."

Chewing, Debra said, "Are there any saddle horses on the place, Grandmother?"

"Two left, I believe. They're getting on, but still able to carry a person around. Why?"

"I'd like to ride over Moraghan, if it's all right with you, and see what changes have taken place."

Brian Moraghan was seething when he left the house. He mounted up and drummed his horse into a gallop, riding toward one of his sawmills to oversee the day's work.

It seemed that his mother wasn't about to forgive him for inheriting under Daddy's will. It was damned unjust, in his opinion. Who had a better right? He was the eldest son, and it was his rightful heritage.

Besides, Kevin would never have been capable of exploiting Moraghan's resources to the fullest. He didn't possess the driving force necessary. He would have been content to farm the land, maybe run a few cattle. It took energy, daring, and imagination to make Moraghan pay the way he, Brian, had. Hell, he was considered one of the foremost timber men in East Texas!

Sure, there were a few who carped about his stripping the land bare. But they were simply envious that they hadn't thought of it first. What was the timber there for, if not to be used?

His mother kept raking him over the coals for "ravaging the land without putting anything back," claiming that Daddy's philosophy had been—take care of the land, and it would take care of you.

Brian laughed harshly. That was fine for his daddy. When Sean Moraghan settled in East Texas, the land was there for cultivating, rich and fertile. Growing cotton and other crops and raising some livestock were sufficient to make a good living. But that was no longer true. To provide for his family, to make his mark, a man had to plow ahead with daring and imagination, be damned to what was left in his wake!

The proof of that was in the respect accorded to one Brian Moraghan in East Texas. He was a man to be reckoned with, he thought, and he was probably the wealthiest man in the Big Thicket. Kevin now, had never been out in the world—certainly Brownsville was not much more worldly than East Texas—but if nothing else, Brian's stint in the Texas Rangers and his service at the siege of Vicksburg during the War Between the States, had taught him a valuable lesson. It was every man for himself. If there was something there for the taking, you took it, before someone else did. If you didn't, you were left sucking hind tit.

He could visualize Brother Kevin grubbing away down there along the Rio Grande, working himself into an early grave just to put bread on the table. And that snippy daughter of his! Where did she get off barging in here uninvited and sneering at him? Could it be that she hoped to sail back up here and somehow lay claim to a part of Moraghan?

If that was her aim, she'd made a long trip for nothing! Except for the big house and the ten acres surrounding it, Moraghan belonged to *him*, and by God it was going to remain his! If she got in his hair, he would damned soon send her scooting back to Brownsville.

Abruptly he laughed, a booming laugh that caused his horse to rear, ears laid back. Viciously yanking the reins, he got the animal under control, but he was still laughing as he rode on.

Wouldn't that little old girl be delighted to know that she was *his* daughter, not Kevin's?

Five

At thirty-five Stony Lieberman was a fine figure of a man—tall, well-built, with a flair for wearing well-tailored clothes. In repose, his dark features had a tendency toward melancholy, his black eyes somber. But those same eyes could twinkle with a sly humor or spark with anger. He enjoyed homespun humor, the jokes often on himself, and just as often exaggerated. Of late years, he had developed a mannerism of pulling at his rather long nose to hide a smile.

Stony had been told that he bore a faint resemblance to Abe Lincoln, and he supposed, in moments of self-analysis, which he was given to more often than was probably good for him, that he cultivated this trait.

Although he was now well-to-do, he lived alone in a log cabin on the outskirts of Nacogdoches. Another attempt to conform to the Lincoln mystique? If so, it was rather risky, since Abraham Lincoln was far from universally admired in East Texas.

He had earned a reputation as an excellent defense lawyer, and his law practice had flourished. His practice was not all that lucrative, however, since many of the clients he defended were more likely to pay him in goods rather than cash. Most of his income was derived from civil law: the writing of wills; handling estates; giving legal advice in business deals, et cetera. But he loved the arena atmosphere of the courtroom, and he considered the adversary system the best means of justice man had yet devised, all the while mindful of its many flaws.

For many years Stony had been the only Jew in Nacogdoches, and it had made him an alien, at least in his own mind. However, he had come to realize that this very strangeness worked to his advantage in the practice of law. East Texans were, by and large, a friendly and tolerant people and allowed a man his eccentricities, if he performed well in his profession; and since Stony was their only Jew, their initial wariness soon diminished, and they viewed his Jewishness as simply an eccentricity, along with his being a confirmed bachelor, living alone in relative isolation, tending to a garden patch, and reading excessively. Of course, Stony was a Jew by race only, having little use for religion of any kind.

This shared skepticism, Stony had often reflected, had been a large factor in drawing Sean Moraghan and him together—a defrocked Catholic priest and a lone Jew among Gentiles. Many were the philosophical discussions the pair had pursued over a jug of whiskey, and Stony calculated that he was the only person in East Texas, aside from Nora, who knew about Sean's former profession.

Now there were two more Jewish families residing in Nacogdoches, both merchants, yet Stony had offended them by refusing to attend the Saturday sabbath held regularly in the home of one, and because of that, he remained Nacogdoches's treasured eccentric and respected lawyer. Such was the esteem in which he was held that he was being courted to stand for election, to run for judge.

Stony had so far avoided giving a direct answer. The idea appealed to him; it was a goal to be cherished by any man with a reverence for the law. On the other hand, it would mean that he would have to forgo the courtroom battles that he loved.

There was another factor that troubled him. These same men who were urging him to run had also hinted, not very subtly, that a married man stood a far better chance at being elected than a single one. It was considered unseemly that any man should still be a bachelor at age thirty-five.

Stony had no aversion to getting married. He had considered it often, but his had been a busy life; furthermore, he had never met a woman he could love. Love, of course, wasn't necessary. Many men married for expediency—a wife to bear their children, to keep their households, to give them standing in the community.

However, he was a hopeless romantic. He thought that love was a necessary ingredient for any marriage. God knows, there had been opportunities galore. Once he had become respected and well-to-do, there were numerous mothers with eligible daughters who were willing to overlook his Jewishness, willing to sacrifice their Baptist heritage, in order to see their daughters well married.

Stony had long since decided that this avid pursuit was one thing that had caused him to shy away. A man should reserve the right to pick and choose his own mate, he believed, and not be exposed to a parade of girls, like cattle at an auction!

So, he kept more to himself than ever, refusing most social invitations, devoting his working hours to the practice of law and his off-hours to his garden and his books.

And such was his life when word reached him that Debra Lee had returned to Moraghan. He remembered Debra Lee across the years—a precocious, vital eleven year old, round eyes clinging embarrassingly to his face at Sean's funeral and later at the reading of the will.

Stony took a day off from his practice, saddled his horse, and rode out to Moraghan.

His visits to Nora Moraghan were a habit now. He had grown quite fond of Nora during the past nine years. In the beginning they had conspired together to

44

find a means of breaking Sean's will. As was customary, the will left everything, except the main house and ten acres, to Sean's eldest son, Brian. But Brian had been believed lost in the war, and Sean had been contemplating changing his will in favor of Kevin. Stony had gathered from things left unsaid that there had been bad feelings between Sean and his youngest son but that they had grown closer after Brian was presumed dead, and Sean had been edging closer to changing his will. Unfortunately, he had been shot dead by Sonny Danker before that had come about.

And then, shortly after Sean's funeral, Brian Moraghan had shown up, alive and well, having been captured at Vicksburg by the Federals and kept a prisoner until the end of the war.

Learning that he had been disinherited, Kevin Moraghan had packed up and left Moraghan forever, only a week after the reading of the will. For months following his departure, Stony and Nora had wrestled with the problem of breaking the will—in those early days of his practice he had had time to spare.

In the end he had said, "It's mostly an intellectual exercise we're indulging in, Nora. Certainly we can take it to court, and I can testify that Sean spoke to me of his intention of changing the will. But an oral statement is not legally binding, especially not when a written document already exists, duly signed and witnessed."

"I'd almost be willing to take it into court, even knowing we couldn't win, just to shake Brian up a mite. He's changed, Stonewall. The war changed him. He was always a little arrogant and conceited, but now he's downright cruel. Not only did he drive Kevin and his family from me, but he's set and determined to get rich by stripping the land of everything. I hate to speak so of my own flesh and blood, but it's the Lord's truth."

"A public trial could get nasty, my dear Nora. It's almost an axiom that a trial involving members of the same family invariably airs dirty linen that otherwise would never see the light of day."

Nora gave a start and peered at him sharply. "What

do you mean by that? What dirty linen? Have you heard something?"

Stony spread his hands. "No, no. I'm only—" His gaze grew intent. "Why? Is there some secret you don't wish to come out?"

"I—" She broke off, her glance sliding away.

He sensed that she was about to confide some dark secret. He said quickly, "Nora, I don't want to hear about it. Whatever it is, keep it to yourself. But if there *is* something, don't get involved in a trial, especially since the likelihood of winning is infinitesimal."

"Yes." Her sudden smile was tinged with melancholy. "You're right, Stonewall. What's done is done, and I reckon I'll have to live with it, as galling as it may be."

And it was left at that, but Stony continued his visits. Nora was aging now, yet her tart wit was still sharp, and her mind was keen as ever. He enjoyed talking with her, and he knew that she was lonely. Oh, she had women friends, and she was still actively engaged with her dramatic productions in the red schoolhouse Sean had built for her so many years before. Her theater productions, many of which she wrote herself, were always well attended, even if often shocking and controversial to her conservative Baptist neighbors. But she had once confided in Stony that she missed men around her, that she had always liked men better than women, anyway, and he knew that her rare meetings with Brian usually ended on an acrimonious note.

It was a warm day when he rode up before the house. Nora was rocking on the front porch. Oddly he felt a pull of disappointment to find her alone. Had Debra Lee cut her visit short?

Stony waved, then dismounted, tied his horse to the rail, and went up the steps.

"She's still here, Stonewall," Nora said dryly. "My granddaughter is out riding somewhere."

"How are you, Nora?" he said, laughing. "Now how do you know that I didn't come out here just to visit with you?"

"Knowing how our word of mouth telegraph works, I

figured the news of Debra Lee's visit had reached Nacogdoches by this time, and you have an itch of curiosity as active as any woman's, Stonewall."

He eased down into the rocker beside her. "Yep, I heard the news. How is Debra Lee, Nora?"

"She's fine and dandy, far as I can tell. Turned into a little beauty, has Debra Lee."

"How long is she staying?"

Nora shrugged thin shoulders. "We haven't spoke much on that subject. She's welcome for as long as she wishes, of course. A young person's laughter, especially that of my own blood, sounds fine in this lonely old house." Her gaze rested on his face. "She asked about you, right off."

"Did she?" he said with forced casualness. "It's a wonder she remembers me at all."

"Now that's the truth, isn't it? I reckon you must have made a good impression on that old girl." She raised her voice. "Maria! Come out here!" Nora cocked her head at him. "A glass of cold lemonade? Or maybe something stronger? Or"—a smile tugged at the corners of her mouth—"maybe you'd like to ride out and look for Debra Lee?"

He hesitated, tempted. "No, I think not. The ride from Nacogdoches is enough for one day. Anyway, I wouldn't know where to find her."

Debra was enjoying herself thoroughly. During her early years on Moraghan Acres, there had always been riding horses available; but down in the valley, there had been only the mule. And who, she thought, could enjoy riding a mule?

The two horses left on the place were no longer young, but they were slick and sassy, and one, a small bay mare, was frisky and still liked to run.

Debra had ridden every day since her arrival. For the first few days, she had confined herself to her grandmother's ten acres, then extended her range to Brian's acreage, always with an eye out for her uncle—she had no wish to encounter him.

47

She was appalled at the destruction he had wrought to the once lush valley. The fields lay fallow, weed-choked, most fences down. But even worse was the wanton destruction of the timber. She saw few trees larger than saplings, and nothing had been replanted to replace those cut down. The only signs of activity were the fat cows grazing the unplowed fields. She could not understand how her uncle could deliberately bring about such utter waste. It was all she could do to keep from thundering over to his house and confronting him.

It was for that reason that she chose a different route. She rode along the river, guiding the mare in and out of the pecan trees along the bank. Before too long she was off Moraghan property entirely, and when the growth along the riverbank grew too thick to ride without injuring the mare, Debra reined her up the gentle bank and onto the dusty wagon track meandering alongside the river.

The mare was sweating freely now. Debra slowed the animal to a walk and rode along in drowsy contentment. It was a lovely day, and she was glad she had come to Moraghan. How different it was here from the Rio Grande Valley!

She came to with a start as the mare shied, snorting. A man sat his horse astride the lane, blocking her way. The sun was directly behind him, forming a golden haze as it filtered through the trees, and Debra couldn't see the man's features. She did notice that he was a big man, dressed all in black, and his mount was a great black stallion. There was an air of menace about the mounted figure, and Debra experienced a chill of dread.

"Well now, I'd just bet my best pair of boots that you'd be the little Moraghan gal I heard just came back to these parts," he said in a sneering voice.

Debra managed to knee the mare off the lane a little, and she could finally focus on the man, without the sun in her eyes.

He was indeed a big man, around thirty, but already he had a big belly that drooped over the saddle horn as he slumped in the saddle. The black, flat planter's hat shadowed his face, yet she could see the big nose, crisscrossed with purplish, broken veins, and small, muddy-brown eyes. His mouth was small, thin-lipped, and it was pursed as if he were about to whistle. Despite the warmth of the day, he wore a long duster, with a vest underneath, and a string tie. As he shifted his bulk in the saddle, the tails of the duster whipped back, and Debra glimpsed a cartridged gunbelt and a holstered pistol on his hip.

Muddy brown eyes. . . . The phrase tickled an uneasy memory.

"I got it right, ain't I?" he said in that same unpleasant voice. "You're a Moraghan?"

She sat up straighter. "Yes, I'm Debra Moraghan. But I'm afraid I don't know you, sir."

"Oh, we ain't met, but I'm certain you'll recognize the name. I'm Tod Danker."

"Danker?" A name to strike terror in Moraghan hearts. "Are you related to Sonny Danker?"

"Yup, he was my daddy." He smiled now, coldly.

"He killed my grandfather and left Daddy with a limp he'll have all his life!"

"And your daddy killed mine. That ain't something I'm likely ever to forget, missy."

"Well, that's all ancient history."

"Not for me, it ain't. We Dankers never forget. My daddy taught me that."

For a long moment their glances locked, and Debra stifled her mounting fear as she realized just how vulnerable she was, out here alone with this man. She doubted that there was anyone within hearing distance, should she call for help.

As though sensing her fear, Tod Danker grinned, then pursed his lips in that rather womanish mannerism. "Well, Miss Moraghan, should you be needing my services, please feel free to call on me."

"Now why on earth should I ever need your services?" she said in astonishment.

"Why, because I'm a servant of the people in this here county." Danker folded the duster back, and Debra saw the star glinting on his vest. "Duly elected sheriff of Nacogdoches County."

"A Danker, elected sheriff!" Debra exclaimed. "I could hardly believe what I was hearing! How could that have come about, Mr. Lieberman?"

Nora gave a humorless laugh, and Stony Lieberman grimaced as he set his glass down. He said, "Well, he ran for the office, and his opponent was a nobody. Danker was elected by only a couple of hundred votes, but he *was* elected."

"But how could people vote for him? His father was a professional gunfighter, a killer, and his grandmother.... Everybody knows what she was!"

Stony said, "Tod Danker is almost as good with guns as his father was. He'd killed a couple of men before he became sheriff. One killing probably helped him get elected. It was a troublemaker in town—"

"You see, that's just what I mean!" Debra interrupted. "This one's cut from the same cloth as his daddy."

"Yes, Debra Lee, I know what you mean," Nora said. "And I agree wholeheartedly. I hated to see a Danker elected sheriff, and I'll never understand it."

"It's a holdover from the frontier days," Stony said reflectively, "although those days are mostly gone around here. But they still exist in other parts. Dodge City, for instance. You see, when violence is an everyday occurrence, people have to fight fire with fire, to use a cliché. At least that is how the thinking goes. So, they hire a badman, a professional killer, to keep the peace. And it works, by and large. Look at Dodge City. Some of the marshals there you wouldn't want for your next-door neighbors. Yet they manage to keep the lid on. The same philosophy still holds around here. Tod Danker is not a man you'd want for a close friend, yet he keeps things under control in the county."

"*What* things under control?" Debra said scornfully. "I'll wager that he's had little more to do than ride that big black horse around, the gun thumping on his hip."

"That's largely true," Stony said with a laugh. "There

hasn't been any outright violence in these parts since the Shelby County war, but we're still a violent people. It's there, under the surface. Don't misconstrue my meaning, Miss Moraghan. I'm not saying that I hold with a Danker for sheriff, but I can understand the reasoning behind his being elected. Knowing of what happened between your father and Sonny Danker, I can also understand your feelings on the matter."

"I gather from what Tod Danker said, Grandmother, that the feud isn't dead. Not so far as he's concerned, anyway. He probably can do you harm, with him being sheriff. Has he done anything to you?"

"What can he do to an old lady, child?" Nora said with a wry smile. "And if he's caused Brian any trouble, Brian hasn't mentioned it. Anyway, Stonewall here, when he's elected judge of this county, will see to it that the sheriff causes us no trouble."

"You're a little premature, Nora," Stony said uncomfortably. "I haven't made up my mind to run yet, and when I do run, *if* I do, I have to get elected."

"Oh, you'll win, Stonewall, never fear."

Debra said, "Grandmother's right, Mr. Lieberman. I'm sure you'll have no trouble winning."

A brief silence fell. Nora had a vague look on her face, as though she were dreaming of the past, and Stony gazed down into his drink. Debra felt suddenly shy, remembering all too vividly her thoughts about this man. When she had ridden back to the house following her encounter with Tod Danker, she had been too indignant to more than merely acknowledge Stony's presence, but now she was acutely aware of it. He was just as attractive and compelling as she remembered, and she was strongly drawn to him.

The feeling her mother had dismissed as a childish fantasy was as strong as ever, and Debra was truly glad that she had come back to Moraghan.

Stony said, "How long are you staying, Debra Lee?"

"Please, Debra. I detest Debra Lee."

"All right, Debra." His dark eyes suddenly danced with mirth. "If, in exchange, you'll call me Stony, instead of Mr. Lieberman."

51

"Won't it sound a touch strange, calling an august judge Stony?" she asked gravely.

"Does that mean you'll be staying that long? The election is over a year away."

Her gaze never left his face. "How long I'll be staying will depend . . . on a number of things."

Six

Tod Danker was in an unusually thoughtful mood after his chance encounter with Debra Moraghan. His feelings were mixed. On the one hand, he was gloating over the terror he had seen leap into her eyes, pleased that the Danker name could still arouse fear in a Moraghan. The few times he had met Brian Moraghan, even after being elected sheriff, the arrogant bastard had looked through him as though he didn't exist. He wrenched his thoughts away from Brian Moraghan—that bastard's time was coming!

Debra Moraghan was a pretty little thing, and his lust had stirred, made even stronger by the fear she had shown. Tod liked his women to fear him; it added spice to any coupling.

On the other hand, meeting a Moraghan face to face had brought the ancient enmity raging to the surface, setting up such a hatred in him that it had taken all his self-control to keep a rein on it. This was a purely visceral emotion, he knew; bitter feuds between families were out of date nowadays. Yet a Moraghan had killed his uncles, and another one had killed his father.

There had to be some way he could get back at the Moraghans. He had power and authority now, as sheriff of Nacogdoches County, more power than he had ever dreamed of. How his daddy would have chortled at a Danker being elected sheriff, he thought.

No one could have been more surprised than Tod himself. When he had been approached by certain people in the county with the proposal that he stand for election, his first inclination had been to hoot with laughter. But when the same people also offered to finance his campaign and seemed really convinced that he could win, he figured that he had little to lose. The campaign fund was large enough so that he could easily siphon off some bucks for himself. And with the office went a fine house in Nacogdoches, far finer than any house a Danker had ever inhabited.

Tod was willing to grant that luck played a part in his getting elected. A local malcontent, crazy drunk, had killed a man outside a saloon in Nacogdoches. Tod had happened to be passing by, and seizing his chance, he stepped in to subdue the man and eventually had to shoot him dead. That little incident had assured his election. Now, the very same people who proposed his election came around once in a while for small favors, nothing big and nothing anyone was likely to notice, but for each favor given, Tod was slipped a little something on the side.

Yes sir, he was living high off the hog these days, and it likely would be foolish to risk it all by trying to get in a few licks against the Moraghans. However, he knew that he would, if the chance presented itself. It was in his blood, he had been born with it, a heritage coming down from Ma Danker like a sickness passed down to each generation. He would have to be sharp about it, that was all.

It was long after dark when he rode into Nacogdoches, cantering along under the great oaks to that fine, two-story house that was his for as long as he was sheriff.

All of a sudden, he remembered something that his daddy had once told him. For the first few years of his life, Tod rarely had seen Sonny Danker. But when his daddy learned that his oldest son had a natural aptitude for handling a gun, the two had grown closer together, and Tod had been made privy to the details of the Danker-Moraghan feud. Sonny had told his son about Sean Moraghan driving the Danker clan off property that should have been theirs, through squatter's rights; after all, they had been there first.

And then Sonny had told his son about that long-ago day when they had gone to the Moraghan house when Sean was off to war. They had staked Nora Moraghan out in the yard, like the Indians used to do to their victims, and Lem and Jed had taken their turn at her, urged on by Ma. Sonny had begged for his turn, but Ma had refused him. But Sonny had remembered every detail, vividly, and had told it to his son, and it had come alive in Tod's mind. And that very night his daddy had taken the boy to his first whore.

Now, riding his horse down alongside the house and to the barn in back, Tod's thoughts moved to the Moraghan girl. How enjoyable it would be to throw her down onto the ground, push her skirts up around her waist, and do to her what his uncles had done to that high-and-mighty grandmother of hers! That would be a fitting way to get back at the Moraghan clan!

Oh, she'd fight, no doubt in his mind about that. She had gumption, he'd seen that in her eyes. But that was just fine, he'd like that. Rap her across the skull a few times with his Colt and she'd quiet down soon enough.

Unsaddling his mount, Tod began to hurry as he felt his groin swell and begin to itch. It was late enough so that he hoped the four kids would be bedded down, for what he had in mind would occupy Sue Anne for a spell. Nowadays, he usually went to some of the shacks on the other side of town for his bit of fun. The nigger gals over there never complained when he whacked them around for a little before he got into the saddle. Who could they complain to? He was the by God sheriff and they didn't dare say him nay!

But it was a half hour's ride over there, Tod thought, and he didn't like to dally when his tallywhacker clamored for attention.

Mouth pursed, he pounded up the steps to the back door and pushed open the screen door to the kitchen.

Sue Anne, having heard him ride up, was just coming into the room.

Always a big woman, bearing four kids in six years had put twenty extra pounds on her large-boned body and left it sagging and bulging in all the wrong places. This was one thing that had driven Tod across town to the nigger gals, but Sue Anne had the same thing between her legs as any other woman, and in his mood his tallywhacker wasn't all that particular.

Her pale blue eyes were dull as she welcomed him. "I didn't know what time you'd drag home, Tod. Supper's warming on the stove. . . ."

"My belly doesn't need attention right now. Something else does. The kids bedded down?"

"For some time . . ." Her eyes widened, and she backed up a step. Coming toward her, Tod was already unbuttoning his trousers. "What in God's name do you think you're doing?"

"What does it look like? You know what I want, old woman."

"But it's hardly dark. It's indecent!"

"So what if it is indecent? That's never bothered you before. Remember the night we moved in here, into this house? We did it right here on the kitchen floor. That night, you couldn't get enough."

"But the children, they're just upstairs! That night, they were staying at my sister's."

He had reached her now, and he dropped a heavy hand onto her shoulder. "I'm not worried about the kids right now. Lay down, woman."

She resisted his push. "We can at least go upstairs!"

"I don't want to wait. Here, right here." He whacked her hard across the mouth with the back of his hand. Blood spurted from her lip where his knuckles had split it.

A spark ignited in her eyes. Sue Anne liked to be whomped on; that was one reason he'd married her. He hit her again, lighter this time. Gasping, she reached with eager hands for his trousers. Undoing them, she sank to the floor, pulling his breeches down around his ankles. She sprawled full-length on her back, hiking her skirts up around her waist.

His gaze fastened on the abundant thicket of dark pubic hair. Then Tod dropped to his knees and grunting, entered her.

They rode along the riverbank, horses speckled with splashes of sunlight coming through the trees. Debra turned a bright smile on Stony.

"I'll race you!"

Without waiting for a response, she kneed the little mare up the slight incline to the road. Drumming her heels into the animal's flanks, she sent her flying. The mare loved to run, and she was in a full gallop within a few yards. In a few moments Debra heard hooves thundering behind her. Hair loose and flying, she turned her head and saw Stony's big chestnut coming all out. Dust boiled up behind them like a storm cloud.

Very quickly he overtook her, the chestnut surging into the lead. One of the many things Debra liked about Stonewall Lieberman was his sense of competitiveness. Many men, she well knew, would have let her win. Not Stony. If she couldn't compete, don't challenge him. He hadn't said that in so many words, but this was the third week he had come out to Moraghan for Sunday supper with Debra and her grandmother, and Debra thought she was getting to know him pretty well.

She liked what she had learned, and she knew for certain that the love that had started when she was eleven wasn't false. But one thing did puzzle her. Was he courting her? If he was, who could tell? The Sunday afternoon rides had become a habit and were the only times they were really alone together, yet he had not once done anything by word or gesture to give her reason to hope. She had no way to fathom what he felt toward her. It was frustrating, and she had even been wondering if she should be so brazen as to poke at him about it.

She knew that her folks would be scandalized at her even thinking such a thing. A young woman of twenty simply did *not* take the initiative!

Yet, Grandmother Nora would not be all that shocked, Debra knew. During the month that she had been there, Debra had learned a great deal about her grandmother. Nora had reminisced about the past, and one of the things she had told Debra had been about meeting Sean Moraghan back in Tennessee. "His name wasn't Moraghan then, of course. Oh . . . I already told you that. Getting forgetful, I am."

Nora went on to tell her that it had, finally, been she who had pushed the issue, leading Sean into proposing marriage. She had never regretted it. So, if it had worked for her grandmother, Debra thought, why couldn't it work for her?

Ahead now, Stony reined in his horse and waited for her, laughing in open delight.

Debra pulled up beside him. "You wouldn't beat me so easily, Mr. Lieberman, if this mare was younger. You've got several years on me."

"I know." He sobered. "Quite a few, in fact."

He wasn't thinking about horses, she realized, and she experienced a surge of elation. He *had* thought about her then!

Carefully concealing her feelings, she slid down off the mare. Letting the reins fall to the ground, she gestured. "Let's walk down by the river."

Stony dismounted. Leaving the two animals grazing on the sparse grass, they strolled down to the sluggishly flowing river. They stood side by side on the bank, a sudden restraint between them.

"About what you said, Stony." Shyly, she touched his hand. "You know what they say about fine wine."

"Wine, yes, but that hardly follows with people, no matter what they say." He glanced down into her eyes from his greater height. His dark eyes seemed shadowed, yet a spark had begun to glow deep within them. "I'm thirty-five, Debra."

"Good heavens, you're practically in your dotage," she said mockingly. "Will I have to help you back onto your horse? . . ."

Her voice died, as their hands inadvertently touched again. Heat flowed from his flesh into hers. His eyes

58

had never left her, and they seemed to grow larger, and she was drowning in them. A feeling of faintness crept over her, and she leaned against him for support. A groan came from deep in his throat. His hand closed around hers almost painfully, and then she was in his arms. His mouth was hard, and then soft, incredibly soft, and she was drowning in the sweet fire of the kiss.

Debra had been kissed a few times by other men, usually a timid peck, or, worse, a greedy, wet, demanding kiss that disgusted her. This was different. Godalmighty, was it different! And no man had ever dared touch her as he was now doing, his hand cupping her breast through the thinness of her shirtwaist. His hand squeezed gently, his thumb rolling across the sudden swelling of her nipple. She yearned toward him, abruptly seized by an ache of wanting that began in the center of her being and swept over her like a fever.

It was a feeling that she had never experienced before but had, sometimes, dreamed about. It set up a trembling in her, and she muttered against his mouth, "Oh, Stony! My darling, how I've longed for this to happen!"

He took his arms from around her and stepped back so abruptly that Debra swayed, almost falling. Stony muttered, "Not right! Not right at all!" He turned away, moving off a few steps.

What was wrong with the man? she thought in exasperation. What was not right about it? Could it be that he was involved with another woman? The thought sent an arrow of pain to her heart.

The question was on her lips, but she swallowed the words. It would be rash to be too greedy at the moment. This was the first time he had taken her into his arms, the first kiss, and she knew from his reaction that he was certainly attracted to her. She decided to be satisfied with that for the time being.

She moved up alongside him, said musingly, "My little brother and I used to swim along here. Several times"—an involuntary giggle escaped her—"we went in without our clothes on." She said artlessly, "Did you ever go swimming without your clothes, Stony?"

He jumped, then moved another step away, as though

fearful she might touch him. Then he laughed, a soft chuckle. "Doesn't everybody?"

"With your sister?"

"No, Debra. I didn't have a sister," he said distantly. "I was an only child. In fact, I didn't swim when I was a boy, naked or otherwise. There were no rivers where I grew up. My father was a tailor in Brooklyn."

"But I've read about New York rivers. What are they called? The Hudson, the East River?"

"Oh, yes, there are rivers, and boys that I knew regularly swam there in summer. But from where we lived, it was a long hike and I. . . . Well, my father had to struggle to make a living for us, and I worked, in his shop, after school."

As he talked Stony's face took on a faraway look, and Debra watched him closely, fascinated, being very careful not to break his stream of reminiscences. This was the first time he had talked of his past, and now she was beginning to understand his reticence. Clearly, many of his memories were not particularly pleasant.

"After I got out of public school, Poppa was adamant about my going to college. Not that he cared much about what I became, just so long as I went into some profession so I could escape the poverty that he had known all his life."

"Then it was your decision to become a lawyer?"

"Yes. Law always appealed to me. The logic of it and"—a half-smile touched his face—"the illogic of it. But even in its worst moments, our system of law is the best so far devised by man, in my opinion. Justice does not always triumph, yet it never fails to thrill me when, through my own efforts, I can triumph."

"One thing I'm curious about . . . your name. Isn't Stonewall a rather unusual name for a Jewish man?"

He laughed. "I agree, it is. My father abhorred violence. He was a gentle man. When I did something wrong, he was more inclined to retire into a hurt silence than to punish me. Yet he harbored an admiration for military men. Why, I have never understood, unless it gave him an opportunity to live a more violent life vicariously. In any event, he was well read about mili-

60

tary men, and one of his favorites was Stonewall Jackson. Hence, Stonewall."

He fell silent again, staring into the shadows of the trees across the river.

Debra said softly, "Your folks . . . are they dead now?"

He nodded. "Yes. My mother died early on, but Poppa at least lived to see me officially an attorney, opening an office in Brooklyn. He died soon after. In a way, it might have been better that way." His mouth had a wry twist.

"Why is that?"

"For the first two years that I practiced law in Brooklyn, I damned near starved to death. That is why I knew I had to get out. After he died, I drifted across the country, always south and west. When I came to Nacogdoches and discovered that there was a paucity of lawyers there, I hung up my shingle, and there I still am."

"Stony, why have you never married?"

He stiffened, his face darkening. "You know, Debra Lee," he said severely, "you can sometimes be a rather forward young lady. Why should my being married or unmarried be any concern of yours?"

Sensing that she had indeed gone too far, Debra said hastily, "It's just that men around these parts unmarried at your age are . . . well, rather unusual, you must admit."

"I'll admit no such thing. Anyway, it's strictly my affair and none of yours, Miss Moraghan."

Her temper flared. "Godalmighty, you're thorny! Excuse me, Mr. Lieberman! If I'd known you were so touchy about it, I wouldn't have asked."

"So now you know."

She spun away, started up the bank. "We'd better be getting back, supper will be ready soon."

She mounted the mare and started up the road without waiting for him. Stony sent the chestnut galloping after her. As he ranged alongside, he said, "For all you know, I may have asked a dozen women to marry me. Did it ever occur to you that no woman would have me?" He tugged at his nose, a touch of laughter in his voice.

When they drew up before the house, Nora was in the rocker on the porch, a tablet and quill pen in her lap. As they mounted the steps, she frowned at them. "It's about time the pair of you got back. Maria's been grumbling for a half hour. Supper is ready and waiting."

"Sorry, Nora, we dallied longer than we should have." Stony slanted a suddenly merry look at Debra. "The thing is, your granddaughter here insisted we have a swim in the river. Without clothes, you understand."

"What? My God, that's—that's—" Nora sat up, at a loss for words.

"Shocking?" he said helpfully. "Is that the word you're looking for? I agree, but Miss Moraghan has a mind of her own."

Debra felt her face grow hot. "It's not true, Grandmother, he's fibbing to you!"

"Sorry, Nora. Just joshing," he said without any indication of contrition in his voice. "But you'll have to admit"—again he slanted a look at Debra—"that you insisted on it."

"I did not! I just mentioned that Michael and I used to. . . . Damn you, Stonewall Lieberman, you're a terrible man!" She struck at his arm with her fist. Laughing, Stony easily caught her fist and held it.

"All right, children," Nora said tolerantly. "I should think you're both a little long in the tooth for such horseplay." She held up the tablet she had been writing on. "Debra Lee, I'm writing a letter to your folks. Anything you'd like me to pass along to them? Or maybe," she added hopefully, "you'd like to include a message of your own?"

Although her heart was singing—he wasn't really upset with her!—Debra put on a sober face. "I'll write something, Grandmother. I feel guilty about not writing for all this time."

Kate was waiting on the veranda when Kevin rode the mule into the yard. She forced patience on herself until he had dismounted and limped toward her. He had gone into Brownsville for the mail, and her heart thudded with hope. They had waited so long for a letter from Debra Lee.

"Well?" she demanded.

He waved the envelopes in his hand. "There's a letter here from Momma."

"How about Debra Lee?"

"No, Kate. I'm sorry. Here, you read Momma's letter." He held it out to her. "I'm afraid to."

Kate quickly opened the letter, then her face bloomed in a smile of delight. "There *is* something from Debra Lee! Along with your mother's letter."

"Well, read it!"

Kate's gaze had already raced down the half-page letter. Now she began to read:

"Dear Mother and Daddy,

I know I should have written sooner. Please forgive me, but I've been trying to get my thoughts in order. Besides, I'm not sure you'll even want to hear from me.

Anyway, your wayward daughter is fine. Grandmother Nora may have already told you in her other letter, but the reason I was a month getting to Grandmother's is because I ran out of money in Corpus Christi, and I waited tables in an eating place for a month. Can you imagine your daughter working at a job? I did fine too, if I do say so myself!

Things are not going too well here. Oh, Grandmother is in good health, considering her age. She has grown old since I was last here. But she and Uncle Brian are not getting along at all well. He has changed, Daddy. He's become greedy and grasping, and he has gotten fat. I used to look up to him, when I was little, but no more.

I know you do not like to hear this, Daddy, but you should have stayed and fought for your share of Moraghan. Uncle Brian is a spoiler. He spoils everything he touches. Moraghan will be ruined forever by the time he is finished with it. All he thinks about is money. I hate him!

I will close now, with a promise to write more often. I cannot tell you how long I will remain here, because I do not know myself. I love you, Mother, and you too, Daddy. If I hurt you by running off, I am deeply sorry.

Give my love to Michael and Lena.

Your wayward daughter,
Debra."

"At least she's all right." Kevin heaved a sigh of relief. He was smiling. "I see she still insists on calling herself Debra."

Kate merely nodded, now reading Nora's letter. In a moment she said, "Listen to this. 'Debra Lee is seeing quite a bit of Stonewall Lieberman. They are together at least once a week. They go riding together, then have Sunday supper with me. Just how far Debra Lee's courtship has progressed, I do not know. I call it her courtship since it seems plain now that she came up here bound and determined to snare the poor man! In point of fact, I hope she does. Stonewall is my best friend, and I must say that I fell in love all over again with Debra Lee. The pair of you have done a fine job raising her. Do not think too harshly of her for running away. It will all be to the good in the end, I am sure.'"

Kevin shook his head. "Poor man indeed! I feel sorry for the fellow. Our Debra Lee does have a way of getting what she wants." He turned serious. "But you know, Kate, maybe Momma's right. It just might be a good thing, if Debra Lee marries this Lieberman fellow."

"But Stonewall's at least fifteen years older."

"In years, perhaps." Kevin was smiling as he came to her, wrapping his arms around her. "But in all other respects, I doubt there's that much difference in their ages. All we can do, dear Kate, is hope for the best."

Seven

The courthouse drowsed under its shade. A norther early in the week had cooled the weather considerably, and leaves were just beginning to turn as Debra tied her horse at the hitching post in front of the courthouse and went up the walk. She had stopped off at Stony's tiny office, and a hand-lettered sign over the door had announced simply: In Court Today.

The interior of the courthouse was as somnolent as the outside. She had no idea what courtroom Stony might be in at the moment, but she didn't want to inquire, so she poked her head into three courtrooms before she located him. He was examining a witness, and Debra slipped in quietly and onto one of the hard benches in the back. There were only about a dozen spectators; most of them were ancient, and about half were dozing. She had been told by Stony that many oldsters watched trials just to pass the time.

"Mostly they sleep," he said, a twinkle in his eye. "Unless it's an important trial, and there aren't that many. Even then, if I'm handling the defense, they sleep through most of it. I'm not what you'd call an inspired crowd-pleaser. I plod along like a plowhorse, winning, when I do win, by sheer persistence and by conviction that my client is innocent as a babe."

Debra didn't believe him for a moment. She was familiar with his professional reputation by now, and she was also aware of his habit of deprecating his ability. She had not warned him of her coming today, thinking that she might surprise him.

Debra noticed that there was one woman in the courtroom, sitting off by herself. About all Debra could see of her was a large, wide-brimmed hat, decorated with an enormous feather.

Debra leaned forward as Stony turned away from the witness and crossed to the defense table. His glance swept the courtroom, but he gave no indication of being aware of her presence—he was capable of total concentration, excluding everything but the matter at hand. Resisting an impish impulse to flap a hand at him, she scrunched down a little in her seat.

Stony picked up a scrap of paper from the table, studied it for a long moment, then returned to the witness—an angry-looking man wearing rumpled clothes and holding a greasy hat in his lap, which he kept turning between big-knuckled hands, warping it out of shape.

Debra's glance went to the small man in the other chair at the defense table. He was a scrawny, furtive-looking individual, as jumpy as a flea, and it struck Debra that he looked capable of almost any crime. Certainly he did not look as innocent as a babe!

"Now, Mr. Welkes," Stony said, "I have here in my hand a bill of sale, stating in no uncertain terms that the horse in question was sold to my client in good faith, for the sum of fifty dollars. At the bottom is a signature, the name of Bob Welkes. That *is* your name, is it not?"

"You know that's my name," the witness said sullenly.

"Well then, I show you this bill of sale. Is that your signature, Mr. Welkes?"

Welkes squirmed. "No, it ain't."

"It's a forgery then, is that what you're telling this court?"

"I don't know about forgery. All I know is I didn't sign that slip of paper!"

"Do you know what perjury is, Mr. Welkes?" Stony

bounced the edge of the paper against his palm. "You swore an oath, sir, when you took the witness stand, an oath to tell the truth. Perjury is a crime, sir. Are you aware of that?"

"If you mean, am I lying, no, I'm not!"

"I see." Stony cocked his head, gave the witness a quizzical glance. "Are you acquainted with a woman by the name of Greta Heinrich, Mr. Welkes?"

Before the witness could respond, the prosecuting attorney popped up. "Your Honor, I object! Whether or not the witness knows this Greta Heinrich, whoever she is, has no bearing on these proceedings."

The judge, seated at a desk instead of an elevated bench, aroused from what seemed to Debra to be a short nap and stared at Stony. "Mr. Lieberman, does this have relevance?"

"It does, Your Honor, it most certainly does."

"Very well, Mr. Lieberman, you may proceed." The judge rapped the desk with his knuckles. "Objection overruled."

"Mr. Welkes, I ask you again. Do you know one Greta Heinrich?"

"I know the widow, yeah."

"The widow?" Stony's eyebrows arched. "Your use of that term implies that you know Mrs. Heinrich rather—intimately, shall we say?"

"Don't know what you mean by that."

"Well then, suppose you tell this court just how well you do know Mrs. Heinrich."

"I know her."

"That is not good enough, Mr. Welkes! Have you been inside her house? Have you broken bread with her? Have you escorted the lady to social affairs?"

"Yes!"

"Yes what, Mr. Welkes?"

"Yes to all them things!" the witness snarled.

"Then let me ask you this, have you been, to put it delicately as possible, romantically involved with her?"

"Your Honor!" The prosecutor was up again. "This is intolerable! Mr. Lieberman has failed to establish any connection whatsoever between the theft of the horse in question, this woman he has suddenly injected into these proceedings, and this witness!"

Debra noticed that the few spectators had suddenly sat up and taken notice when the name of Greta Heinrich had been mentioned. A few snickers were heard now. The judge glowered out at the spectators, and they fell quiet.

Stony was speaking, "Your Honor, I will establish the connection to the court's satisfaction, if I may now call the next defense witness, and I reserve the right to recall Mr. Welkes to the stand for further cross-examination."

The judge peered at him. "Your next witness is present in the courtroom?"

"Yes, Your Honor."

"Very well, Mr. Lieberman." He rapped the desk with his knuckles. "The witness may step down, subject to recall. Do not leave this courtroom, Mr. Welkes."

Stony faced around. "Defense calls Mrs. Greta Heinrich to the stand."

The lone woman got to her feet and made her way to the front, the focus of all eyes. She was rather buxom and wore a tight-fitting dress of lurid velvet. The feather atop her head bobbed like a bird in erratic flight.

She was sworn in, responding to the court clerk's bored questions in a husky voice. She sat down in the chair, arranging her long skirts decorously around her feet. Her plump, pretty face was powdered and rouged.

Stony said, "Will you state your name, please?"

Before she could respond, the judge said irritably, "Madam, will you please remove that confounded hat?"

"Oops, sorry, judge." Greta removed the hat, flashed a bright smile at the judge.

Stony pulled at his nose, hiding his smile. "Now, state your name, please, for the record."

Greta tossed her hair—long, to her shoulders, black as tar, except for a dramatic streak of white extending back from her wide forehead. "I'm Greta Heinrich."

"You are married, Mrs. Heinrich?"

"Was. I'm a widow." She assumed a pious expression. "Poor Carl passed on, five years back."

"I see. And what do you do for a livelihood, Mrs. Heinrich?"

"I take in washing, clean house for the rich." She tossed her head. "Not many ways a widow woman can earn a living."

"I'm sure," Stony said dryly. "How do you get to the houses you clean, Mrs. Heinrich?"

"Walk, up until a month ago." She flashed a dimpled smile at the defense table.

"And what happened a month ago?"

"I got myself a horse and buggy. It was given to me by—"

"Just a moment, please." Stony held up a hand. "Before we get to that, do you know the defendant in this case?"

"You mean Jonesy? Sure, I know him."

"Is he in this courtroom?"

"Certainly is."

"Would you point him out to the court, please?"

Greta leveled a forefinger. "That's him right there, at that table."

"Indicating Clem Jones, the defendant. Am I correct?"

"That's him."

"Now, Mrs. Heinrich, you are also familiar with Robert Welkes?"

"Bob? Sure, I know Bob Welkes."

"He is the man who just vacated the witness stand?"

Greta giggled. "That's him, yeah."

"How well do you know Mr. Welkes?"

"Pretty well." She lowered her eyes demurely.

"Just how well? Were you ever intimate with him?"

The prosecutor roared, "Your Honor!"

"Mr. Lieberman, is this line of questioning germane?"

"It is, Your Honor, very much so, and I will so prove, if allowed to continue."

"Very well, Mr. Lieberman. Objection overruled." The judge sighed. "You may continue."

Stony faced the witness squarely. "Now, Mrs. Heinrich, my next question may be somewhat embarrassing for you, and I apologize for that, but it cannot be helped. Have you ever known Mr. Welkes in the Biblical sense?"

She looked at him intently, said gravely, "Do you mean, have I bedded him?"

Stony cleared his throat. "That is what I mean, yes."

"Yes, sir, I bedded him, regularly for some time."

"You speak in the past tense, Mrs. Heinrich. May we take that to mean that you are no longer—uh, intimate with Mr. Welkes?"

"You may," she said, grinning.

"Would you please tell the court what, if anything, happened to end the relationship?"

"Jonesy, that's what happened. Jonesy came along."

"You are speaking of Clem Jones, the accused?"

"That's the fellow. Jonesy ain't stingy. Bob Welkes now, it pained him to even take a girl out to supper."

"In essence, what you are saying is, that Clem Jones took Bob Welkes's place in your affections?"

"That's what I'm saying, yep."

"And Mr. Welkes, how did he take to this?"

"He didn't take to it at all. He stomped around, threatening me and Jonesy. He couldn't understand, he said, why I'd take to a little fellow like Jonesy. And I told him that Jonesy might be little in some ways, but not in all departments. No, sirree!" She laughed, and the spectators laughed with her.

The judge rapped the desk severely with his knuckles. "Order in the courtroom! If you do not cease this disturbance at once, I shall order the courtroom cleared!"

The courtroom quieted immediately. Debra shot a glance at the table where the young prosecutor sat, with Bob Welkes alongside him. Welkes was red in the face, and his hands were clenching and unclenching, as if he wished Greta's neck were between his hands.

"Now, Mrs. Heinrich, going back a little. You started to discuss your various jobs, stating that you walked to the houses you cleaned until recently. What happened to change that, if indeed such a change took place?"

"I got a horse and buggy, that's what happened," she said proudly.

"And just how did you come about this horse and buggy?"

"Jonesy gave them to me, for my birthday. Jonesy is a real generous fellow!"

"The horse that you now have—is it a roan, with a white spot roughly in the shape of a star, between the eyes. A horse called Star?"

She was nodding eagerly. "Yeah, that's the one!"

"The accused gave you this horse for a present. Do you have any personal knowledge as to where he might have acquired this horse?"

"Why, he bought it from Bob Welkes, paid him—"

The prosecutor said wearily, "Hearsay, Your Honor. The witness cannot know this of her own knowledge, not having witnessed this so-called transaction."

"I withdraw the question, Your Honor." To Greta, Stony said, "You may step down, Mrs. Heinrich."

"Just a minute now!" The prosecutor shot to his feet. "I wish to cross-examine this witness! I have a great many questions for her, you may be sure of that!"

"Your Honor," Stony said, "I move for a dismissal of the charge against my client at this time."

"On what grounds, Mr. Lieberman?"

"On the grounds that the prosecution has failed to prove a case against the accused. If I may have a few moments to speak freely, Your Honor, since we dispensed with the jury and the verdict rests with you?"

The judge leaned back. "Proceed, Mr. Lieberman."

"What happened here is glaringly obvious. We have the classic case of a romantic triangle. A spurned lover, thwarted in his passion, spitefully tries to get back at his rival. There is a bill of sale, which even the prosecution cannot deny, showing that the animal in question was bought and paid for.

"Mr. Welkes denies that the signature on the bill of sale is his, claiming that the horse was stolen by the accused. Yet this witness just testified that the horse *was* sold to Clem Jones, who in turn made her a present of the animal. My client has also testified that he purchased the horse. The question remains, who is to be believed? Two witnesses against one, Your Honor. In my opinion, Mr. Welkes sold the horse to my client in good faith, then was outraged when he discovered that the animal was purchased as a gift to his former paramour, so he resorted to the only course that, in his estimation at least, was left to him.

"Now, we can continue this trial, if Your Honor so wishes and if the prosecution so desires. But it is my belief that it will degenerate into a farce, like those so beloved by the French dramatists, should it be allowed to continue. I certainly intend to pursue a probing cross-examination of Mr. Welkes, and in the end he will be humiliated, to say the least.

"So, on those grounds, Your Honor, I move that this trial be terminated here and now, and that the charge against my client be dismissed."

The judge glanced over at the prosecution table. "Mr. Benson, does the prosecution have any comment to make to this motion?"

"If I may have a minute with Mr. Welkes, Your Honor?"

At the judge's nod, the prosecutor huddled with Robert Welkes. From where she sat, Debra could see Welkes wagging his head from side to side, but the prosecutor pressed his argument in a furious whisper. Finally, Welkes gave a reluctant nod, his broad shoulders sagging.

The young prosecutor got to his feet. "Your Honor, if it please the court, the prosecution agrees to the dismissal of the charge lodged against Clem Jones."

The judge rapped his knuckles. "It is so moved then. The charge against the defendant is dismissed. This court stands adjourned."

The instant the judge left the courtroom, Clem Jones let out a whoop and hastened toward the witness chair. Greta went to embrace him, burying his face against her large bosom. He was at least three inches shorter, Debra noted.

Now the little man broke free of Greta's clutches and hurried to Stony, who was at the table stuffing papers into a scuffed case. Jones shook Stony's hand happily, then returned to Greta, took her arm, and they sailed down the aisle and out of the courtroom, which was now deserted except for Debra and Stony.

Debra got to her feet uncertainly, suddenly wondering if she should slip out before he spotted her. Then it was too late. Smiling broadly, he was striding toward her.

"I didn't think you realized I was here," she said a little shyly.

"Oh, I saw you. In fact, for a moment I was so startled that I lost my train of thought." He took her hand.

"Are you angry with me?"

"Angry? Of course not. Why should I be? I'm flattered that you came."

"I came by your office and saw your sign, so I thought I would like to catch a glimpse of the future judge in action."

He arched an eyebrow amusedly. "So, what did you think?"

"I thought you gave a great performance."

"Performance? I'm not sure how to take that. I did have right on my side, after all, and a few facts to present. Admitted, a lawyer in a courtroom is somewhat akin to an actor on stage."

Debra flushed. "I'm sorry, I didn't mean it the way it sounded. What I meant was, you really showed the other man up, the prosecutor."

"It wasn't all that hard." He shrugged, then took her arm, and they started out of the courtroom. "Benson is young, also ambitious as hell. He operates under what I call the buckshot theory. He seldom bothers to investigate much when he receives a complaint. He figures that he'll go to court and win most of the time, with the law of averages tipped in the prosecution's favor. He didn't even talk to my client, just took Welkes's word, and he never saw that bill of sale until today. Even if he had, he might still have gone into court with it. But even a neophyte could have won that case today for Jonesy."

They were outside the courthouse now. He paused, gazing down at her. "To what do I owe the honor of this visit today? There's nothing wrong, I hope?"

73

"Oh, no! I just took it into my head to ride into town, and while I was here, I thought I'd look you up."

Even to her own ears, it sounded thin, and she was sure that Stony knew she'd come into Nacogdoches just to see him. Looking at him covertly, she saw that he was tugging at his nose, hiding his mouth.

"Well, since you *are* here, I'll take you to supper. That's the least I can do."

As they started down the steps, Debra said, "I was a little surprised that that woman, the widow, would admit before God and everybody that she had been bedding two men."

"Greta Heinrich hasn't the best reputation in town. I talked it over with her, before asking her to testify, afraid that the prosecutor would rip into her. He probably would have, too, trying to destroy her credibility, if I hadn't managed to get the charge dismissed before he could get at her. But Greta assured me that she didn't care, she'd do anything to save Clem Jones. She says he's the only man who's treated her decent since she became a widow. I gather that her late husband was no great shakes, either."

"It always annoys me, the attitude men have toward widows. They seem to think that all widows are fair game."

Stony shrugged. "It's the way of small towns, I suppose. A widow has only two ways to go, stay aloof and be very particular about her men friends, or choose Greta's way."

He pulled her to a stop before a restaurant, May's Place. The sign outside read: The Best There Is. Stony said, "The sign is a slight exaggeration, but the food is excellent. May is a fine cook."

It was still early for the supper hour, and the place was not crowded. A waitress led them to a table in the back. The restaurant was sparkling clean. The tables were covered with red-and-white tablecloths, and a slate menu hung on the wall, the choices written in chalk.

They both ordered chicken-fried steak, and the food was good and ample—tender steak smothered in thick gravy, fluffy biscuits right from the oven, black-eyed

74

Eight

All the way out of town Debra resolutely kept her face forward. She would not look back, she *would* not!

Yet her anger gave way to dismay before she was far along the road. It had been a stupid quarrel, and mostly her doing. She had said some hateful things that she wished she could take back.

Worst of all, she had probably left Stony with the impression that she wasn't a virgin. Then her anger blazed up again. Men! What right did they have to expect the women they married to be virgins, while they could have bedded dozens of women and be thought none the less for it? In fact, just the opposite. For a man of Stony's age to still be celibate would subject him to suspicion and ridicule.

It wasn't fair! Which, in a way, was just what Stony had said.

Debra recalled something that Kate Moraghan had said once, during one of their mother-daughter talks: "Face it, Debra Lee, it's a man's world, in more ways than one. We are supposed to be seen not heard, never go counter to the male viewpoint, no matter how asinine it might be, and we're supposed to come to the marriage bed immaculate as the first snow. And for a woman to enjoy the marriage bed, much less the *unmarried* bed, if there is such a thing . . . heaven forbid! At least that's the way most men look at it. Fortunately, Kevin isn't. . . . But never mind that. The thing is, if you should enter the marriage chamber less than immaculate, try not to let your husband know it. I'm not making a stand for or against keeping your virginity intact. Just don't let him know, if you're not. Maybe it'll be different some day, but I doubt that either of us will live to see that blessed day. And don't talk to me about fair or unfair, that's the way of it."

All of a sudden, Debra felt a poignant longing for her mother. She had never appreciated Kate so much as she did right now. How many mothers would talk so frankly to their daughters? Godalmighty few, she was certain of that.

She rode on, deep in thought. It was quite late now. Most of the farmhouses she passed were dark, and they were growing farther and farther apart. Now and then a dog howled at her passing, a lonely sound in the still night. It would be nearly morning before she reached Moraghan. She had told Nora that she intended to stay the night in Nacogdoches, at the hotel. There had been a brazen hope in her mind that she might spend the night with Stony. But that had been made impossible, and she had needed to get as far away from him as she could.

Once, she thought she heard hoofbeats behind her, and she reined in the mare, heart thudding in sudden fear. Then she decided she must have heard an echo. There was little traffic on the road late at night, but if there were any riders out, they likely were up to no good. She had been rash, riding all this distance late at night. She resisted an urge to kick the mare into a gallop; it was still a long ride, and she knew the mare could not run all that distance.

Debra rode on, letting the mare set her own pace. The monotony of the long ride and her weariness had a soporific effect, and Debra began to doze, head falling onto her chest.

Suddenly the mare shied, snorting in fear. Startled awake, Debra had to grab at the saddle horn to keep from falling from the horse, and then her heart began to race as she saw, in the faint starlight, a horse and rider alongside her. The rider leaned across and snatched the reins from her grip and began to lead the mare off the road toward the trees along the riverbank.

"Who are you?" she demanded. "What do you want?"

A harsh laugh was her only answer.

The rider stopped and slid to the ground. He looped the reins of both horses to a low-hanging branch and came to stand by Debra's stirrup. She still could not make out his face, could only hear his harsh breathing.

"If you're planning to rob me, I don't have any money!" she said wildly.

"It's not your money I'm after, missy."

The voice belonged to Tod Danker!

"You! What do you think you're doing?"

"I'm going to have me some sport, that's what. Just the way my uncles did with that grandmother of yours."

He closed a hand around her arm and yanked. Debra came off the horse like a bundle of old clothes. She struck the ground so hard that she was momentarily stunned. By the time she could think clearly again, he had her skirts up around her waist and had ripped away her drawers.

Kneeling between her spread thighs, his trousers down, the duster pushed back, Danker clamped both hands around her breasts and held her pinned to the ground.

"You'll pay for this!" she gasped out.

His cruel laughter was taunting. "Oh, I think not. Who'll do anything? Your grandma? That high-and-mighty uncle of yours? He wouldn't care what happened to you, he's too busy getting rich. Besides, I'm the sheriff. It'd be your word against mine. People will think you're making it all up, just to get back at us Dankers."

"I'll make you pay," she said in a whisper. "When I get the chance, I will kill you myself!"

"Oh, my goodness! Don't frighten me so, missy, you'll make me pee my britches. Anyway, you may like it. Most women do like it when they get a little taste of my tallywhacker."

81

He moved his hips, and Debra shuddered with revulsion as she felt his rigid organ against her inner thigh. She began to fight, insensate with rage and disgust. She kicked and kneed and rained blows with her fists about his head and shoulders. Her body bucked and writhed.

For just a moment she thought she had torn free, as Danker, taken by surprise, was thrown half off her. Then he was back, laughing, his huge bulk pinning her, almost smothering her.

"A regular little wildcat, ain't you? I like that."

"You filthy, rotten sonofabitch!"

"Goodness me!" His laughter mocked her. "You ain't such a lady, after all!"

She became silent, drew a deep breath, and then turned wild, going right to the edge of her strength, determined that this disgusting man would not have his way.

"Enough's enough, bitch!" he snarled.

Debra saw his arm raised against the starlight and the outline of something in his hand. Then she was given a stunning blow on the temple. Excruciating pain exploded in her head, and a great rush of blackness seized her, and she went with it, dimly grateful.

When Debra came to, she was alone. How much time had elapsed she had no way of knowing, but enough for her body to have been violated—that was immediately apparent. She was sore all over, and her vagina throbbed like a wound. Her skirts were still rucked up around her waist.

Her hand crept, like a frightened animal, down to her pubic region and then recoiled in revulsion as she encountered the stickiness of blood and semen.

Such vileness! Dear God, how could this have happened?

Without warning, her stomach heaved, and she turned her head aside just in time to spew bitter vomit out onto the ground. She retched for a long time, her mind retreating from the awfulness of what had happened.

After a while she sat up. Something moved beside her in the dark, and she cried out in fright. Then she recognized the mare, still tied to the tree. She fumbled for the stirrup, speaking in a broken, soothing voice to the animal as she painfully pulled herself erect. Finally she was on her feet, leaning against the mare for support.

And then full knowledge finally crashed in on her. She was no longer a virgin! Godalmighty, had this been some sort of retribution for what she had led Stony to believe? How would she ever be able to tell him about this? The knowledge was like a bruise in her mind, which she kept shying away from. And what if the man had infected her with some loathsome disease? Worse, what if he had impregnated her?

In that moment she knew that she would have killed Tod Danker without a qualm, if he were here and she had the means. How could she tell *anyone* about what had happened? She certainly could not tell Stony. She felt dirty and shamed, and if she ever told him, forever after, whenever he looked at her, she would wonder if he was thinking about Tod Danker.

She managed to climb onto the mare, then let the animal pick her own way home. Debra rode slumped in the saddle, sunk deep into apathy.

It was long after sunrise when she rode into the yard. Nora was on the porch in the rocker, wrapped in a shawl against the morning's chill.

She came to her feet and hurried down the steps as Debra slid off the horse. "Good heavens, child! Whatever happened to you? You look absolutely dreadful!"

"Some night animal spooked the mare, and I was thrown, Grandmother." Up until that moment Debra hadn't known what story she was going to tell, and the lie came out without forethought. She knew in that moment that Tod Danker's ravishment would remain her own secret.

"Are you all right?" Nora asked anxiously. She touched Debra's temple where Danker's pistol had rapped her. "That's an awful-looking bruise. Should I send for a doctor, Debra Lee?"

"No, no, I'll be fine," Debra said hastily. The last thing she wanted was a doctor's examination. "My head struck a boulder when I was thrown. I was unconscious for a time, but there's no permanent damage." Bitter mirth howled like a mocking wind through her head. No permanent damage? She would never be the same woman again! "Right now, the thing I most need in this world is a long soak in a hot tub."

"I'll tell Maria to heat a tub of water for you."

They started into the house together. "I thought you were staying overnight in town, Debra Lee?"

"I changed my mind," Debra said curtly.

"Stonewall—did you see him?" Nora asked in an off-hand manner.

"Yes, I saw Mr. Lieberman. We had supper together." She placed her hand on Nora's arm. "Grandmother, I don't wish to discuss it right now. We'll talk at supper, all right? After I've had a bath and some sleep. I've never been so exhausted."

"Why, yes, of course, Debra Lee."

Inside the house Debra trudged upstairs. Nora stood for a moment, staring after her, a look of concern on her face. Then she sighed and went to find Maria.

Debra soaked for a long time in the tub, scrubbing at herself until her skin burned. She washed her private parts again and again, convinced that she would never be able to scrub away the stain Tod Danker had left on her, in her.

When she finally crept into bed, she doubted that she would be able to sleep, but her exhausted, bruised body ruled over her mind, and she sank into a deep, healing sleep. It was dusk when she awoke, and her frame of mind had improved. She awoke knowing exactly what she would do, what she *had* to do.

At the supper table she announced without preamble, "Grandmother, I'm leaving."

Nora stared across the table at her. "I see. When, Debra Lee?"

"Before the week is out. Tomorrow, or the next day."

"Before Sunday and Stonewall comes to visit, is that it?"

Debra flushed. "Partly, but that's not all of it. I came here with the wrong idea in mind. Oh, not that I'm not glad I came to visit you, Grandmother Nora." She reached across to squeeze Nora's hand. "But I came here with some childhood fantasy in mind. It was foolish of me."

"You and Stonewall have a spat yesterday?"

"Well, yes, sort of," Debra admitted. "But he's not going to ask me to marry him, as I came here expecting, and certainly not after—" She bit off her words. "Anyway, I'm leaving."

"It's never good to act in anger, child," Nora said slowly. "My advice to you is to wait, at least until you see him again."

"No, no." Debra was shaking her head. The very thought of facing Stony made her cringe inside. "I'm going before Sunday, and nothing you can say will change my mind."

Nora peered at her. "I have a suspicion that something else has happened for you to make up your mind so suddenly. But you're a grown woman and should know your own mind. Where are you going, would you tell me that? Back home to Brownsville?"

"Oh, no!" Debra shook her head emphatically. "I couldn't go back there, with my tail dragging. Even if not for that, I wouldn't go home. There's nothing for me there, Grandmother."

"Where then?"

"I don't know. . . ." Even as she spoke, a decision formed in Debra's mind, but she didn't deem it wise to let her grandmother know, yet, where she was going. "But wherever it is, I'll let you know. And my folks, too, eventually."

"But you have no money, child. You told me."

"I'll manage. If nothing else, I've learned that I can always manage."

"I have some money, money Brian doesn't know about." Nora smiled. "You'll have to go through Nacogdoches, no matter what your destination. I'll give you a note to my banker there, instructing him to let you have a thousand dollars."

"No, Grandmother! It's very generous of you, but I couldn't take money from you. You'll need it."

"Nonsense, Debra Lee," Nora said briskly. "Whatever do I need money for? Besides, if I can't help one of my own, of what use is it? Now, I'll hear no argument. The money's yours, to do with as you wish. If it'll make you feel better, call it a loan. Pay me back when you can, without interest. If you can't pay me back, I'll be losing no sleep over it. You know I've always felt bad about Kevin leaving here with nothing. This will make me feel better, knowing that at least one of his has something from Moraghan."

"Thank you, Grandmother," Debra said with a fond smile. "You're a nice person, you know that? And I love you."

Nora was on the porch when Stony rode into the yard that Sunday, early in the afternoon.

He dismounted and came toward her. "Good afternoon, Nora." His gaze went past her, probing the shadows of the house.

"She isn't here, Stonewall."

"Isn't here? You mean she's out riding already?"

"No, that's not what I mean." Nora sighed. "She packed up and left three days ago."

His face registered dismay. "Oh, hell and damnation! I had a sort of feeling and ignored it. Where did she go, Nora?"

"She wouldn't tell me, Stonewall. Could be she didn't even know herself. She did promise to write when she got settled. Sit." She motioned to the rocker beside her. "You two had a fight in town the other day, didn't you?"

He sat down heavily. "Not exactly a fight, just a silly spat. What did she tell you about it?"

"Nothing. She wouldn't talk about it, but I knew something had happened."

"But it wasn't that serious, for God's sake! It certainly was no cause for her to take flight." In terse terms he told her the essence of the quarrel with Debra.

Nora said thoughtfully, "I agree, that hardly seems enough to send her kiting off. Something else happened, I'm sure of it, but I can't imagine what, and she wouldn't talk of it. Her clothing was torn, and she was scratched and bleeding, and there was a large bruise on her forehead. She said the mare spooked and threw her, but I didn't believe her. What time did she leave Nacogdoches, Stonewall?"

"Not too late. I didn't check my watch, but I'd say around eight, no later than nine, I'm sure."

"And she didn't get home until long after sunrise. It shouldn't have taken her all that long to get here. Something delayed her, but for the life of me I can't imagine what." She looked off. "Well, maybe she'll write and tell me whatever it was."

"Goddamnit, I don't understand any of this!" Stony pounded his fist on his knee.

"Nor do I, Stonewall. Tell me . . . do you love the girl?"

"I'm not sure how to answer that, Nora. I think so, but then I've never been in love before."

"When you fall in love, you'll know it."

"Well, I can tell you this much. Now that I find her gone, I feel a great loss, and that's something I've never felt before. You will tell me the minute you hear?"

"You'll be the first to know, my solemn promise."

Nine

After picking up Nora's thousand dollars in Nacogdoches, Debra headed for Corpus Christi. This destination had come to her while talking to Nora. It was the only place she was at all familiar with, and she had decided to look for another job as a waitress, if nothing else was available. That had been before Nora offered her the money. Debra still didn't know what she would do, but with that much money to depend on, she could take her time. Surely there was some sort of business she could buy, or start, with that money.

Most lone women opened a dress shop, or a clothing repair, but Debra had never learned more than the rudiments of sewing. She considered sewing the most boring activity in the world.

Maybe she could open a restaurant, she thought. She was not a very good cook, either, but at least she had learned something about how an eating establishment was operated.

Come to think of it, she mused, she was deficient in most talents women were supposed to have.

Of course, she could become one of Rose Sharon's girls. What would Mr. Lieberman think of *that*? It was an amusing thought, but she knew she would never follow it up. Whoring struck her as the most degrading profession a woman could take up, no matter how dire the circumstances.

However, when she reached Corpus Christi, the first place she made for was Rose's house. Although she hadn't remained there but the one night, she had visited with Rose a number of times during her sojourn in Corpus Christi, and they had become good friends. Debra enjoyed Rose's biting wit and was constantly amused at the combination of piety and bawdiness in the woman. Moreover, Rose knew just about everything that went on in Corpus Christi, and if there was a business opportunity open for a young woman with energy, ambition, and a thousand dollars, Rose would know about it.

Since it was mid-afternoon, Debra wasn't surprised at the absence of horses at the hitching rail, yet all the curtains were drawn, and she had to knock for several minutes before she heard the shuffle of footsteps behind the door.

Belle opened the door. She had a distraught air, and her eyes were swollen and red. She burst into fresh tears at the sight of Debra.

"What's wrong, Belle?"

"Aw, honey! It's Rose, she's sick bad!" She stood back for Debra to enter.

"What's wrong with her?" Debra asked.

Before Belle could speak, a grumpy male voice from behind her said, "Belle, didn't I tell you no visitors?"

"This ain't a caller, Doc. This is Debra Moraghan, she's a friend of Rose's."

A short, thin man emerged from the shadows behind Belle. He was ancient, with rheumy gray eyes, a long nose, and a scraggly, graying goatee. He held a glass in his hand, and whiskey fumes rolled toward Debra.

"I'm Dr. Price," he said in a clogged voice. "You're a friend of Rose's? Now how did that come about, young lady? From the looks of you, I'd say you're not in the business."

"No, I'm not in the business," Debra said curtly. "How I know Rose isn't important, and none of your affair, I might add. What's wrong with her?"

"She has a heart condition. She had rheumatic fever as

89

a child, and it weakened her heart. Now it's finally giving out."

Debra, remembering what Rose had told her about this man, studied him dubiously. His clothing was wrinkled and stained, his open collar frayed.

His gray eyes sharpened. "I know what you're thinking, young lady. I'm a toper, everybody knows that, but I'm still a damned good doctor. I know my business. I'm perfectly willing for Rose to call in another doctor, but she refuses. Hell, Rose is my friend, as well as my patient."

"How is she? Can I see her?"

"I've confined her to bed and told her to stay there, if I have to tie her down. No reason you can't see her, young lady. Just don't excite her or tell her that she's dying."

"She doesn't know? Not that I would tell her."

"She may realize it. Rose is a shrewd woman." Dr. Price shrugged, took a drink. "But I haven't told her, not in so many words."

Debra went up the stairs and down the hall to Rose's bedroom. She knocked softly, not wishing to wake the woman if she was sleeping.

"Come in," Rose said faintly.

Debra opened the door and went in. The room, opulently furnished, was dim. She could barely make out the big four-poster bed.

"Debra! What a pleasant surprise!"

Rose stirred, sat up against the pillows propped against the headboard. An open Bible slid off her lap. Debra approached, appalled at the change in the woman. She was pale and drawn, and she seemed to have lost considerable weight. Yet those eyes still held their indomitable sparkle.

"Sit, girl!" Rose gestured with a blue-veined hand to a nearby chair. "And tell me what you're doing back here in Corpus."

Debra pulled the chair close to the bed and perched on the edge. "I visited my grandmother, as I intended. It was a nice visit, but things weren't what I expected, so I decided to return here."

"This fellow you told me about. . . . He wasn't interested in marriage?"

"Not to me, at any rate."

"Men, who can ever figure them? But I'm glad you're
here, girl, before I pass on to the bosom of the
Lord. . . ."

"Rose, don't say that!" Debra said in distress.

"Debra, I never lie to myself. I know my time is near.
I've had a good life, in most respects, with few regrets.
The thing is, I feel like you're family, one of my own."
She reached out to squeeze Debra's hand. "And that's
funny, come to think about it. I left my own family all
those years ago, down in Savannah. Of course," she
added, her smile a parody of its former bawdiness, "they
would have disowned me if I hadn't beat them to it."

"Are any of your folks still living, back in Savannah?"

"Oh, must be. It's been almost twenty years since I've
been in touch, but since I had a wagonload of relatives,
many must still be around." Her smile turned wistful.
"I've been thinking of going home to die, but I have a
problem with that."

"What's that, Rose?"

"This place, and the girls." She gestured vaguely. "The
house is mine, free and clear, and I could sell it easily
enough, I reckon, but the girls. . . . They're like my
children, and they *are* children, in many ways. What
will happen to them? I don't need much money, thanks
to the Lord, but there's nobody I can trust to run this
place, except into the ground. Belle's the only one with a
thimble of sense, and she'd take off with the first fancy
man she took a shine to. I don't know how many times
I've had to practically hogtie her to keep her from making a fool of herself."

Suddenly seized by an idea, Debra leaned forward ex-
citedly. "Rose . . . my grandmother loaned me a
thousand dollars. I came to Corpus Christi with the idea
of getting into some kind of business. Why not this
one?"

Rose reared up, a look of incredulity on her face.
"*You*, running a sporting house? Girl, are you out of
your mind?"

91

"Why not?" Debra said defiantly. "I know I've had no experience, and I'm young, but with some advice from you and with Belle's help, I'm willing to try."

"But why? Why do you want to do it?"

"Because I have to earn a living some way. And, as someone said to me recently, there aren't all that many ways for a woman to earn money." Debra remembered her resolve never to become a whore, yet she could run the place without becoming one, couldn't she?

Rose was silent for a long moment, studying Debra shrewdly. "That's not much of an answer, girl. You're trying to get back at someone, ain't you? Who, your family? This man who wasn't interested in wedding bells?"

Taken aback by the woman's perceptiveness, Debra looked away. "I hadn't thought of it that way. Perhaps you're right. But what does it matter, my reasons?"

"Like I said once, girl, you've got brass. Do you have any idea what you'll be letting yourself in for? The decent folk, not to mention your own folks, will shun you like a plague. Once you've taken such a step, it will never be easy to get accepted again."

"I'll take that risk."

"If you ever get around to thinking of marriage, any man will think twice about marrying a brothel madam."

"Maybe I never will get married."

Rose scowled. "Don't talk foolishness, Debra!"

"You've never gotten married."

"Now that's where you're wrong. I've gone to the altar three times. None of the three was worth a gob of spit."

Disconcerted, Debra said, "I'm sorry, I didn't know that. I suppose you're right, I will get married in time. But if the man I marry isn't tolerant enough to accept me for what I am, he wouldn't be the sort of man I'd want."

"Debra, Debra! You *do* have a lot to learn." Rose shook her head chidingly. "And there's another thing you must consider. Are you willing to lay on your back for just any man who comes along?"

"Why would that be necessary? I can run this place without being one of the girls, can't I?"

"It's possible, but not easy. You're young and juicy, and they'll be after you. The good Lord must have known what He was doing when He put that thing between a man's legs, but He neglected to give it a conscience. You'll have to fend them off time after time."

Debra's thoughts swung to Tod Danker and that night by the river. She said grimly, "No man will ever lay a hand on me again, unless I'm ready and willing. I can promise you that, Rose."

"Promises, promises! How many times have *I* said that?" She sighed. Then she sat up a little, her gaze sharpening. "Wait. You said 'again.' What do you mean by that? Did something nasty happen to you while you were in East Texas?"

Thrown into confusion, Debra sat back. She had sworn to herself that she would never tell a soul about Tod Danker. She muttered, "It's nothing, Rose."

"Now come on, girl. I thought there was something odd about you, the minute you came in here. Come on, tell Rose. It's just between us girls."

To her astonishment Debra found herself telling Rose about it. But after she was well launched, she realized that she had been aching to relate it, and when she was done, she experienced an immense relief.

"What a rotten sonofabitch that Danker must be! And a sheriff yet. Wasn't there someone you could go to about what happened?"

Debra shook her head. "Not really. It would have only brought trouble, probably caused that old feud to flare up again, and God knows who might have been killed. Besides, nothing would erase the fact that it happened." Anger threaded her voice as she added, "Some day, I'll get even with Tod Danker. I promised him, and myself, that after it was over."

Rose heaved a sigh. "The good Lord certainly placed a burden on us women. If it's any consolation, girl, I've been raped at least three times in my life, and it doesn't hurt so much after the first time, but you never feel any less degraded and violated." Her gaze was keen, probing. "And that's another thing you have to consider. I've always catered to gentlemen in this place, and I'm sure you will as well, but if you say hands off to the gents, in time one of them will get too much liquor in his gut and try to take you by force."

"It will never happen again," Debra said vehemently. "If need be, I'll arm myself."

Rose shook her head. "You do indeed have a lot to learn, girl. There's an old saying. You can't roll in the dirt and expect to get up clean as a whistle. Still, it seems you're bound and determined, and it does solve the problem that's been nagging at me. Now I can go home with an easy conscience, unless it begins to nag at me about you."

"Don't worry about me, Rose. I'll be fine."

"That's it then." Rose slapped her hand down onto the bed. "I won't need any of your thousand dollars, I have more than enough. You can pay me for the place out of your profits, if there are any, and I'll pray hard to the good Lord for that to happen. My advice would be to use your money to fix the place up some. I've let everything go of late, since I've been feeling puny."

Debra said eagerly, "Will you help me, Rose? With advice, I mean?"

Rose shook her head. "Nope. You're on your own, Debra. The minute I get my strength back, enough to get on a boat, I'm heading home, to Savannah. Besides, you don't want advice from an old tart like me." The bawdy grin was back. "You'll have your own ideas. Give the place a touch of class, girl."

Rose Sharon boarded a ship two days later, against the advice of Dr. Price. Debra and all the girls were there to see her off, and a great many tears were shed. Debra's own eyes were wet; she was sure she would never see Rose again. It was strange how such a strong affection could have developed between them after only such a short acquaintance.

Debra didn't fail to notice that the girls all stood slightly apart from her, grouped together as if for protection, and from time to time one eyed her askance. Rose had gathered them all together the evening before and informed them that henceforth the place belonged to Debra; and if they all knew what side their bread was buttered on, they would obey her orders. Debra had overheard two of the girls whispering together about where they should go, but so far none had made the move.

When she had reported what she'd overheard to Rose, the older woman had snorted. "Hell, girl, they ain't going anywhere! They're always talking about moving on, but they almost never do, unless they fall for some galoot and go off with him. This is their home, the only place they know. Unless you let the place fall apart, they'll stick with you. What choice do they have?"

Privately Debra had doubts about that. She knew they considered her young and inexperienced—all too true—and if she didn't take a firm hold at once, she would soon have a house without girls.

Consequently, when they returned from seeing Rose off, Debra called them together in the front parlor. With a confidence she was far from feeling, she said, "Rose has told you that I am in charge now. Now, *I* am telling you. But we're going to remain closed for a couple more weeks. I intend to make many changes. The house will be redecorated, inside and out.

"I know that men from all over Texas come to Corpus Christi in the winter, and in the summer, men of great wealth, important men. I intend to cater to their trade, exclusively if at all possible. If I have my way, this place will be known far and wide, all across Texas, as a place of refinement, a place of class, where gentlemen can come and relax without fear of demeaning themselves. In the end, I hope to turn it into a private club. The change will extend to you girls as well." She held up her hand at a mutter of protest. "I'm not bad-mouthing any of you. All I'm saying is that I expect a more discreet attitude from all of you. The men I hope to attract will be given gentility, as well as pleasure.

"One change that will take place immediately is a name for the place. In honor of Rose, it will be called Rose's Emporium."

Belle was frowning. "But Debra, I thought emporium meant some kind of a store?"

"It does," Debra said with a sudden grin. "And that's what we have here, in a manner of speaking. We have something to sell, don't we?"

A titter of laughter swept through the girls, and Debra relaxed a bit—they were with her now. She said, "Only I intend to have a high-toned store, with classy packaging."

"Some of us are a little long in the tooth, including me, to be considered classy," Sally said. "Which means that we will be kicked out on our tails."

"No," Debra said instantly. "So long as I am running this place, and so long as you follow my instructions to the letter, this will always be your home. You have my promise. If we do as well as I hope, I will likely employ other girls, but not as replacements for you." Even as she spoke, she wondered if perhaps she wasn't promising too much. Yet it was a promise she knew she had to make, if she was to expect their loyalty and cooperation.

"How about you, then?" Sally asked boldly. "You going to be one of us?"

"No! I am not for sale, and I want all of you to remember that."

A great change took place in Rose's Emporium during the next two weeks. Debra spent most of her thousand dollars on redecorating the house, inside and out; much of the money was spent on paint, material to recover the furniture, and crisp white curtains for all the windows. She didn't have enough money to spare for new furniture.

She had the painters do the outside in sparkling white—"for virginity," she told Belle, laughing—and had a single red rose painted on the front-door panel.

Another portion of the money went for new clothes for the girls, items as decorous as those of a schoolteacher, yet attractive and appealing, the only concession to the girls' profession being a plunging neckline on the dresses.

The last item she purchased was a battered upright piano, which she placed in the parlor. After the delivery men left, Debra stood back, surveying it, then gave a pleased nod. "It's somewhat beat-up, but it'll do until I have the money for a new one. Maybe a baby grand, who knows?" She grinned at Belle and Sally. "Now I have to find a man to play it."

Sally Hopkins said shyly, "I can play a piano, Debra. Quite well, in fact."

Debra arched an eyebrow at the woman in astonishment.

"You can play the piano? How did that come about?"

"My folks gave me lessons until I was eighteen."

"Then how did you become? . . ."

"A whore?" Sally finished for her. "I married a no-good who left me without a penny after two years. I had to make a living some way, and I figured I might as well sell what I had been giving away to him."

They all seemed to have the same story, Debra thought; they all had been brought to ruin by a man.

Belle was speaking. "Never heard of a place with a woman piano player. It's always a man. Somehow, it don't seem right, a woman."

"Just because it's not usually done is no reason I can't do it here," Debra retorted. "I intend to break several rules. Sally, when we reopen next week, you'll be at the piano."

At that moment Rose's Emporium was the subject of a rather heated discussion in the home of T.J. Dillon up on the hill. From the window of his parlor Dillon could look down upon the newly painted house, its pristine white standing out like a beacon among its dingy neighbors.

"Gentlemen, I say we must do something about Debra Moraghan and her house of abomination," Dillon said emphatically. "I thought when Rose Sharon got sick that she'd close it up and we'd be rid of that element for good."

One of the other three men in the room was Bradford Carpenter, an elderly man with snow-white hair and a goatee to match. As he looked down at the white house, there was an impish twinkle in his gray eyes. "From here, I'd say she's made a considerable improvement in the place."

Dillon stirred, his florid face scowling. "You know that's not what I'm talking about, Bradford. It's what goes on *inside* that house that is the shame of Corpus Christi." He became pompous. "We're growing, and many important people are coming here. Why, I even heard that the governor is thinking of buying a summer home here."

"Maybe he heard about Rose's Emporium, did you ever think of that?" Carpenter said with a sly grin.

Dillon said stiffly, "That's blasphemy, man! The governor is a Christian, a proper husband, a God-fearing man."

"It's been my experience that those are the kind who sneak in and out of sporting houses in the dark of the night."

"Damnit, Bradford, it's no use talking to you when you're like this!" Dillon slammed a fist against his fleshy thigh. "I called you all here for a serious discussion. If you can't be serious, you might as well leave."

"Oh, I suppose I can dispense with the levity for a spell." Carpenter settled his spare frame in a wing chair. "But I fear that I can't get too excited about a brothel, T.J."

The four men in the room were the power elite of Corpus Christi. The charge had been made that they, in effect, ran the town, and there was a great deal of truth to the charge. All four were wealthy men and retired from their respective professions or businesses, with the exception of Judge Jonathon Ross, who still sat on the bench, but all four still had various business investments that required their supervision. As Carpenter often commented irreverently, they needed "something to do to pass the time, which usually means trouble, or at the very least mischief, for some Corpus Christians." He had labeled them the "Council of Four," a name that had stuck despite all of Dillon's efforts to the contrary.

T.J. Dillon was their self-appointed leader, and they accepted his leadership, since Dillon was aggressive, a mover and a doer. At fifty, a few years younger than the others, Dillon had made his fortune in sheep and cattle; his acreage did not nearly approach that of the vast Rancho Santa Gertudis spread, but his holdings were substantial. He had moved from his ranch headquarters to Corpus Christi several years before. He much envied the promoter Uriah Lott, who had been instrumental in starting construction on the Corpus Christi & Rio Grande Valley Railroad to Laredo, and Captain Richard King, and he fully intended to become as powerful and well-known as those two individuals. So far, he had been unsuccessful.

But there was one area of little concern to either Lott or Captain King—the inner-city politics of Corpus Christi. Uriah Lott was busy carrying out grandiose plans for the area as a whole, and Captain King was primarily concerned with his ranch. So that left Dillon with a free hand to work behind the scenes, to grasp what he considered the real power.

Bradford Carpenter once said, "You may have to settle for being a little frog in a big pond, T.J.—King and Lott have the big frog thrones nailed down."

Carpenter was a prickly thorn in Dillon's side, and he would gladly have eliminated him from the Council of Four, but Carpenter was a shrewd fellow and respected and well-liked by the other two members.

Now Carpenter said, "So, what is it you have in mind, T.J.?"

"I'd like to see to it that that den of iniquity is closed down!"

"Den of iniquity?" Carpenter murmured. "I don't remember when I've last heard that expression."

"Well, damnit, that's what it is!" Dillon pounded his fist on his thigh.

"It's not going to be that easy. Its closure would not affect me personally, you understand," Carpenter said grinning, "since I'm past the age for its attractions. But there are many gents around who use the, uh, conveniences offered. Also, we don't have any enforceable red light laws on the books."

"Then we should get some passed," Dillon said.

Judge Ross stirred, said ponderously, "I am much in

99

favor of that. I have tried to push for strict city laws against prostitution, but I am usually greeted with snickers of amusement."

Carpenter looked with ill-concealed disfavor at Judge Ross. In his opinion, Judge Ross was an anachronism, as blue-nosed as any of the old New England puritans; and if he had his way, witch trials—with him presiding, a guillotine blade for a gavel—would again be popular.

The fourth member of the group, Jack Thomas, looked doubtful. "If we start pushing for something like that, T.J., we'll be stepping on a lot of toes and upset a lot of people."

Dillon grunted contemptuously. "You should know by this time, Jack, that toes have to be stepped on to get anything done. They'll all be grateful after we've accomplished what we set out to do."

"The voice of God, T.J.?" Carpenter wagged his head. "Just how are you going about this business? And what do you expect from us?"

"I expect you to support me, in trying to get a law passed to close that place down."

"That won't be easy. The judge here has already explained that. Many people think that a brothel helps to bring people into Corpus."

"At least we can try. If we can't get the law we want, there are other ways."

"Such as?"

"We can intimidate her. I understand this new madam is young, fresh to this rotten business. She should be easily frightened off. We can drop a word to her customers. And even if we don't have laws on the books for that specific purpose, she must break any number of laws every day."

Carpenter said dryly, "Like spitting on the sidewalk?"

"Yes! And we can have a word with the shopkeepers in town, tell them not to sell to her."

"That's harassment, T.J. It's not only petty, it's illegal, and I'll have no part of it. I don't understand you, don't understand why you're stirring up so much dust over something like a whorehouse in town. Hell, it's been here forever, it seems."

Dillon scowled angrily. "I happen to think that a brothel is not only a sin against God, but an offense to the decent people in this town! If you can't see that, I'm disappointed in you, Bradford. I can see there's no use discussing it further with you, so I'm going to call for a vote. All in favor, raise your hand." Dillon raised his hand, and Judge Ross followed suit. Dillon looked over at Thomas. "Jack?"

Jack Thomas said slowly, "I'm sorry, T.J., but I have to go along with Bradford on this issue. I think it's something that could turn sour on us."

"Looks like we've come to an impasse, T.J." Carpenter laughed softly. "Now I have to go, I have things to do. So long, fellows." He raised a hand and started out.

"Bradford!"

Carpenter turned back. "Yes, T.J.?"

"This isn't the last of it. I'm going to bring it up again."

"Oh, I figured that, knowing you like I do," Carpenter said dryly. "Well, you just go right on ahead now."

The other two, made uneasy by the unpleasant scene, soon followed, leaving Dillon alone. He sat for a time, seething with frustration. He was going to have to get rid of Bradford Carpenter, he had put up with his insolence long enough! It had been a mistake to have taken him into the Four. Yet Dillon knew that it would be difficult to get rid of him now. Carpenter was a respected man in Corpus Christi, intimate of the Kings, Uriah Lott, and others of equal power and influence. There seemed to be only one way to cope with Bradford Carpenter—add a fifth member to the Council of Four, a man Dillon could count on to vote with him, no matter what the issue.

There was a powerful reason behind his determination to rid Corpus Christi of Debra Moraghan and her stable of whores. Dillon hated all whores with a passion, for there was a dark secret he hugged to his breast, a secret that he only looked at in moments like this, poking at it as a man will inadvertently probe with his tongue at a sore tooth. His mother had been a whore. Born of a whore mother in the French Quarter in New Orleans, he had never known his father; he seriously doubted that his mother had known, either. Times beyond counting he had lain in their miserable room in the dark, listening to his mother and a customer rutting in the bed across the way.

He had to wait until he was twelve before he could escape, begging a job as a cabin boy on a riverboat plying the Mississippi, taking a new name for himself, one that he considered had a little class. He didn't know if his mother was still alive; he had never tried to find out. He had made two vows that long-ago day when he had departed the French Quarter—to become so rich and powerful that nobody would deny him what he wanted and to work toward eliminating whores and whoredom. In the first he had succeeded, and now was the time to begin work on the second.

He cringed to think of the derision that would pour from Bradford Carpenter should he ever learn about his, Dillon's, origins. No one must ever know. That was one reason he had never married.

His obsession had grown so over the years that he had come to believe that all women were whores, if not in actual practice, at the very least in their hearts. If nothing else, he would see to it that no whore-woman would ever get her greedy claws on the money he had worked so hard to accumulate!

Anyway, he didn't need Carpenter's agreement in the matter of Debra Moraghan. There were many things he could do on his own, and he would put them into operation at once. It was only a matter of time before the woman and her split-tails would be only too glad to leave Corpus Christi.

As always, when his thoughts ran in this direction, he had a strong physical reaction. He moved uncomfortably on the divan as his groin swelled.

He raised his voice to a bellow. "Consuela! Get your ass in here!"

When Consuela, the plump, middle-aged housekeeper, entered the room, he was already unbuttoning his trousers.

"Yes, Señor Dillon . . ." Consuela's voice died when

she saw his swollen member protruding from his trousers.

"You know what to do." He gestured graphically. "Get on with it!"

Her dark face took on a look of weary resignation, and she approached the sofa. She lifted her voluminous skirts—Consuela never wore drawers in this house, never knowing when she'd be asked to attend to his needs—straddled him on the sofa, and shimmied down. He groaned aloud as she began to move rhythmically.

Ten

Dear Grandmother Nora,

I have decided that it is time to write and let you know what has happened to me. After I tell you, you may very well disown me.

I used your thousand dollars, Grandmother, to take over a brothel in Corpus Christi. It is the place I stayed the first night I was in Corpus Christi. Rose Sharon, the women who owns it, is in failing health, and she turned it over to me in return for my promise to pay her back in installments. The thousand dollars I used to renovate it, and I am proud of it!

Does that shock you, Grandmother, my being proud of a whorehouse? I sincerely hope that this does not drive us apart, but I cannot find it in myself to feel that what I am doing is terribly wrong. One bitter lesson I have already learned is that men are ruled by their animal lusts and see women as a means of slaking their desires. So it seems to me a matter of practicality to turn this fact of their nature to a commercial advantage.

I well know that few people would agree with this attitude. Certainly many here in Corpus Christi do

stone wall?" At the unconscious pun, Kate began to laugh helplessly.

Kevin gave her a look of disgust and limped out of the house. It was a full minute before Kate got her laughter under control. Then she collapsed into a kitchen chair, the letter in her lap. The laughter was partially a hysterical reaction to the news of Debra Lee's new calling, plus relief that she was all right. She couldn't expect Kevin to understand that, in his present mood, and he certainly would not agree that the girl was all right.

It was high noon. The sun scorched the already dry ground, and the constant wind blew dust like smoke.

Kevin limped along, head bent, cursing the dry ground, the heat, and the dust, and his daughter. . . . No, she wasn't *his* daughter! She was his brother's bastard child! What else could he expect with Brian's blood in her?

Then he felt a hot shame. In every way except blood, Debra Lee was his daughter, and he loved her just as much as if she had sprung from his own seed.

Stooping, he picked up a handful of the dry earth and let it trickle through his fingers. Water, it always came back to that. He had wracked his brain for a way to drill down to the water under the earth.

He determined to redouble his efforts. If he could get water to the thirsty land, his acres could become a Garden of Eden. If he prospered, he could make Debra Lee proud of him. No longer would she be ashamed of his poverty and scorn him for spurning his heritage.

Laughing harshly, he flung the last of the dirt into the wind and stood unblinking when it blew back into his face.

Only a short time ago he had been furious with Debra Lee for becoming a brothel madam, and now he was thinking of a way in which he could make her proud of him! But then Kate was right—she was their daughter and they must love her no matter what she did. If a man didn't stand tall before his children, of what value was his brief time on earth?

After her initial astonishment, Nora Moraghan began to laugh when she had finished her granddaughter's letter.

Her thousand dollars had been used to set Debra Lee up in a whorehouse! If alive, Sean would have been outraged, but Nora was sure that he would have seen the humor in it in the end.

She felt a certain sympathy for Kevin and Kate. She fully realized what a cruel shock it must be to them, especially Kevin, who had an unfortunate tendency toward being too straitlaced in matters of this sort.

And Brian, oh, how outraged he would be! Nora had heard the rumors of his roistering when away from the immediate vicinity—he was a patron of whorehouses. He was a hypocrite, as well, like most men of her experience, when it came to sexual matters. In his view a man could do as he damned well pleased, but a woman should always hold herself inviolate from activities that men could converse about freely among themselves but that women were not supposed to even think about, much less discuss or indulge in. For all of his being straightlaced, Kevin was at least tolerant and understanding. Brian was not, he was as unforgiving as a statue of anything going counter to his beliefs.

Oh, was she going to enjoy reporting to Brian the contents of Debra Lee's letter! And he would roar like an enraged bull when she told him that his own mother had financed his niece in her endeavor. Nora certainly intended to tell him. Any victory over Brian these days was to be cherished.

As it happened, the first one she told was Stonewall Lieberman. The letter arrived on Friday, and Stony still rode out to have supper with her on Sundays. Nora debated with herself about telling him, but she had promised to let him know the instant she learned Debra Lee's whereabouts. She supposed she could lie by omission and not tell him of the brothel, but if Debra Lee had chosen not to lie, why should she?

It was a chill day, dripping rain. Stony had brought along a bottle of wine, and they drank it before the fireplace in the parlor, while Nora read Debra Lee's letter in its entirety.

Stony was silent for a moment after she was finished, staring into the leaping flames, turning the wineglass back and forth between his hands.

"Well, Stonewall? What do you think?"

"What's to think, Nora?" He looked over at her, shrugged. "If you expect me to show shock, I'm not going to. I'm disappointed, true, but not really surprised, not after second thoughts. During the short time I knew her, I learned never to be surprised at anything Debra might take into her head to do. I'm just wondering. . . ." He broke off, staring into the flames.

"Wondering what?"

"Well, I don't think I told you all that we talked about that last night. She mentioned staying in that brothel in Corpus Christi, and I expressed disapproval. That was probably a mistake. Hindsight is great, isn't it?"

"It probably was a mistake, Stonewall. Are you thinking that might have brought this about?"

"Oh, not really." He shrugged again. "I hardly think I'm that important in Debra's life."

"You could be wrong about that. I don't think I told you, but she had a crush on you all those years she was away. That's the real reason she ran off from home and came here, just to see you again."

He raised and lowered one hand. "It was nothing more than a girlish crush. I'm certain of that, after all that's happened."

"Well, at least you know where she is now. You could always go to see her."

He was silent for a moment, then shook his head slowly. "No, I don't think that would be the thing to do."

"Why? Because she's running a whorehouse?" Nora said bluntly.

Stony winced. "Touché. I deserved that, I suppose. But that's not the real reason, Nora. You notice that she didn't once mention me in her letter."

"Of course she didn't! She feels that you've rejected her, and she has that stiff-necked Moraghan pride. She

111

got that from Sean, passed down through Kevin. But for Kevin's damnable pride, he would still be here, where he belongs."

"Damnit, Nora, I didn't reject her! It never came down to that. If anything, it's the other way around." His smile took on a twist. "I told you once that I wasn't sure about being in love. It could be that I've been a bachelor too long to ever marry any woman."

"And it certainly wouldn't look good for a future judge to marry a whorehouse madam, would it, Stonewall?" she said with more tartness that she had intended.

He gave her a dark look, got to his feet. "I would have expected better of you than that, Nora." He reached for his hat, jammed it on his head. "I'll say good night now."

"Going so soon, Stonewall?" she said in dismay. "You haven't had your supper yet."

"I've suddenly discovered that I'm not hungry. If I stay, we may get into it and say something we'll both regret. I'll see you next Sunday, Nora."

After he was gone, Nora sat looking into the fire. It always amazed her how contrary humans could be, how they could allow pride to break their own hearts as well as others. It was obvious to her that Stonewall and Debra Lee were in love with each other, and because of a few harsh words spoken in anger, any hope of the culmination of that love seemed doomed.

She wondered if she should try to bring about a settlement of their differences by writing to Debra Lee. She decided it would not be wise, at least not at this time. It had been her experience that meddling by an outsider into a private quarrel usually resulted in disaster, no matter how good the meddler's intention.

Her memory winged back down the years to that moment when Sean learned that she was pregnant by one of the Danker brothers, who had raped her. It had taken a long time for Sean's pride to bend enough to allow him to touch her in love, and it had taken him years after the birth of Kevin, the child of that rape, until after they had been led to believe that Brian was dead, before Sean thawed enough to allow himself to love Kevin.

* * *

Brian's reaction to Debra Lee's letter was pretty much what Nora had anticipated. He rode by the morning after Stony's visit. Brian and Nora were in the sunroom having coffee when Brian glanced around and asked, with elaborate casualness, "Where's Debra Lee?"

"She left near a month ago."

"Has it been that long since I've been by?"

"It has, Brian. If you'd come by more often, you'd know what was going on."

"I'm a busy man, Momma." He took a sip of coffee. "Hightailed it back home to her folks, did she?"

"Nope. She's in Corpus Christi."

"Oh? How's she getting by? Waiting on tables, like she was before?"

"As a matter of fact, no." With a quiver of satisfaction, Nora took Debra Lee's letter from her apron pocket. "She's doing rather well for herself, is Debra Lee. I got a letter from her last week."

"Is she now?" He raised an eyebrow. "So what is she doing?"

"She's operating a whorehouse, Son."

"She's what!" Brian almost strangled on his coffee. Eyes bulging, he set the cup down with a clatter. "Momma, is this your way of having fun with me?"

"No, Brian. It's true."

"A daughter of. . . . My niece, operating a whorehouse! I don't believe I'm hearing this!"

Nora said dryly, "Believe it, Brian. It's true."

"But this will bring shame down on the Moraghan name. How can you take it so calmly, Momma?"

She shrugged. "I suppose, at my age and with the things I've seen in my life, nothing can disturb me too much. There's some things in our back history that do little honor to the Moraghan name, beginning with the fact that Moraghan was not Sean's name, but one taken to conceal the fact that he was defrocked by the Catholic Church when he married me."

"I don't want to hear it!" He knocked the cup and saucer from the table with a swipe of his hand. Coffee splattered across the floor, and the cup and saucer shattered against the far wall. "Jesus Christ, what a thing to learn about one of your own family, running a whore-house . . . Wait a minute!" He stared hard at his mother. "How did Debra Lee happen into that? She had to have some *money*, and according to what you told me, Momma, she didn't have a penny."

"I loaned her a thousand dollars, Son."

"*You* loaned—!" His face turned red, and his neck thickened until Nora feared a blood vessel would burst. "Momma, you did that just to spite me!" He thrust his face at her. There was a lingering odor of liquor on his breath. "Didn't you, Momma?"

Suddenly Nora was sorry for opening up this Pandora's box, and the triumph she thought she would feel had turned rancid. "No, Brian," she said, a tremor in her voice. "Debra Lee was leaving here without any money. I couldn't let her do that. I had no inkling that she would use it in such a manner."

"Oh, yes, you did," he said through gritted teeth. "Ever since Kevin left Moraghan, you've been on the outs with me. You'd do anything to make me feel bad. Well, I hope you're happy now, Momma. You've made me feel like a piece of shit!"

He turned on his heel and stomped out.

For all his bluster and arrogance, Brian had never before used foul language around her. Nora wondered what she had set in motion. One thing was certain—she had certainly succeeded in driving her oldest son even further away from her.

And he's right, she thought dully; I did it purely out of spite, an old woman's spite.

Eleven

By the time the anniversary of the reopening of Rose's Emporium rolled around, Debra calculated that her new venture had been a roaring success, far beyond her expectations.

She had doubled the number of girls, bringing in young, pretty ones, being very selective. To all newcomers she emphasized that decorum was to be desired at all times. Once behind a closed door, the girls could do whatever their personal standards permitted them to do to please their customers, but in the parlor, and especially outside of the house, they would be proper ladies at all times. If they were at any time brazen enough to call undue attention to themselves, they would be sent packing at once. But once they learned that Debra meant what she said, there were very few incidents requiring such measures. Since the reputation of Rose's Emporium had grown throughout Texas, there were working girls galore clamoring to get into the place.

Of Rose's original seven, only three remained. Belle was no longer working; instead, she had been elevated to Debra's assistant, overseeing the girls with a firm hand. Sally was still playing the piano, and she had proven Debra's instinct correct—she had become a prime attraction. Aside from playing beautifully, she also had a good singing voice. When she sang sentimental songs, of home and mother, of lost loves, strong men well into their cups wept unashamedly, and still weeping, went upstairs with girls on their arms.

Only once did Debra encounter any problems with the girls, and that was with one of the last pair she took into the house. June Blount was twenty-five. She had a ripe figure, long raven hair, and hot brown eyes. She also had an insolent, slouching manner that irritated Debra, but her baby face had a pouting, depraved sexuality about it that Debra knew would soon make her a favorite with the customers.

Debra accepted her reluctantly and regretted her decision that very first evening. June was late coming downstairs, and the parlor had a half-dozen men in it when she finally made her entrance—and entrance it was!

Debra was standing at the bar across the room, her back to the beaded doorway, when she became aware that utter silence had fallen.

She turned quickly. June Blount stood just inside the entrance, hip-shot, one hand raised to her hair, and all male eyes were riveted on her. It was easy to understand why. She had on a low-cut blouse about as substantial as smoke, and the light from the hallway behind her blatantly outlined the shape of her figure.

Debra was already in motion. She took June by the arm and propelled her out into the hall and back out of sight of the parlor. "Just what the devil do you think you're doing?" she whispered furiously. "Wearing a blouse like that?"

"What's wrong with it?" June said innocently. She stroked her palms down over her breasts, and Debra could see the nipples standing out prominently.

"You know very well what's wrong with it. With that blouse you might as well be naked from the waist up."

June shrugged. "That's what it's all about, ain't it? I've been taught to display the merchandise."

"I don't care what you've been taught," Debra said coldly. "In here, at least in front of the customers, you

116

don't wear anything that revealing. When there are no men in here, you can go around stark for all I care."

"Goodness, you're proper." June sneered. "And I suppose you feel you're too good to work on your back, like the rest of us."

"You suppose right."

June gave her a calculating look. "Maybe you're one of those who like women, instead of men? Is that it, honey?"

Debra brought her open hand up and whacked the woman hard across the face.

June fell back against the staircase, her hand going to her cheek. Her eyes teared. "You hit me! Nobody has ever hit me before."

"Oh, I'm sure you've been hit before and will again, with that snippy manner of yours. Now you can do one of two things. You can march right upstairs and put on something decent and never wear that blouse again before a man. Or you can pack your things and leave right now."

"I have no place to go," June said in a whining voice.

"Then you don't have much choice, do you?" Debra stepped back and motioned up the stairs.

June gave her a look of burning hatred, but she turned away and trudged up the stairs.

Debra now had enough steady customers so that she could afford to institute her private club policy. To gain admittance now, a man had to be a member of the Rose Club, with the privilege of bringing a friend, so long as said friend observed decorum and generally behaved himself.

Debra charged a membership fee, and a man in good standing could charge his drinks and the girl's fee. It was a policy that paid excellent dividends and had the added advantage of keeping out the riffraff.

The efforts of the man on the hill, T.J. Dillon, had so far been frustrated. He had tried twice to get a law on the books closing down the place but had been unsuccessful. He had tried other tactics, such as trying to get storekeepers to deny Debra and her girls patronage.

This had worked with about half the storekeepers, but the others were more than happy to serve them. Dillon had tried to discourage her customers, even threatening blackmail in a few instances, but in that he had failed as well.

Debra was naturally pleased by this development, but she was also mystified. In the beginning she had been afraid that Dillon would succeed in either closing her down or driving her customers away.

She talked of this with Doc Price during the anniversary party. She had closed the doors for the evening, bought a case of champagne, and a huge cake, with a rose and one candle in the center, and given the girls a well-deserved evening of relaxation.

The only man present, and the only outside guest, was Doc Price. She had grown quite fond of the doctor, realizing after only a short acquaintance that he was a competent doctor when sober, and he was usually reasonably sober—he had an amazing capacity for alcohol. Also, he had no family and was a lonely man, yearning toward her friendship. He had a cynical wit and had become not only her fast friend but confidant as well.

As she sat with him in the parlor, watching the girls literally let their hair down, she turned to him. "It's been a good year, Doc, a Godalmighty lot better than I ever expected."

He nodded, drawing on one of the foul-smelling cigars he smoked when in his cups. "You run a respectable, clean house, Debra. You've done a good job."

She laughed. "Respectable? How many people would agree with that, I wonder?"

"There's respectable, and there's respectable. As bawdy houses go, my dear, yours is more than a notch above average." He grinned. "I speak from experience. I've seen a few in my time, both as a customer and a medical man."

Debra took a sip of champagne. "The one thing that I can't understand is how I've managed to keep operating, with T.J. Dillon preaching fire and brimstone against me."

"T.J. is an ass, in spades." Doc Price made a face.

"He's doing his damnedest to become a big man in Corpus, barking up every tree like a loony dog."

"I know all that, but he does have some influence. I was running scared for six months, sure that he'd manage to force me to shut the doors here. But he doesn't seem to have that much effect. I'm puzzled."

"It's simple, my dear. You're in the sin business, and since the war, the cattle business and the sin business have been in a boom period. A cowman, out on the range for months on end with nothing to look at but the hind end of a cow, hankers for a woman's well-rounded bottom to look at instead, not only to look at but to pat. The wilder, the wetter, the wickeder a town is, the better to their liking.

"The astute businessmen recognize this indisputable fact, so they began catering to the cowboys. In line with that, most towns legalized the saloons and bawdy houses by licensing them. This served two purposes. It made fancy houses legitimate, and the license fees took some of the tax burden off the backs of the good Christians.

"Texans developed a tolerance for such wickedness, not only a tolerance but a liking for it. If it was good enough for the cattlemen, it was good enough for them. That is why T.J. Dillon isn't having much success in arousing what he thinks should be the proper civic indignation."

"But why is he so incensed? I'm doing nothing to hurt him in any way."

Doc Price took a pull of his drink. "From what I hear about Dillon, it's not how much harm you can do him, but how much good you'll do for him, if he manages to chase you out of town. It'll be a means of showing his power. So if I were you, Debra, I wouldn't relax my guard. It's been my experience that when a man hungry for recognition and power is frustrated, he tends to redouble his efforts instead of letting up."

"I can't think of much else he can do."

"Oh, there are other things. So far, he's been within the law, more or less. I wouldn't put it past him to go beyond the law."

She stared at him. "Such as?"

"He could pay some bully boys to come in here and stir up a ruckus or two. If there's enough trouble stirred up in your place, then he might be able to get the powers that be to listen to him and close you down as a public nuisance."

Debra stirred uneasily. "Surely he wouldn't go to such lengths!"

"I wouldn't put it past him. Bradford Carpenter is a member of that Council of Four," his lip curled, "as they like to call themselves. Bradford is a friend of mine. A number of years back, when I was still trusted by Corpus Christians, I saved a daughter of his when she was given up for dead. Bradford tells me that T.J. Dillon seems obsessed by this thing. Even Bradford is puzzled by it."

"It sounds as though I should hire a bodyguard."

To Debra's surprise Doc Price took her remark seriously. "I agree, that would be a good idea. A house like this should always have a man around. A bouncer, as it were."

Just then Belle called Debra over to officiate at the cutting of the cake, and she immediately forgot about the discussion.

The following week, she came to see the truth of Doc Price's warning. It was a Saturday night, usually their busiest night, and this one was no exception.

Business began to slow down around midnight, and Debra had a few minutes to relax. She was in the kitchen having a sandwich and a cup of coffee, when Belle hurried in, looking worried.

"Honey, you'd better come out here. I smell trouble brewing."

Debra sighed and stood up. "What's wrong now?"

"One of the regulars, a gent by the name of Peter Howard, you know, the fellow from Austin, something to do with state government?"

"Yes, yes, I know who you mean, Belle," Debra said impatiently. "What about him? As I remember him, he seems well behaved, never causes any fuss."

"Oh, it ain't Mr. Howard, it's a friend he brought

120

Debra and scooted out the door. His hasty departure brought about a chorus of relieved sighs, and conversation became general. Bill Longley dipped his head at Debra, smiled slightly, and crossed the room to sit beside one of the girls.

Debra stepped to the piano. In a low voice she said, "Are you all right, Sally?"

Sally straightened up, her face still showing traces of fright. She said shakily, "Now I am. But I have to tell you, Debra, that I was scared out of my drawers there for a few minutes!"

"So was I, Sally, Godalmighty scared. Do you feel up to playing and singing?" At the girl's nod, Debra said, "Then give us a song. Something bright and cheerful, see if we can't perk this crowd up a little."

As Sally began to play a lively melody, Peter Howard, a hangdog expression on his face, approached Debra. "Miss Moraghan, I wish to apologize. I had no idea that Farnum would stir up a ruckus. You can be sure that I'll never invite him again."

It was on the tip of Debra's tongue to remind him that bringing along a guest who caused trouble was enough to revoke his club privileges. She changed her mind, however, and said instead, "Since it turned out all right, thanks to Bill Longley, we'll let it pass this time. But I would appreciate it if you'd tell me about Farnum. Who is he, and how did you come to invite him?"

"Until two days ago, I didn't know him from Adam," Howard said sheepishly. "A man in Austin asked a favor of me. He asked me to invite Farnum to your place as my guest. The man who asked the favor is high up in state government, but it'll be a cold day in hell before he'll get another favor of me!"

"T.J. Dillon had nothing to do with your bringing Farnum here?"

"T.J. who?" He stared. "Oh, you mean the fellow up on the bluff? Not so far as I know, Miss Moraghan. I've never even met Dillon. Why do you think he had anything to do with this?"

"It's a long story, and one I doubt you'd be interested in. Anyway, I may be wrong. But Mr. Howard, just be more careful who you bring here in the future, all right?" She smiled forgivingly.

"You have my word on that," he said fervently.

Debra saw that Bill Longley was alone for the moment. She excused herself and crossed the room. "Mr. Longley?"

Those cold eyes came up, and he got to his feet. "Miss—Oh, Moraghan, is it?"

"Yes, I'm Debra Moraghan. I do want to thank you for rescuing me from what could easily have turned into a nasty situation."

"You are most welcome, ma'am." Humor touched his face. "A man's reputation, one like mine anyway, comes in handy sometimes."

"I see your glass is empty, Mr. Longley. May I join you in a drink?"

"It would be my pleasure, Miss Moraghan," he said.

Debra beckoned to the girl serving drinks and ordered a glass of wine for herself and a whiskey for Bill Longley.

Longley held up his glass. "To your good health, ma'am."

"Thank you, Mr. Longley."

They drank, and when Debra set her wineglass down, she caught Longley looking at her speculatively.

"I won't say that I'm surprised to find a lady such as yourself, one of good breeding, running a place like this. I've seen stranger things in my travels across the west, all the way up to the Dakota Territory. But what does surprise me is your drinking with a man of my reputation."

Debra shrugged. "I've learned never to take people for what other people say they are, Mr. Longley."

"Oh, what they say is mostly true, Miss Moraghan. I've killed a great many men—most of them deserved it," he said with a certain pride. "Of course, I'm not counting niggers. . . ."

Debra winced inwardly, but let nothing show, suspecting that he was testing for a reaction. One thing could be said for the Moraghans, except possibly her Uncle Brian—they had never bred prejudice into their children.

124

Debra was quite familiar with the story of Nora Moraghan defying her neighbors' prejudices and producing a version of *Uncle Tom's Cabin* in her little schoolhouse, to the outrage of the audience, who walked out en masse. Yet the Civil War was too fresh in the minds of most Texans, and feeling against the Negro still ran high across the state.

Longley was going on, ". . . . I was fifteen when I killed my first nigger. A lawman he was, if you can feature that. He was riding down the street threatening decent white folks with a rifle. He threatened to gun down my pa. I shot him dead, and folks buried him on the quiet, and nobody else ever knew what happened to him."

He chuckled reminiscently and took a drink. "I've been many things since then. Cowboy, gambler, saloon keeper. I even stooped to chopping cotton for a spell. But I always had my iron on my hip. I wandered all over the west. There was no law at all. It was simply the rule of claw and tooth and fang, and the weakest went to the wall. The only law was the rope. When folks got real down on a man, they strung him up and retired to the nearest saloon to celebrate with a few drinks."

His glass was empty, and Debra gestured to the girl to refill it. Debra wondered why Longley was so garrulous. Of course, he probably had few friends or confidants.

What he said next confirmed her surmise. "I was asked once why I was never caught or gunned down. The answer is simple, I never had any confidence in anybody." He accepted the fresh glass of whiskey, drank. "I've also been asked if I regretted killing any of those men. Only one. I was camping with a feller once, years back. I'd had a hard day and wanted to go to sleep. Now this feller kept watching me across the campfire, and there wasn't no way I was going to close my eyes with him eyeballing me. Well, along about midnight, tuckered out as I was, I got enough of it, so I shot him in the head and went to sleep. The next day I found out that this feller was on the dodge, just like me, so I've always felt kinda sorry I shot him."

Longley was smiling coldly, and Debra wondered just how sorry he was. She felt a shiver of revulsion, but she concealed it. She had been raised on stories of the bad men of the West but had never expected to meet one face to face. Still, she reasoned, Bill Longley was a product of his times and probably no better or worse than others of his ilk. After all, he had extricated her from a potentially explosive situation. Whether from good motives, or simply from the need to show just how much fear his name would evoke, did not really matter—the results were the same.

An idea came to her, and she mulled it over during a few minutes of silence. She recalled a remark Rose had made: "You can't roll in the dirt and expect to get up as clean as a whistle." On the other hand, she already had a bad name in Corpus, so how much worse could it be?

She said, "If I'm not being too personal, Mr. Longley, how do you happen to be in Corpus?"

He shrugged, unoffended. "Laying low for a spell. I got into a spot of trouble up north and had to hightail it. I figure this is as good a place as any to wait until things cool down. Thing is, I'm running low on dinero. Another week or so and I'm going to have to scout around for something."

"I just may have a solution." She added quickly, "It's only temporary, of course."

"Temporary is fine with me. I never stay in one place for long, it ain't healthy." He drank. "What did you have in mind, Miss Moraghan?"

She took a deep breath. "There is a man here in Corpus, T.J. Dillon, who is trying everything he can think of to get me closed down. Although I have no way of proving it, I'm convinced he paid this man Farnum to come in here tonight and stir up trouble. If there had been a bad ruckus, Dillon could probably have me closed down as a public nuisance. I'm sure he'll try again. But if you're here, to keep things under control, he'll have trouble finding someone to go up against you. I can't pay too much, but there is an empty room you can use, and you can take your meals here. Also"—she looked away—"you can enjoy the privileges of the house."

"Watchdog for a fancy house?" Longley looked amused. "That I've never done before. It might be good for a few laughs. But I warn you, I will be moving on. A couple of weeks at the most."

"That will be fine, Mr. Longley." Debra was already wondering if she was making a mistake. There was always the possibility that Bill Longley might cause more trouble than he would prevent. However, for all his reputation, he seemed in command of himself, and she had the feeling that, no matter how much liquor he consumed, he would never let it get out of hand. A drunken gunfighter was an easy target for anyone eager to have the reputation of being the man who gunned down Bill Longley.

"We have a bargain then?" Longley raised his glass.

"We have a bargain, Mr. Longley." She clicked her glass against his.

". . . Bill Longley, Mr. Dillon," Farnum said. "No way I'm going up against him. Lord knows how many men he's gunned down. He's deadlier'n a rattlesnake whose tail you just tromped on."

T.J. Dillon contemptuously studied the sweating man. "I went to a lot of trouble to get you in there, pulling some strings in the state government, and I paid you well. Now you come whining to me with empty hands. Well, you'll just have to go back when Longley isn't around."

"That woman'll never let me in again. Besides, ain't you heard?"

"Heard what?" Dillon snarled.

"Seems she's paying Longley to stick around. He's even staying there."

Dillon stirred his bulk, excitement gnawing at him. "That should be enough right there to have the authorities close her down, harboring a wanted man, an infamous killer."

"Naw." Farnum was shaking his head. "You're blowing air, Mr. Dillon. Bill Longley ain't wanted in these parts. He's careful not to shit in his own backyard. Folks in

127

this part of Texas figure him for one of their own. No local law is going to go after him."

Dillon felt a rise of bile. "Damn it to hell, there must be some fellow around who's not afraid of Bill Longley!"

"The only one I know who ain't might be the Piper."

"Who?"

"Blackie Piper. He ain't afraid of God nor man, the way I hear it. Some say he's part nigger. He's sure as hell black enough. Onliest difference between Blackie and Bill Longley is that Blackie only kills for money. Longley now, he'll gun a man down for looking at him cross-eyed, or just for the hell of it. Longley's got a temper like a stick of dynamite, whilst Blackie's cold as a piece of ice. It's said that he never lost his temper in his life."

Dillon leaned forward eagerly. "Do you know how to get in touch with this Blackie?"

Farnum hesitated. "Last I heard, he was up around Fort Worth somewhere."

"You get him to come down here and face this Longley, and I calculate you'll earn the money I've already paid you."

"It'll cost you. Blackie doesn't come cheap."

Dillon waved a hand. "That's no matter."

"Bill Longley's probably faster, if'n he don't lose his temper. He might win a shoot-out."

Dillon scowled. "What do I care which one is killed? They can kill each other, for all I care. All I want is trouble in that bawdy house, enough trouble to get her closed down."

Twelve

Debra had felt some apprehension about hiring Bill Longley, fearful that his mere presence might frighten customers away. The contrary happened. Business picked up considerably.

"Curiosity, my dear," Doc Price told her through a brown screen of smoke from his cheroot. "William Longley's name is well-known, true, but many people have never laid eyes on him. Consequently, the gents all figure this is as good a chance as they'll ever get. As for being afraid of him, most of them probably are scared spitless. But this gives them a secondhand thrill. Besides," he grinned slyly, "haven't you ever heard that fear enhances the sex drive?"

She laughed. "No, Doc, I can't say I've ever heard that, but I'll take your word for it, since you've had so much experience with bawdy houses."

"Also, Bill Longley is considered a Texan, one of our own. And all men, even the meekest of us, often dream of being a badman. They're our heroes, in this time and place. Not good examples, I'll admit, but we make do with what we have."

Whether or not the doctor's analysis of the situation was correct, Debra was happy with her decision to employ Bill Longley. Her one fear, up until two days ago, had been that he might wish to remain indefinitely, and *that* she could not stomach. But she had noted his growing restlessness, and two nights before, he had confided in her, "I've been here almost three weeks, Miss Moraghan. That's usually longer than I stay in one place. My feet are beginning to itch. Despite the comforts offered here"—a wintry smile curved his mouth under the mustache—"I'll be moving on in a day or so."

Debra knew little more of Bill Longley than she had after that first night. He was not a particularly communicative man and had not confided in her after that one conversation. But he was unfailingly polite to the girls, soft-spoken, and although he drank heavily every night, he never once got out of line. Doc Price had told her that he was famous for his quick temper, yet Debra had not once seen any evidence of it.

After the episode with Peter Howard and Farnum, she had given a wary eye to any new faces. Consequently, when one of her regular customers came in with a stranger in tow, Debra took the customer aside. "Zeke, who's the gent with you? I'm being extra careful these days about strange men. Maybe you heard about an unpleasant experience I had three weeks ago?"

"Yes, Miss Moraghan, I heard about it. But this fellow now, he's gentle as a lamb. He'll give you no trouble."

There was something about Zeke's manner, however, that left Debra with an uneasy feeling. But there was little she could do about it. If she told Zeke, a regular customer, to ask his friend to leave, it would likely cause an unpleasant scene. She did decide to warn Bill Longley. Looking around the parlor, she didn't see him. He was always present in the evenings, but Debra had discovered that he had a weak bladder and had to make frequent trips to the outhouse in back.

One of the girls came up just then to ask her a question, and the stranger's presence escaped Debra's mind for a few moments. When she looked around again, she noted that Zeke had disappeared. The sense of impending trouble returned full force. Her glance sought out the stranger. He was tall, very dark, and thin as a skeleton. At the moment he was across the room, leaning up against a wall, a glass in his hand. He was dressed all in black, including his hat, which he wore tipped down, hiding his face. She saw that the whiskey glass was full and he was not drinking from it.

At that moment Bill Longley entered the parlor from the hall, and Debra heaved a sigh of relief. She took two steps toward him but halted as she saw the stranger step away from the wall, angling across the room toward Longley. He maneuvered until he was in the middle of the room. There he stopped, feet planted wide apart. He tipped his hat up, and his right hand brushed his coat back. Debra saw light wink off the holstered gun on his hip.

"Bill Longley?" His voice had a rusty, unused quality.

Longley stopped, his gaze on the stranger's face. "Yup, I'm Bill Longley. Do I know you, friend?"

"Blackie Piper."

"The Piper?" Longley's eyes widened a trifle. "I've wondered if our paths would ever cross by chance. But then, I reckon it ain't by chance, is it, Piper? Not if what I've heard about you is true."

"You know what you are, Longley?" Piper said in that grating voice. "You're a low-life sonofabitch, lower'n a snake's belly! You're yellow through and through!"

"Trying to get me riled, are you, Piper? I reckon you've heard about my temper. But I've been called just about every name in the book, names don't bother me much nowadays. Who paid you to come looking for me, Piper? And how much? I always like to know what I'm worth to some yellow belly without the guts to face me on his own."

"Now I know why you've killed so many men. You talked 'em to death!"

"I wouldn't bet your wad on that, Piper." Longley raised his voice. "What was the name of that feller's been after you, Miss Moraghan? I reckon he's paying the Piper." He laughed softly. "Little joke there, Piper. Course, being a nigger like you are, I reckon you don't have much of a sense of humor."

What happened next happened so quickly that Debra was never quite clear in her mind about it.

She saw Piper's right hand start for his hip. Her position was such that she could also see Longley on the periphery of her vision. His own right hand was a blur, so fast did it move. His pistol fired as it came up, and a second shot sounded an instant later.

The distance between the two men was about fifteen feet. Piper's weapon had just cleared the holster as the two bullets struck him. He managed to fire once, the bullet gouging splinters from the floor. At such close range the force of the bullets striking his chest hurled him all the way across the room. His stumbling body knocked over a table, and one of the girls jumped screaming out of his way. He struck the wall and slid down. Two spots of wetness appeared on his chest and spread, like scarlet flowers blossoming.

The room stank of gunpowder and still reverberated with the booming of the gunshots. An eerie silence fell as the sound faded away.

Debra was shocked and sickened by the raw, primitive violence. And in a way, she had triggered it. If she hadn't asked Longley to stay around, this would never have happened. She knew, with stunning clarity, that this was a moment she would never forget. It would cause her many sleepless nights.

A murmur grew as people began to talk together in shocked voices. As one in a daze, Debra made her way toward Bill Longley.

The gunfighter still had the revolver in his hand, his face frozen in a smile like a rictus, his gaze on the inert body of Blackie Piper. He gave a start as Debra came up. After blowing the last wisps of smoke from the Colt, he quickly inserted two fresh cartridges and holstered it.

"The sonofabitch thought he'd rile me," he said calmly. "They all think that, thinking it'll give them an edge. My temper, Miss Moraghan, ain't near as bad as I've made it out to be. But fellers believing I'm that touchy gives me an advantage. In my kind of work, a man needs all the advantages he can get. It's helped keep me alive."

Debra said tonelessly, "I never dreamed that it would come down to this."

"Didn't you now?" he said. "Next time you'll know.

When you have a man like me around, death is always close, me or the other feller's."

Debra shook her head, her mind beginning to function again. "What you said just before, asking me for Dillon's name. Do you think—?"

"Think he hired the Piper to come after me? Somebody sure as hell did. You can bet on it, Miss Moraghan. Blackie Piper was a gun for hire. He would never come gunning for someone unless he was paid to. This means I have to be on my way, soon as I can pack up and git. What happened here will be all over Texas in a matter of days. If the law up north learns my whereabouts, they'll come looking. So, it's adios, Miss Moraghan. It's been a pleasure knowing you, a real pleasure."

"It's probably just as well, your leaving now," she said dejectedly. "After I call the law in here and word gets around about what happened, they'll likely close me down. If the law doesn't move in that direction, I'm sure that T.J. Dillon will see that they do."

T.J. Dillon chortled to himself and took a drink of bourbon in celebration. Word had just reached him about the gun battle at the Emporium. He had the lever he needed now to close the place down. If the authorities didn't act at once, he thought, he'd by God see that they moved against that house of sin. The people of Corpus Christi would be outraged over an infamous gunfighter killing a man in a brothel in their city. It would give the town a bad name throughout Texas. All those high-and-mighty bigwigs from Austin and elsewhere would no longer dare come to her defense and keep her place open.

He took another swallow of his drink, just as Consuela came into the study. He glared at her. "What do you want? I didn't call you."

"There is a man here to see you, Señor Dillon."

"Who is he?"

"He did not tell me his name, but he said that it would be to your benefit to see him."

"All right," Dillon said irritably. "Send him in."

Consuela ushered in a tall, goateed man, and left

133

them alone. Dillon scowled at the stranger. "Who the hell are you?"

The man's eyes glinted coldly. "We haven't met, but I think you'll recognize my name. I'm Bill Longley."

His right hand pushed back the tail of his long coat, and Dillon saw the gun on his hip. Dillon's guts froze in terror.

"I just killed a man I believe you hired to gun me down. That don't matter a whole lot. It's happened before, and it'll doubtless happen again. The reason I'm here is to deliver a warning."

"A warning?" Dillon croaked.

"Yeah. I'm leaving Corpus, but there's a little lady by the name of Debra Moraghan you seem to have it in for. Now I don't like that, I purely don't. She's a fine lady, and I wouldn't like to hear that anything's happened to her, like her place being closed down on account of you. I have friends in Corpus, who always know how to get in touch with me. If I hear from them that you've caused her more trouble, I'll head right back to Corpus and gun you down like I would a mad dog in the street. I want you to understand that I mean what I say, Mr. Dillon."

His arm moved, and the gun was in his hand, aimed directly at Dillon's heart. Dillon cringed as he saw the hammer drawn back. Then the muzzle shifted a fraction, and a shot blew apart the whiskey glass in his hand. Dillon stared stupidly at the glass fragments on his desk. One shard had slashed open his thumb, and blood flowed freely from the cut.

Longley said tautly, "Is my message loud and clear, Mr. Dillon?"

Dillon felt warm liquid stain the crotch of his trousers. He had pissed himself. He nodded mutely, unable to speak.

Thirteen

Bill Longley's estimate of widespread news coverage of the shooting at Rose's Emporium was an understatement, if anything.

The news raced like a prairie fire across Texas and beyond, and the newspapers seized on it hungrily.

Headlines blared: "Shoot-Out in Brothel"; "Infamous Gunfighter Kills Man in Corpus Christi Whorehouse"; "Bill Longley Adds Another Notch to His Gun"; "Bill Longley Versus The Piper: Piper Loses Bout"; "Outrage in Sporting House." And so on, and so on.

The front page news stories were pretty much the same:

Bill Longley, hired as a protector for Rose's Emporium, a notorious sporting house in Corpus Christi, Gulf Coast resort city, gunned down a man late Tuesday evening. His victim was another well-known killer for hire, Blackie Piper, known familiarly as The Piper, and his death certainly will not be mourned as any monumental loss by our decent citizens.

How long will the state of Texas remain a haven for badmen? The wild and woolly days of the shoot-em-up West are gone forever, or should be.

But how can they be gone when incidents of violence such as this continue unabated?

It is long past time for all decent-minded citizens to rise up in righteous wrath and let their elected representatives know that such outlawry, such arrogant defiance of law and order, will no longer be tolerated.

It is also time for the legal closure of houses of ill-repute such as Rose's Emporium in Corpus Christi, operated by Debra Moraghan. Your reporter has investigated Debra Moraghan's background and discovered that she comes from good stock. Her grandfather, Sean Moraghan, was a respected citizen of Nacogdoches, Texas. His eldest son, Brian Moraghan, is today an upstanding citizen in his own right, one of the foremost timber men in East Texas. Debra Moraghan's father, Kevin Moraghan, is at the present time a farmer in the Rio Grande Valley, just outside of Brownsville.

It is a cause for alarm when a woman of such good lineage can sink so low as to become the madam of a notorious brothel. The answer as to why such a thing should come to pass is not known by your reporter, but it is much to be deplored. For shame, Debra Moraghan!

"Oh, my dear God!" Kate muttered in horror as she read the week-old newspaper.

Fortunately, she was alone in the house at the moment. Michael and Lena were outside and Kevin, after bringing the mail pouch in from Brownsville, had gone out to the fields after learning there was no important mail.

"I'll read the paper before supper tonight," he'd said. "There's usually nothing but bad news, anyway."

Kate sighed, dreading his reaction when he read the paper. She even toyed with the thought of destroying the newspaper before he saw it, telling him that she'd burned it by mistake. But that would not do; he was sure to learn eventually, and probably from a neighbor, which would only make it worse.

136

"I'm not so sure about that," he said, a distant look on his face.

"I'd advise you to stay out of it, Brian. In fact, I forbid you to do it."

"You *forbid*, Momma?" He sneered. "You've long since forfeited the right to forbid me anything. If I decide to go see Debra Lee, I'll go."

By the time Stonewall Lieberman rode out for Sunday supper with Nora, he had already read the article. "I guess you've seen the paper?"

Nora nodded. "I have. Not only that, but I've had neighbors dropping by, people I haven't seen in years, just to make damned sure I've heard the news." She grinned wickedly. "I do believe some of them were surprised to find me still alive. I don't know whether they thought age might have taken me or the shock and shame of it may have killed me. Whatever, I can't say I'm sorry to disappoint them."

"It doesn't upset you?"

She shrugged. "Not all that much, Stonewall."

"You're a remarkable woman, Nora."

"Brian is upset enough to make up for both of us. He's even talking of going down there to chew on her." She added dryly, "It's too bad Debra Lee is his niece, he might turn it into an enjoyable time, since he knows his way around a whorehouse. But I don't think even Brian would indulge himself with a relative running the place."

They were silent for a long moment, Nora surreptitiously studying Stony's frowning countenance. "I gather that you are somewhat upset, Stonewall?"

He nodded glumly. "I'm upset for Debra's sake. I do feel sorry for her."

"I doubt she needs your sympathy all that much. Besides, you can always say she brought it on herself."

"Well, damnit, she did bring it on herself, Nora!" he said angrily.

"Yes, in a manner of speaking, to the extent that any person brings trouble on themselves by simply living."

141

"Nora—" He stood up. "She doesn't have to live in a brothel! That was her own choice."

"There are all too many people in this world who have little or no choice about the life they live," she said mildly. "What she did takes courage, you have to admit that. Courage to defy tradition and courage to risk social and family disapproval. She chose to live her life on her terms, not spend it bending to the will of a husband."

He peered at her suspiciously. "Meaning me, I suppose?"

"If you wish to take it that way, yes."

"Nora, you had a good life as wife to a man, didn't you? Have you regretted any of it?"

"Yes, I had a good life. But I had no real choice in the matter. Of course I loved Sean, but in a way I had to go after him, just as Debra Lee set her cap for you. But something happened there, and she gave up on you."

"Damnit, are you trying to make me feel guilty?"

She said dryly, "There's a saying, if the shoe fits. . . ."

"No!" He pounded his fist into his palm. "I refuse to accept the responsibility! It was her own choice."

"Stonewall," she said quietly, "do you love the girl?"

"Yes, damnit, I do!" he shouted. "There, is that what you wanted to hear? Are you satisfied now?"

She ignored his outburst. "Then I think you should go to her, tell her so."

"And what good would that do?" He paced back and forth, then said in a subdued voice, "It's official now, Nora. I've been asked to run for judge. I agreed, and my name goes on the ballot. As it stands now, I have no effective opposition. Do you have any idea what an honor it is for a lawyer to become a judge? It's what most lawyers dream about all their lives."

"I'm sure it's a great honor, Stonewall, and I'm happy for you. If you go to Corpus Christi and see Debra Lee, that would give them some dirt to throw at you, wouldn't it?"

"It could easily cost me the election. I suppose you think that's selfish of me, but I would even take the risk if I thought it would do any good. But by running off like that, Debra made it quite plain where I stand with

142

her. By now she may know other men." A spasm of agony tightened his face. "I would only embarrass her, embarrass both of us."

Nora was sure that she knew what he was thinking. Despite Debra Lee's disclaimer to the contrary in her letter, it was clear that by "other men," Stonewall meant a whore's customers.

She sighed, said, "Stonewall, you do what you have to do. I'll think none the less of you for it. There are times in this world when a person has no choice but to think of himself first."

Despite what he had said to Nora, Brian wavered for several days. Maybe it would be better to let it rest in the hope that talk would die down and people would forget about it. The plain fact was, he dreaded a confrontation with Debra Lee. How could a man lay down the law to his own daughter, when she didn't know she was his daughter? And he had to admit that she had inherited his stubbornness, if nothing else, and such a confrontation might very well come to nothing in the end, anyway.

However, his mind was definitely made up for him later in the week when he had occasion to go into Nacogdoches to see Tod Danker. He saw as little of Sheriff Danker as possible. Brian had not been one of the men behind the scenes manipulating Danker into the sheriff's office. Although he was not a man to let old enmities get in the way of a dollar, Brian still felt his blood boil at the mention of the Danker name. Tod Danker's daddy *had* killed Sean Moraghan, and Brian had loved his father, probably the only person he had ever truly loved in his life.

Aside from that, he considered Danker a slimy fellow, as crooked as they came, going with whichever favorable wind blew his way. And at the time Danker's election to the sheriff's office had been broached, Brian could not see his way clear to supporting him—openly, secretly with campaign funds, or in any other way.

However, Brian had to admit that Danker had his uses. Ask a favor, slip him fifty or a hundred dollars under the table, and the favor was usually granted. Brian had bought favors only a couple of times before. Now he was having a problem with timber thieves. Recently he had leased the timber rights to a hundred acres east of Nacogdoches, virgin timber that should yield him a large margin of profit by the time it was cleared off. He had erected a temporary sawmill on the property so the logs could be sawed before being hauled into town. Four times over the past few weeks, when the crew came to work at the sawmill in the morning, they had found lumber missing. By a rough estimate, Brian figured he had lost a half-dozen loads of lumber. It had to be stopped. He could hire a couple of men to guard the sawmill at night, by why go to that much expense when Danker's services were available?

He found Tod Danker in his office in the courthouse, booted feet propped upon his scarred desk. He was wearing a yellow duster. It was a brisk winter day, but it seemed strange for him to be wearing the duster indoors. Thinking back, Brian realized that he had never seen Danker without it.

Danker took his time about removing his feet from the desk and getting up. "Well, Mr. Moraghan! Ain't often you drop by to see me. To what do I owe the pleasure?"

His tone was servile enough, but Brian thought he detected a hint of sly mockery in his voice. He said, "I have a situation at one of my sawmills. . . ." He went on to explain the problem.

Danker nodded. "I'll take care of it, Mr. Moraghan, you can depend on it. I'll stake the place out, me and one of my deputies. Anybody comes sneaking around, we'll blow a load of buckshot up their ass. If that don't do it, we'll plant 'em in the ground, so they'll never steal your lumber again. I reckon you don't care much how we do it, so long as it's done?" His grin was knowing.

Brian tried unsuccessfully to hide a spasm of distaste. "How you handle it is your business, Sheriff." He took an envelope from his pocket and passed it across the desk. "Christmas will be around soon. Here's a little something for your Christmas stocking."

Danker said, "I'm mighty grateful to you, Mr. Mor-

144

aghan." He took the envelope and quickly slid it into his desk, making of it a furtive gesture.

Brian said coolly, "I'll say good day then, Sheriff."

Danker waited until he got to the door before saying, "Mr. Moraghan?"

"Yes?"

"Too bad about your niece, ain't it?"

Brian went rigid. "What do you mean?"

With a straight face Danker said, "Oh, all that trouble she's in down in Corpus Christi. Leastways, if what I hear is true, she's in a mess. Course, maybe that's all so much wind. People do like to gossip about people who're better'n they are, now don't they?"

Brian throttled back a rise of anger, said tightly, "And that seems to include you, doesn't it, Danker?"

Danker's muddy eyes widened in a pretense of innocence. "I reckon I don't understand, Mr. Moraghan."

"Oh, you understand well enough. You're pleased as a toad that gossip is fouling the Moraghan name." He stepped to the desk, leaned on it on his hands, and thrust his face at the sheriff. "If I hear that you're dirtying the Moraghan name with your tongue, I'll personally see to it that you rue the day. I've got a lot of push in this part of Texas, Danker, and I'll use whatever I have to to shut your mouth!"

Danker's eyes went flat, but he didn't seem intimidated in the least. "I meant no disrespect. I was just passing on the gossip."

Brian said grimly, "You just see that it stops here, in this office, and I'll see that it stops elsewhere."

"Just how you going to do that, Mr. Moraghan?"

Brian straightened up, his decision made in that instant. "I'm leaving for Corpus Christi. I'll see for myself just how much truth there is to all this bullshit floating around, and straighten everything out."

He turned on his heel and strode out.

Danker called after him, "Well, good luck to you, Mr. Moraghan."

Tod Danker waited until Brian Moraghan had slammed the door behind him before reaching down into the bottom drawer of his desk for the bottle he kept there. He took a long suck at it. The bite of the fiery liquor only fueled his smoldering fury.

The highfalutin' sonofabitch! All the Moraghans thought their shit smelled like French perfume. Well, he had dirtied one, the girl. Now *her* shit probably smelled like whorehouse perfume!

He laughed coarsely at the thought. He had meant to humiliate her when he'd raped her that night, rub a little mud on her, but never in his wildest imaginings had he dreamed it would turn her into a whore! Now this scandal was icing on the cake.

He cackled with glee, took another drink. His rage receded, and his thoughts fell more into order. It was long past time he was putting the Danker stamp on Mr. Brian Moraghan. There had to be a way, there was always a way. But he wanted it to be more permanent than what he'd inflicted on the girl.

He sat up straight as an idea came to him. He examined it carefully, his smile growing. If he handled it right, he could accomplish his purpose, and he could get away with it, with no one the wiser.

Fourteen

Belle stuck her head in the door, said in a breathless voice, "Honey, there's someone here to see you."

Debra tensed and turned around at her desk, where she was totaling up some bills. "Who is it? The law?"

"Nope." Belle smiled suddenly. "It's a woman, says she's your mother."

"Mother! Godalmighty!" Debra shot to her feet. She started to run from the room, then stopped in mid-stride. "Tell her to come up, Belle."

Belle nodded and turned away, leaving the door open. Debra, jittery as a new bride, flew to her dressing table and snatched up the hand mirror. She looked a holy mess, she thought. After tucking in a stray hair, she searched frantically through the confusion on the table-top for powder and rouge. Then she gave a snort and straightened up. Whatever her mother wanted, she wouldn't be much concerned with how she looked!

Debra moved into the center of the room, trying to look composed and in command of herself. She heard light footsteps in the hallway outside and managed to retain her composure until Kate Moraghan appeared in the doorway.

Her mother smiled tentatively, said softly, questioningly, "Debra Lee?"

Debra went at a stumbling run into her arms. "Oh, Mother!" The tears came then, in a flood, the first tears she had shed since the shoot-out.

Kate held her tenderly, murmuring nonsense words of love. Finally, with a determined effort, Debra stepped back, dashing away the tears with her knuckles. "I'm sorry, Mother, for the waterworks. You know I'm not a weeper, but it's just seeing you, and so unexpectedly, when I feared you and Daddy might never want to speak to me again." She craned to look past Kate's shoulder. "Where is Daddy, downstairs?"

"He didn't come, dear."

Debra stiffened. "I should have known!"

"Now don't go leaping to conclusions," Kate said sharply. "We couldn't both very well come, without bringing the children, and I'm sure even you will agree that this is hardly the place to bring children. Kevin thought it best that I come alone, but he wanted me to assure you that he loves you as much as ever and that you have his best wishes."

Debra laughed shakily. "Best wishes! I find that hard to believe, sending best wishes to his daughter who is running a whorehouse!"

"Which means you don't know him as well as you thought. Kevin was afraid you wouldn't understand. To tell the truth, I thought he would fly into a rage, myself, when he read that newspaper article." Kate smiled slightly. "But he didn't, so I don't know him so well, either. You know the first thing he said? He said that Brian would undoubtedly roar like a maddened bull when he read the article."

"I'm sure he did. I thought of Uncle Brian, too," Debra said with a laugh. "I've been expecting to hear from Grandmother Nora. Mother, why are you here? Don't misunderstand, I'm glad to see you. You'll never know what a lift it gives me. But if you've come all the way here to try and talk me into—"

"Debra Lee, I haven't come to talk you into anything. I thought you would like to know that we're behind you, no matter what. Of course, if you *should* like to come

148

home, Kevin and I would be most happy. But I suppose—"

"No, Mother," Debra said grimly. "I wouldn't tuck my tail between my legs and run home now. Godalmighty, no! I'm sticking."

"That figures." Kate sighed. "What has been happening since the shooting?"

"Nothing really, and that surprises me. Oh, more of the townspeople than before are turning their noses up when I walk by. But I expected some effort would be made to close me down. I wrote you about T.J. Dillon. I'm sure he was behind the shooting. He sent Blackie Piper in here to cause trouble, intending to use it to have the city close me down. But there hasn't been a whisper. And business has been better than ever. I suppose the men are coming largely out of curiosity." She laughed at Kate's shocked look. "I'm sorry, Mother, I know that's not news to make you joyful, my increased business."

"This business does take some getting used to," Kate said ruefully. "But I'll adjust."

"How long are you going to stay, Mother?"

"I can stay as long as you need me. I had planned on staying at least a week."

"There are several good hotels in town. Or"—Debra's look was probing—"I have a room for you here. It's up to you."

Kate smiled palely. "I think I can stay here without getting contaminated, my darling daughter."

Belle rapped lightly on the doorjamb, then stuck her head into the room. "Miss Moraghan," she said primly, "supper is on the table. And you know Lupe, if we don't eat while it's hot, she pouts for days."

"Mother—" Debra touched Kate's arm. "Will you have supper with us? One thing we do have is good food. Lupe is a fine cook."

"Debra Lee, if you keep mincing around the mulberry bush about me being here, it's going to be an uncomfortable week for both of us. I will sleep here, I will eat here. One thing I will not do"—her laughter was a burst of sound—"is work here."

Debra nodded. "You're right, Mother. I won't tiptoe around it anymore. Belle, tell Lupe to set another plate for supper. We're having company."

In the beginning it was an uneasy meal. Aside from an occasional male—Doc Price, Bill Longley, et cetera— this was the first time an outside person had eaten with them. Instead of the usual chatter among the girls, there was an awkward silence, and they all avoided looking directly at Kate. For some minutes the only sounds were the noises of cutlery and china. Debra was beginning to wonder if it had been a mistake to ask her mother to eat with them, but she would be damned if she would apologize to the girls!

Then Kate said to June Blount, "That's a lovely blouse you're wearing—June, is it? Did you make it yourself?"

June looked startled and at a loss for words. Then gulped. "No'm, I can't sew for shit—uh, pardon me!" She turned red as fire. "I bought it before I came here."

Tactfully Kate turned to the girl to her right and commented on the weather. Debra hid a smile behind her hand. The blouse in question, of course, was the same one that she had forbidden June to wear in the presence of customers, and Debra was sure that her mother thought of it as a slut's garment.

The ice had been broken, and conversation became general around the table, the girls including Kate in it. Soon, they were accepting her as readily as if she'd been there for years. Debra realized what she should already have known—Kate was gracious and charming, and there was a sincerity about her that was unmistakable. Debra chided herself for misjudging her mother; after all their years together, she should have known Kate better than that. Evidently there was a core of truth in the old saw, familiarity breeds contempt, she reflected wryly.

After supper she said, "I have to do some shopping before all the stores close, Mother. Order some groceries for morning delivery. You like to go along with me?"

Kate gave her a penetrating look. She said slowly, "I'd be happy to go along, Debra Lee."

It was dark when they left the house, and the salt air

off the Gulf was damp and chilly. They walked briskly, wraps drawn tightly around their shoulders. The streets were mostly empty under the flickering gaslights, and they met few people, none that Debra knew.

Several blocks from the house, Debra turned into Jackson's General Store. There were no customers in the place. Sam Jackson, a graying, portly man in his early sixties, greeted Debra warmly. "You ain't been in in a coon's age, Debra."

"I haven't been getting out much, Mr. Jackson. I figured it was about time I did, so folks wouldn't think I had left town."

"Aw, hell!" The storekeeper waved a beefy hand. "Don't let it fret you none, it'll all blow over soon enough. Just give it time."

Debra gave him a slip of paper. "Here's a list of things for you to deliver in the morning, Mr. Jackson."

Kate stepped up. "Since she forgot to introduce me, Mr. Jackson, I'm Kate Moraghan, Debra Lee's mother." She put her arm around Debra's shoulders. "I'm up from Brownsville for a visit with her."

"I'm sure you're proud of—" The storekeeper stumbled to a halt, his face flaming.

"Proud of her? Yes, Mr. Jackson, I am proud of my daughter," Kate said steadily. "Very proud indeed, both her father and I."

Debra shrank from her mother's smile, suddenly feeling very small. She said quickly, "You have the list, Mr. Jackson. You can fill it without me, and I'll expect the order in the morning."

Outside the store, Debra said, "I want you to know that I am proud of you, too, Mother." Tears sprang to her eyes. "That took courage in there."

"Courage is as courage does, as Nora might say." Kate took Debra's hand and enfolded it in hers. "If you have other stores to make, we'd better hurry before they close."

The rest of Kate's stay went smoothly. She became friends with most of the girls. "I've read about housemothers in schools. That's about what I feel like here.

But I must tell you one thing, Debra Lee. Most of these girls are friendly, nice, if maybe not the smartest I've ever known, and I can warm up to them. But there are three or four that I can't bring myself to deal with. They're selfish, grasping, and cold as ice. June Blount, for one. It's like they never had human feelings, either born without them or what they've endured has frozen them inside."

Debra laughed. "There's a few I don't care for, either, but I don't have all that much choice. To pick only girls that I like would leave me with slim pickings. You have to realize something, Mother. Most of these girls *are* stupid, else they wouldn't be whores in the first place. Oh, not all of them by any means. Circumstances have driven some of them into the business."

Kate was frowning. "I don't think it's because they're stupid that they're not likable, Debra Lee. There are a couple of your girls with no more brains than a flea, yet I can't help but warm to them."

"I agree. Being brainless doesn't mean that you have no feelings. I think many of them are born that way. They're born without any feeling of love in them, and I've found that most of them really hate men, with a vengeance. Every one has some story or other about how they became whores because some man, or men plural, abused them or turned them into whores to make money off them. But it seems to me that if you can't feel or return love, you *invite* abuse by men."

Kate gave her a look of astonishment. "That's an insight I wouldn't expect from you, Debra Lee. It seems that my little girl *has* grown up." She took Debra's hand, looked into her eyes. "Tell me, is that why you have never loved a man? Because you can't return love? I find that a little hard to believe, but then something must have happened between you and Stonewall Lieberman—"

Debra flushed angrily, snatched her hand away. "You're not only being personal, Mother, but offensive as well."

"Well, I'm sorry about that, but if a mother can't inquire into a daughter's private life, who can? For years you've talked of nothing but Stony Lieberman, and I know that's why you went to Moraghan. I think I'm entitled to know what happened."

"All right, I'll tell you, Mother!" Debra drew a steadying breath. "Stony Lieberman didn't want me. Now, does that satisfy you?"

"Didn't want you?" Kate was thoughtful. "Didn't want you or didn't love you?"

Debra shrugged. "What's the difference?"

"There is a great deal of difference, Debra Lee. Did you love him?"

"I thought I did. But what does it matter? It all came to nothing."

Kate touched her hand. "Debra Lee, I know it's almost a joke, a mother always after her daughter to get married, but both Kevin and I would be happy to see you married. Is there any man you're seeing, anyone courting you?"

"Hardly, Mother." Debra laughed. "This would not exactly be the place to find a suitable husband, now would it?"

"I can't argue with that. And of course, for me to ask when you're giving all this up, would only get your dander up."

"You're exactly right, Mother. I have no intention of giving up here, not until I have made the money I expect to make. And I wouldn't cave in under all the pressure now, Godalmighty, no! Nobody is about to frighten me away from here before I'm ready to leave."

The afternoon after Kate left for Brownsville, something happened that caused Debra to wonder if it was by design—the Moraghans coming at her from all sides.

She was in her room when Belle knocked lightly and opened the door. "Honey, there's somebody downstairs to see you. A man, this time."

Debra, at her dressing table getting ready for the evening's business, turned about. "Who is it?"

Belle shrugged. "It's nobody I know, and he refused to give me his name. All he'd say was that you would know him when you saw him."

153

Could it be her father? Debra dismissed that thought at once. For a moment she considered telling Belle to turn whoever it was away, but she finally nodded. "All right, send him up, Belle."

Debra quickly put on a dress and composed herself to wait, leaving her door open. When footsteps stopped before the door and she saw Brian Moraghan in the doorway, Debra wasn't really surprised. It was inevitable that the newspaper stories would draw him here.

"Hello, Uncle Brian," she said evenly. "I suppose I was subconsciously expecting you to show up."

"I'll just bet you were," he said, with a sneer. He came into the room, slamming the door behind him. "A real fancy place you've got here."

"Yes, it is. And that's what it is, a fancy house."

"Don't be flippant with me, young lady." His voice was loud, carrying, and she abruptly realized that he had been drinking heavily.

"Did you have to get drunk to face me?"

"I had a few drinks, yes. The shame of it would drive any decent man to drink. And speaking of shame, I should think you would be ashamed to face me."

"I feel no shame." Her head went back in defiance.

"Well, you damned well should! Unless you've become so corrupt that your soul has rotted away!"

"The condition of my soul is no concern of yours, Uncle Brian. Why are you here?"

"To see to it that you close this place down. I refuse to have the name of Moraghan connected with a whorehouse!"

"You have nothing at all to say about it. My mother was just here—"

"Kate was *here*?" His eyes widened.

"She was. And if *she* was ashamed of me, she hid it very well. She came to give me support, and she said that Daddy sends his love. So, if my own parents aren't ashamed of me, why should you be?"

He batted a hand in the air. "What does it matter to Kevin what gets around about you? He's nothing but a damned dirt farmer! Gossip can't do him any harm. But

154

me, I'm a man of substance in East Texas. I don't want filth smeared on my name."

"Man of substance, are you?" she said contemptuously. "Godalmighty, you're not half the man Daddy is. He's working his fingers raw down there, trying to make something of the land, while you're raping it."

His face went red and ugly. He took a step toward her, hand upraised. He staggered and had to wave his arms in the air for balance. "You have no right to badmouth me! You, a whorehouse madam! But I'm not here to argue the point with you. I'm here to see to it that you close this place down."

"Then you made the trip for nothing, for I have no intention of closing, and you can't make me."

"I damned well can! If you won't listen to me, I'll go to people in town here who will."

"They won't listen to you, either, Uncle Brian. You may be a big man in East Texas, but you don't amount to a hill of beans here. And you have no authority to tell me what to do or what not to do."

"Oh, yes, I do." His eyes seemed to lose focus for a moment, and he lurched two steps toward the bed.

"Why do you say that? What authority?"

"Because I'm your father, that's why!" he roared. "*I* am your daddy, not Kevin. That's what gives me the right to tell you what to do!"

The enormity of what he was saying was such that Debra literally staggered, as if from a blow. Hands at her throat, she gasped out, "I don't believe you! You're lying! For what reason I don't know, but you're lying."

"No, girl, I'm not lying," he said through gritted teeth. He modulated his voice slightly. "I'm purely sorry that you had to learn it this way, but the circumstances demanded it. I know how hard this is for you to believe. But ask your mother, ask Kate. Kevin, ask Kevin. It happened before they were married, you see. At the time, for good reason, I couldn't marry Kate. So, to have a father for you, she married Kevin."

"Then if what you say is true, how come Daddy knows?" Debra marveled at herself for discussing this in a perfectly normal fashion, as though she truly believed him.

"She said she had to tell him. Kate has always been so goddamned honorable," he said with an old bitterness.

"He married her anyway?"

"Yeah. How about that? I reckon old Kevin was so far gone on Kate that he would have married her no matter what."

Debra was staring at him with loathing. Hate rose in her, so virulent that she feared she would choke on it. She had thought that she would never hate another man as much as she did Tod Danker. She had been wrong.

Brian was saying, "So, you see, I have the right to tell you what to do, the right of a father—"

"Why? Because you and Mother rolled together in bed? Because you left your seed in her? You think that entitles you to boss me? You think that makes you my father? All it does is make you your bastard!" She spat the words at him. "Godalmighty, all that does is make me hate and despise you. Come to think of it, maybe you raped Mother, just like you do everything else in this world!"

Brian's face paled, and he took on a stunned look. "I swear to you, Debra Lee, that it wasn't rape, Kate wanted me as much as I wanted her."

"You lie!" she hissed venomously.

"I swear! Ask Kate, she'll tell you."

"If what you've just told me is true, I hate her, too." Hot tears flooded her eyes now, scalding her cheeks.

He took two faltering steps toward her, still wearing that dazed expression. "Girl, listen to me. You must listen to me, Daughter—"

"Don't call me that! Don't you ever call me that!" She was screaming now. "I'll kill you, you bastard, before I let you tell anyone I'm your daughter."

Close now, he reached out his arms. Debra placed her hands flat against chest and pushed with all her strength. He stumbled backward. The backs of his knees struck the bed, and he fell across it.

"Did you hear me, I'll kill you before I let you spread that story around!"

Brian lay without moving, head turned to one side, eyes closed. In a frenzy of rage, Debra seized his shoulder and shook him. He muttered something but did not otherwise respond to her shaking. He had passed out.

Blinded by tears, Debra stood back, trembling. She had to get out, she simply couldn't remain in the same room with him. Without even thinking about a wrap, she started out of the room.

Belle, at the sound of Debra's footsteps coming toward the door, fled down the hall. She opened the first door she came to and ducked inside. Fortunately the room was empty. She closed the door just in time and stood with her ear to the panel, listening to Debra's hurrying footsteps.

In all the time Debra had been at Rose's Emporium, she had never once had a man in her room, and now she had admitted a stranger! The temptation had been too much to resist, and Belle had listened, with a numb fascination, to the shouting voices inside.

She had liked Debra from the beginning, yet one thing had always rankled her—Debra's refusal to work like the other girls. Rose hadn't, of course, but then Rose had been well past her prime.

By listening, Belle had hoped to hear the sounds of two bodies going at it on Debra's bed. Now, she wished she had not eavesdropped, and she wished with all her soul that she could forget what she had just heard.

It was hard to believe that any man could be so uncaring as to keep his own daughter in ignorance of his fatherhood for all this time and then only reveal it when he was displeased with something she had done. Belle wouldn't blame Debra in the least if she did kill the bastard.

Men! They were all alike, fathers, husbands, lovers—worthless from the word go. She should know, Belle reflected sourly; she'd known enough men in her life.

She eased the door open, peering along the hall. Debra was gone. Belle could hear a hubbub of voices downstairs—the evening's customers were arriving.

She went down to tend to business, determined to forget everything she had heard at Debra's door, yet knowing in her heart that she never would.

Debra walked for a long time. As quickly as she could, she got off the streets and made her way down to the beach, where she walked along the sand. The night was damp and cold, but Debra scarcely felt the chill, even without a wrap, so angry was she.

She walked, going over and over the words that Brian Moraghan had thrown at her like hurting stones. She wanted desperately to disbelieve that he was her real father, yet she knew that it was true. He was an innately selfish man, and he would not concoct such a lie, for it would leave him vulnerable to her demands for the rest of his life—financial demands, demands for love, et cetera.

Love! Her dry laughter was painful, slicing across her nerve ends like a dull knife. Whatever happened, she would never, never demand love from him.

For the first time, her anger cooling a trifle, she considered her parents—the two people she had always thought were her parents. Why hadn't they ever told her the truth?

But would she have been happy knowing that she was Brian Moraghan's daughter? Debra knew that she would not have been; perhaps she might have hated him less, but that would be the extent of it. And what other benefits would have come from her knowing? Few, Godalmighty few. Was that the reason they had never told her? Or had they simply postponed it until it was too late? That seemed the most likely.

And whatever else, she thought, Daddy had proven himself admirable, in marrying her mother knowing that she was pregnant with his brother's child and in loving her, Debra, all these years. Casting her thoughts back, it seemed to Debra that he had always treated her with the same love that he showed to Michael and Lena. No, she could not complain on that score.

She knew, now, that she would always think of Kevin Moraghan as her father.

With that thought she slowed her steps and looked

around. She had walked some distance out of town; the lights of Corpus Christi were a blur behind her in the misty night. Since she wasn't carrying a watch, she did not know the time, but she had the feeling that it was quite late—she had a vague sense of walking for hours.

Surely Brian would be gone by now.

She turned back toward town and walked at a fast pace. She was exhausted, emotionally and physically, by the time she reached the Emporium; she must have walked for miles. From the relatively small number of horses and vehicles before the house, she knew that it was indeed quite late.

She let herself in quietly. There was still the sound of merriment from the parlor. She tried to sneak past the door, but Belle, lurking near, spotted her and came running.

"Honey, I've been waiting for you. I've been worried sick! Where on earth have you been?"

"Walking, just walking." Debra gestured vaguely. "My—uncle and I had a quarrel. He was drunk, and I left him passed out in my room. Did you see him leave?"

"Nope, honey, he's still there." Belle shook her head. "I sneaked a peek in your room about an hour ago. He was still passed out on your bed."

"Damn that man!" Debra's anger renewed itself. "I thought he would be long gone by now. Well, I'll fix him," she said grimly, clenching her fists. "You can be Godalmighty sure of that!" She started past Belle.

Belle stopped her with a hand on her arm. "You want me to go up with you, honey? Or maybe one of the men? Doc Price is here. He's a little soused, but he could lend a hand. . . ."

"Never mind, Belle." Debra brushed past her. "I don't need help handling him." She went up the stairs two at a time.

At the top her resolve faltered, and she hesitated at the closed door for a few moments. Then she drew a deep breath and pushed the door open, not bothering to be quiet. There was no lamp burning in her room, the only light a rectangle of yellow from the open door,

159

falling across the foot of the bed. All she could see was Brian's booted feet; the rest of him was in shadow.

She started resolutely toward the bed. "Uncle Brian, I want you out of here, now! And if you think I'm going to call you Daddy, think again."

He didn't move. She was close enough now to see that that he was lying on his back. Bending over him, she shook his shoulder. His body struck her as being oddly slack and limp.

Her eyes somewhat adjusted to the dimness now, Debra saw something protruding from his chest. Leaning farther down, she realized that it was a knife, a butcher knife that some part of her mind recognized as coming from the kitchen downstairs.

Then her mind ceased to function, and her hand moved, without a command from her and closed around the knife. It came out easily. The handle was wet and slippery, and as her hand fell into the spill of light from the door, Debra saw that it was dark with blood.

A shrill scream ripped from her throat. She fell to her knees beside the bed and screamed again, as she stared in dawning comprehension at the still figure of her father.

She was still on her knees, the butcher knife clasped in her hand, when figures crowded into the room.

Debra turned a blind face toward him. "He's dead," she said in a raw voice. "Uncle Brian is dead."

Fifteen

Stonewall Lieberman brought the news to Nora.

It was a cold day, and she was inside the house when she heard racing hoofbeats and went to the door to look out. A chill struck her heart when she saw who it was. Stonewall never pushed a horse very hard, and now his mount was lathered, sides heaving, as the attorney slid off and pounded up the steps to the porch.

"It's bad, isn't it, Stonewall?"

He nodded gravely. "I'm afraid so, Nora."

"Who is it?"

"It's Debra. It's not in the papers yet, but the news came in by telegram, and it's all over Nacogdoches." At her stricken look he hurried on. "Oh, she hasn't been harmed, not physically. I'm sorry, I should have told you that first off."

She motioned him in. "I've got a pot of coffee on the sunporch, Stonewall. Come on back."

When they both had a cup of coffee and were seated across from each other at the table, she said, "Now. Tell me."

"I know very little, Nora. Debra apparently killed someone in her place, and she's been arrested for murder."

161

"Murder!" Nora sucked in her breath. "It's not possible that she would kill someone!"

"I find it hard to believe that Debra is capable of murder myself, but the fact is that she is in jail at this very moment. But that is not all of it. . . . Brace yourself. The person she is supposed to have killed is Brian."

Nora rocked back in her seat. "Brian! But that can't be! He's here, on Moraghan—" She clapped a hand to her mouth. "Oh, my God, I just remembered. He threatened to go to Corpus Christi. He must have gone, tried to get Debra Lee out of there, and they quarreled. But kill, Debra Lee? If it happened, it must have been an accident."

"Not according to the telegram. She's charged with first-degree murder. If it had been an accident, the charge would be different. Of course the telegram had no more details, so we shouldn't jump to conclusions until we know all the facts."

Another thought struck Nora. "Anna, Anna and the children. Do you suppose they know?"

"I understand that was who the telegram was directed to, so I can only assume that it has been delivered by now. I intend to go by, but I thought I should tell you first."

"We'll both go." Nora got to her feet. "I haven't been in that house since Kevin left Moraghan, but this is not a time to stand on ceremony. If this is all true, they will need me. Will you hitch up a buggy for me, Stonewall?"

Stony rose. "Of course, Nora, right away."

"Wait." She detained him with a hand on his arm. "I have to also think about Debra Lee. The girl will be needing me—" She broke off, staring inward. "You know something, Stonewall? I seem to be thinking about everybody but Brian, my own son. I suppose it'll hit me hard later, but maybe because I've been on the outs with him for so long, I've even stopped thinking about him as mine. But he is dead, isn't he?"

"Yes, Nora, he is," he said uncomfortably. "But as they say, we do have to think of the living."

"Yes." She gave her head a brisk shake. "But about Debra Lee. I must think of going down."

"I have already made arrangements to go. If you wish, you can go with me, Nora. If you feel up to it."

"Oh, I can make it. There's a lot of spit left in this old gal yet. But you, you're going?"

He said simply, "She will need a lawyer, Nora. If she will have me—to handle her defense, that is."

"What about the election, Stonewall? If you were worried about going to Corpus Christi to see her before, how about now? Visiting a whorehouse madam is one thing, but defending a whorehouse madam is another thing entirely. It would more than likely cost you the election."

"That can't be helped. If she needs me, I will defend her, no matter what," he said. "If I turned my back on her, I could never live with myself. I'm meeting in the morning with the people who are behind the move to elect me. If they back off, so be it. Oh, I'm still going to run. It's too late to take my name off the ballot anyway."

"You are a nice man, Stonewall Lieberman." She kissed him warmly on the cheek. "I don't know how Debra Lee is fixed for money, but I will stand your fee."

"No, no." He batted a hand at her. "My fee is the least of my concerns in this. You get ready, and I'll go hitch up the buggy, Nora. I'll leave my horse here and ride over with you."

As they drove up before the big house Brian had built for his family, the place seemed deserted, and as fancy as it was, the house struck Nora as desolate.

"I think the telegram has reached Anna," she said.

"It looks that way."

Stony got down and helped Nora out of the buggy. Lending her his arm, they went up the walk and across the broad porch. Stony rapped on the door with his knuckles. There was no sound from inside. He knocked again, louder.

He gave Nora a questioning look. "Do you suppose there's anybody home?"

Before she could answer, they heard the drag of footsteps beyond the door. It swung open, and Anna Moraghan stood in the doorway. A Junoesque woman when Brian had married her, she had grown heavier with the years and become slovenly in her personal appearance. Her eyes were red and swollen from weeping, and they blazed with sudden hatred when she saw Nora.

"What do you want here?"

"You—" Nora cleared her throat. "You know about Brian then?"

"I know that my husband is dead, murdered by that slut of a granddaughter of yours. It's all your blame, you meddling old woman." Her voice burned like a splash of acid.

"I know you're upset, Anna, but recriminations will do you little good," Nora said steadily. "We are family, after all."

"We're not *your* family, me or mine, not anymore. You turned your back on us years ago."

"That's not true, Anna. It's true we haven't been close, but all the blame isn't mine."

"You think I don't know about your granddaughter, that you gave her money to open a whorehouse? Brian told me all about it. And now, because of you, he's dead. He went down there to put a stop to it, and now he's dead." Tears began to run silently down her face. "If I had my way, I would change my name from Moraghan, as well as both my children."

"Anna, regardless of how you feel, they are my grandchildren, you can't deny them that."

"I damn well can, if I can make it legal!"

Nora sighed. "You're sure there's nothing I can do for you or the children?"

"Haven't you done enough? Just go."

"How about Brian—his body? We'll want to bury him here, on Moraghan."

"I'll take care of it. He was my husband, more than he was your son. Now, I'll thank you to get off my property!"

Anna slammed the door. Nora stared helplessly at the closed door. For the first time since Stonewall had brought the bad news, she began to weep. She had never felt so alone in her life.

She looked at him, her eyes filled with tears. "I don't

164

really know whether I'm crying for Brian or for myself. I feel so alone, Stonewall. I have nobody."

"You have me, Nora, and Debra." He took her arm and started her down the steps. "Come along, Nora. I'll take you home."

The meeting with his backers the next morning, in Stony's office in Nacogdoches, was acrimonious. The three men all lived in Nacogdoches and were powerful men with money and influence. Barton was in the timber business, a close rival to Brian Moraghan. Barton owned a lumberyard in town, as well as many acres of prime timber. Garth owned a Nacogdoches bank, and Peters had a dozen farms, all run by sharecroppers.

Garth, the banker, was the leader and generally the spokesman for the trio. He loved power even more than he did money, and Stony had never liked the man. But Stony was well aware of the practicalities of politics, and this type of man was always found in any political structure.

Garth spoke around a thick cigar. "What's this all about, Lieberman? If you're looking for more campaign funds, I thought we'd worked out a final budget at our last meeting."

"It's not money, Mr. Garth. As I'm sure you all know, I have been a close friend to Nora Moraghan going back to Sean's time."

"What does that have to do with the price of ducks?" Garth growled. "Nora Moraghan is an old woman, and right now the name of Moraghan is mud in Texas. Brian now, he had a little influence, and he knew what bread to butter, but he's dead."

"His death is why I called this meeting, gentlemen. I am going to Corpus Christi with Nora, to see what we can do for her granddaughter."

"For Christ's sweet sake, Lieberman!" Garth said. "You shouldn't touch that girl with an outhouse pole! Do, and you're going to wind up covered with shit!"

Stony did not waver. "I'm sorry, but that's the way it is, gentlemen. I'm attorney for the Moraghans, and Nora wishes me to defend her granddaughter." He figured that Nora would forgive him a small lie.

Barton, skinny as a seasoned fence post and about as tough, glared at him out of angry eyes. "I heard talk about you being sweet on that little gal, squiring her around when she was up here. That have anything to do with this fandango you're fixing to dance?"

"I wasn't sweet on her, Mr. Barton, as you so nicely put it. Even if I was, it would have nothing to do with it."

"A piece of tail then," Barton snarled. "Lord's sake, boy, if you're randy, I can lead you to some nice poontang. You don't have to traipse all the way to Corpus and try to get some gal out of the pokey."

Stony said tautly, "You're being offensive, Mr. Barton, and I don't have to sit still for it."

"The hell you don't, boy. You're our boy, we've forked over good money to see you in that judge's seat. Now you're fixing to blow it all away."

"I am *not* your boy, sir!"

"All right, all right, let's settle down now." Garth waved his hands placatingly. "We're getting away from the point here, and it's true your personal relationship with this Moraghan girl is none of our business, except that it bears on the matter at hand. Unfortunately, it does, Lieberman. You go down there and defend her, it's goodbye election. Christ's sake, man, she's a murderess! She killed her uncle, her own blood, and a man well thought of in the community, to boot."

"She's entitled to a defense, even if she's guilty," Stony said stiffly. "And you don't know that she's guilty, you only have a few words in a telegram to go on, and secondhand at that."

"Shitfire, boy," Barton said, "you know she's guilty. Who else would have a reason to kill Brian? He was a good old boy."

"That's a matter of opinion," Stony retorted. "I've heard different views on that."

"Her being guilty or not is unimportant," Garth said. "The important thing is that she's a whore charged with murder, and the voters won't take kindly to your han-

166

dling her case. Now, I'd advise you to back off, Lieberman. You need this like you need a hole in the head."

"I'm sorry if it affects the election, if it upsets you gentlemen, but there is such a thing as professional ethics. Nora is my client, and I told her I'd handle the defense."

"Hell, break a leg, come down with the pox, anything to get out of it."

"No, Mr. Garth," Stony said stubbornly. "I'm going, and that's final."

"You're betraying our trust, Lieberman," Garth said. "We've backed you all the way, and now you're throwing the election down the privy."

"Aw, hell," Peters said in disgust. "Why argue with the shitpoke? That's what comes of dealing with a Jew, we should have known better!"

Garth said harshly, "I know one thing. If it wasn't too late, I'd see to it that your name was yanked off the ballot. And I'm going to let people know that we're no longer actively backing you. We'll start a write-in campaign. It may be too late for us to elect a man that way, but by Christ it'll take votes away from you, what few votes are left after the news of this gets around!"

Sunk in thought, Stony sat at his desk for a time after the three men had stormed out. Surprisingly enough, he didn't feel as badly as he had anticipated. True, there was a feeling of melancholy in him at the thought of losing the election. He had really yearned toward being a judge. In a community such as this, a judge was accorded more respect, generally, than the state governor.

However, there was a good side to it. Aside from the fact that he would have felt guilty for the rest of his life for not having gone to Debra's aid, he realized, a little belatedly perhaps, that if he had been elected with the support of the three men who'd just left his office, he would have always been in their debt and that they would have found ways to call in that debt. That was inevitable, being the kind of men they had just revealed themselves to be. And he would have tried, short of illegality, to repay that debt.

Now he was free of them, no matter what happened. If by some major miracle he was elected after all, he would owe them nothing.

Finally he stirred and got to his feet. He had a busy day ahead, with several matters to attend to, mainly seeking postponements on several cases he had pending. There was no way of knowing how long he would be gone.

He had promised Nora that he would be at Moraghan early in the morning and they would leave for Corpus Christi. They had agreed that it would be best not to wire Debra of their pending arrival. It was quite possible that she would refuse to see either of them if she knew they were coming.

If they caught her by surprise, at least they should be able to get in to see her.

In Corpus Christi, the Council of Four was meeting in T.J. Dillon's house.

The focus of Dillon's attention was Judge Ross. "Jonathon, you'll be presiding over this Moraghan woman's trial, is that correct?"

Judge Ross coughed behind his hand. "So I'm given to understand, T.J."

"Good!" Dillon nodded in satisfacion. "I'm depending on you to see that the harlot gets what is coming to her."

Judge Ross seemed to swell with self-importance. "I'll do my best, T.J."

"Now wait just a damned minute here!" Bradford Carpenter said explosively. "What's going on? The woman isn't even on trial yet, and you two've got her hung already!"

"Don't you think she's guilty, Bradford? They caught her with the knife in her hand, blood all over her."

Carpenter said, "I don't know if she's guilty or not. That's for a jury to decide. Hell, if I had seen her kill her uncle with my own eyes, I'd still think she was entitled to a fair trial."

Dillon smiled tightly. "I'm sure she'll get a fair trial. Unless you're trying to say that Jonathon here is not a fair and impartial judge. Is that what you're saying, Bradford?"

"Well, the way the pair of you are talking, it sure as hell doesn't sound much like he's all that impartial."

Judge Ross said with swelling indignation, "Now see here, Carpenter, I won't have you impugning my honesty!"

Dillon batted a hand at him, said, "Don't get excited, Jonathon. You know how Bradford carries on. I'm sure he means nothing by that."

Carpenter scowled. "I always speak my mind, T.J., if that's what you mean by my carrying on. Maybe I shake a few sacred trees that way, but let the nuts fall on whoever's head is underneath."

Dillon continued smoothly. "All I'm concerned about is that some slick lawyer doesn't come in here, for a fat fee, and try to pull all kinds of legal shenanigans. I just want to make sure that Jonathon is on his mettle, on the lookout for something like that."

"It strikes me that you're trying the shenanigans, T.J. You think I don't remember the other times you've tried to get us to go along with your little schemes to roust her? Speaking of which, you've been quiet as a little field mouse for some weeks now about Debra Moraghan and her funhouse. You were ready to do just about anything to close her down. What happened?"

Dillon remembered Bill Longley's threat, and he felt a chill. He said tightly, "Since I received little cooperation from you, Bradford, and others, I decided to let matters rock along for a little, sure that something would happen to prove me right. Now it has. This wouldn't have happened, if you'd listened to me earlier. I'm sure you'll agree with that?"

"T.J., I've about decided it's never wise to agree with you about anything."

"Then since you feel that way, I'd suggest you leave, you and Jack there. I'd like a private word with Jonathon."

After the pair had left, Dillon leaned forward and said in an ingratiating voice, "I'm sure we're traveling along the same streambed, Jonathon. We want to see that strumpet convicted, so we can be rid of her, for good and all. Are we agreed?"

Judge Ross said primly, "We are agreed, T.J."

Still in that soft voice, Dillon said, "You do everything you can to grease the wheels of justice, and I'll see to it that you won't be sorry. I know you have ambitions beyond being a judge. Am I right?"

Judge Ross got an eager look. "Any man worth his salt his ambitions to better himself."

"Of course. Now, you know I have strong connections up in Austin. You do for me, and I'll do for you. I'll put in a good word for you with the politicians who run the state of Texas. Who knows what will come of it? And the fact that you're presiding over a well-publicized trial like this one is sure to be a big boost for you. . . ."

Sixteen

At least they had given her a jail cell all to herself.
Debra didn't think she could have borne it if she'd had a
cellmate. For that matter, she was the only person in the
small jail at the moment. The second night of her confinement, a Saturday, a drunk had been thrown in
around midnight, and released early the following morning.

Being in jail was bad enough in itself. Debra had always liked to walk at least part of the day; simply being
confined inside a house, no matter how roomy, had always bothered her. Here, she could walk only about
eight feet one way, six feet the other.

The cell was furnished with a cot, two blankets, a slop
jar and a washbasin. One tiny barred window looked out
on the blank adobe wall of the building next door. At
least the window let in light, but she couldn't open it for
fresh air.

She had been in the cell a full week now. For the first
few days she had been so deep in despair that little beyond her own bleak thoughts registered on her. She had
seen only three people—the jailer, a fat slob by the name
of Browne, who came to feed her twice a day and to
empty the slop jar; Belle, who came every day; and Doc
Price, who had been to see her twice.

For the first few days of her confinement, Debra took little heed of the comings and goings, but the shell the shock had built around her slowly began to slough away, and she took notice again.

Browne, for all his coarseness, was innately a kindly man, if a touch on the stupid side, and he tried, awkwardly, to ease her situation somewhat.

Every time Belle came she tried, alternately, to cheer Debra up and to make her aware of how dire her situation was.

Finally, on the seventh day, Debra began to listen when Belle, in a fit of exasperation, shook her by the shoulders. "Honey, if you don't snap out of it, they're going to have a noose around your neck and the trap sprung before you even know what's happening!"

"All right, Belle, all right!" Debra said sharply.

She pushed the woman away and ran her fingers through her hair. They came away gummy. Her hair was a tangled mess, and filthy. She looked at her hands. They were gray with grime, each nail a half-moon of dirt, and she had on the same dress she'd been wearing when the police came for her. It was wrinkled and stained, and Debra had been sleeping in it; she hadn't removed it once during the time she'd been in here. There were even bloodstains on it, Brian's blood.

"Godalmighty, I'm filthy," she said with a grimace, "and I must smell like a sewer. How can you stand to be around me, Belle?"

"Debra, the way you smell is the least of your worries right now. But as far as that is concerned, I have fresh clothes, soap, and towels, here in the jail. I brought them all over days ago, but you weren't listening to anything I said."

"Well, I'm listening now. I'll tell Browne to bring them in when you leave. Now—how are the girls?"

"They're still there. Nervous as chickens in a hailstorm, but still there."

"You might as well send them on their way. Rose's Emporium is finally and officially closed." Debra's laughter was short and bitter. "It took something like this to finally do it, after T.J. Dillon tried his damnedest and failed."

"Aw, honey! You sure?" Belle looked stricken.

"I'm sure. Belle, I have no choice. God only knows when I'll get out of here, if ever. I'll sign a bank draft before you leave today. You draw out the money and give them all fifty dollars apiece and send them on their way."

"You don't have to do that, honey. You don't owe us a thing. We've all, most of us anyway, had places closed down around us before. What money you've got, you're going to need for a lawyer."

"No, Belle, I wouldn't feel right if they had to go off with nothing in their pockets. Tell me"—her gaze grew intent—"do they believe I killed my—my uncle?"

"Of course they don't, honey! At least none has dared to say so to me." Belle's face flushed, and her glance slid away. "I know you didn't kill him, Debra."

"I don't know how *you* know, Belle. You were the first one in that room, saw me with the knife and his blood on my hands."

"Aw-w, honey, you couldn't kill anybody."

"I was mad enough at him to kill him, but I didn't." Debra began to pace. "The thing is, who did kill him?" She halted, a look of wonder on her face. "You know, that's the first time I've ever really given any thought to that? Belle—were there any strange men in the Emporium that night?"

"Not that I saw, honey, nobody that I didn't already know. But I'm willing to testify that I saw a strange man slip in and out, if that'd help you any," Belle said earnestly.

"Thank you, Belle. That's sweet of you." She patted the other woman's hand. "But a lie wouldn't help me. A clever lawyer could trip you up, and that would only make it worse, for both of us. But it's weird. Who could have killed him?" She shook her head, brow puckered in thought. "He had enemies enough, but all back in East Texas, as far as I know. Another thing just occurred to me—I haven't seen a soul aside from you, Doc Price, and the jailer since they arrested me. No one has been in to

173

tell me what I'm charged with, nobody in to ask questions. Of course, they asked me enough questions that night. It went on until after sunup, before they threw me in here, like a sack of dirty laundry. But do you suppose they suspect someone else and are looking into it?"

Belle shook her head dolefully. "Honey, don't get yourself all het up over that idea. They're convinced you did it, and they've got all they need to stick you with it. Everybody in Corpus thinks you killed him—oh!" She clapped a hand to her mouth. "Me and my big mouth!"

"It's all right, Belle. It's time I was facing up to the truth and deciding what to do. But then, what *can* I do, stuck away in here?"

"One thing you should do, should already have done, is hire yourself a good lawyer. At least then you'll have someone on your side. The way things are, they'll soon haul you into court, and you'll stand there all alone."

"There's one trouble with that, Belle. I don't even know any lawyers."

"There are a few in town, but I don't know how good they are, or if you can trust 'em worth spit. But Austin is full of lawyers. I could probably find one there who would be willing to do his all for you."

"Belle, you're a good person. I hate to load all this on you, but—"

"What are friends for, honey?" Eyes suddenly moist, Belle hugged her. "If you give me the word, I'll catch the morning stage to Austin."

"All right, Belle, and thank you."

After Belle left, Debra asked Browne to fetch the things Belle had brought, along with a tub of hot water. "I need a bath, I stink. Please, pretty please?" She managed a smile for him.

Browne grumbled, but he grudgingly complied. Debra's spirits had been raised a little by Belle's visit. The future still looked bleak, but at least she was functioning again. She might not know what was going on outside the jail, but she was once more aware of herself.

She took the blankets from the cot and rigged a makeshift screen around one corner of the cell—she had a suspicion that Browne had agreed to bring the wooden tub of water just so he could peek at her naked.

The water were merely tepid, but the soap, a thorough scrubbing, and a vigorous toweling afterward made her feel much better. Dressed in fresh clothing, she took down the blankets and shouted for Browne.

Her earlier suspicions were confirmed when he hauled the tub through the cell door. As he set it down to relock the door, he said sourly, "For a whore, you're pretty particular who sees you bare-assed."

"Why, Browne, I didn't think you were interested," she said mockingly. "You should have told me, and I'd've named a price for you to watch. You know a whore doesn't do anything for free, even if it's just a show and no action."

He banged the big iron key against the bars. "All right for you, Miss Snotty. Just wait til you ask me for hot water again and see what it gets you."

"Maybe I won't be here that long, did you ever think of that?"

"You'll be here, missy, until they take you out and hang you."

His prediction failed to depress her, in her happiness at being clean and presentable again. She scarcely had time to comb out her hair when Browne was back again. "Some folks here to see you."

She bounced up from the cot. One thing had been bothering her more than anything else—it had been a week, and she had heard nothing from her parents. This must be them! She refused to think of the fact that Kevin wasn't her father. She said eagerly, "Who is it?"

"I don't know, strangers to me." He shrugged. "A man and a woman, that's all I can say ."

It *had* to be them. "Well, send them back."

She had her back to the cell door, fastening her dress, when a voice said, "Well, Debra Lee. A fine mess, I must say."

"Grandmother Nora!" she said, already turning. "I didn't think you would ever want to see me again. . . ." Her voice died as she saw Stony Lieberman. "No! I don't want to see you!" She stepped up to grip the bars as

Browne started to unlock the cell door. "Browne, don't let that man in, I don't want to see him!"

"Now, Debra Lee," Nora said in a scolding voice. "After he came all the way from Nacogdoches, you won't even talk to him? Foolish girl!"

"Debra," Stony said, "listen to me. Whatever our personal differences are, and I'm not even sure what they are, we have to put them aside for now. You're in deep trouble, and you need an attorney. You don't have one yet, do you?"

"No, not yet." She looked directly at him for the first time, and she felt a wrench of love. She ached to reach through the bars and touch his face.

"Then you need me. You must admit than I am a better than capable attorney, whatever else you may think of me."

Nora said sternly, "Stonewall is throwing away his chances of being elected judge by coming here, Debra Lee. If you turn him away, you deserve whatever happens to you."

"Oh, no!" Debra said, stricken. "I don't want you to do that, Stony. I know how badly you want to be judge."

"It's too late. I've burned my bridges, as the saying goes." His features relaxed, and he smiled tentatively. He reached through the bars for her hand. "It's settled then? You'll let me defend you?"

Debra felt warmth course from his hand, spreading through her blood like a strengthening drug. She smiled crookedly. "I don't seem to have much choice, do I? And, Stony . . . I *am* glad you're here."

"So what do I do, missy?" Browne said, banging the key on the bars. "Let them in or not?"

"Let them in, let them in," she said. "And can't you bring in a couple of chairs?"

"No chairs to spare," he said sullenly. He unlocked the door, let Stony and Nora in, then relocked the door and stood staring into the cell.

"Go away, Browne." Debra motioned. "We want to talk. Privately."

When Browne made no move to depart, Stony said in a crisp voice, "I am an attorney, jailer, retained by Deb-

176

ra Moraghan to defend her. According to law, I am entitled to confer with my client in private. If necessary, I can get a court order to that effect."

Browne gave him a dour look, then slouched off. When the door at the end of the short corridor had clanged shut, Stony said, "Has he been giving you any trouble, Debra?"

"Browne? Oh, no, he's not a bad sort, given what he is. If you mean has he tried to molest me, I don't think he has quite enough guts." She laughed suddenly, the first time she had laughed freely since being arrested. "The most he can do is try to peek at me taking a bath, and since today's the first bath I've taken, that's been no problem."

Stony took her hand, looked down into her eyes. "The first thing I'll try to do is get you out of here on bail."

"Do you think you can? I would like to get out of this place," she said fervently.

"I'll do my damnedest. It's hard to get a judge to set bail on a murder charge, but you being a woman, I just might be able to manage it. Now, sit down on the cot, you and Nora, and tell me what happened. Try to remember every little thing, you never know what tiny detail might turn out to be important."

Nora and Debra sat down side by side. Debra took her grandmother's hand in hers. "Grandmother, you can't know how glad I am that you came. I was afraid that when you heard I was supposed to have killed Uncle Brian, you would never want to see me again." As she spoke, Debra wondered if her grandmother had any inkling that Brian had been her real father.

"Child, you should never have doubted that I'd come to you," Nora said. "Do you think for a minute that I believe you killed Brian?"

"You're about the only one who doesn't." Debra's face was grim. "Daddy and Mother . . . I haven't heard a word from them." Unexpectedly, a sob caught in her throat.

"I'm sure they'll be here, Debra Lee. Maybe they haven't heard yet. Did you let them know?"

Debra shook her head. "To tell the truth, I've been in

177

a fog since it happened. I haven't thought much of anybody but myself. But they must know. The papers are full of it, I understand."

"They'll be here, depend on it." Nora patted her hand. "Now, tell us. Stonewall is waiting."

Debra told them what had happened, in detail, omitting only what Brian had told her about being her father. Stony paced as he listened, frowning at certain points, but he did not interrupt until she was finished.

He said slowly, "Then you did threaten to kill him?"

"Yes, I did. I was absolutely furious with him. He was drunk, overbearing, obnoxious . . . Sorry, Grandmother."

"No need, girl," Nora said. "Brian could be trying, how well I know."

"The point is," Stony said, "did anyone overhear you making the threats?"

"Not that I know of, but then there's always a great amount of coming and going along the hall outside my door. And I was screaming at the top of my lungs, I'll have to admit that."

"We have to assume that someone did overhear. It's always best to assume that the worst will come out. I'll question everyone who was there, of course, but they may hide the truth, then come out with it on the witness stand. The next question is, who was in that house who could have killed Brian after you stormed out?"

"Nobody that I can think of. I've wracked my brain and can't come up with anyone. The girls, why would they kill him? They didn't even know him."

"To get back at you, maybe? Kill him and hope the blame would land on you? As it has, unfortunately."

"That seems a little extreme, Stony."

He shrugged. "In a murder case, nothing is too extreme, no motive too small. You'd be surprised. Now, as to the others in the place. . . . You say this doctor—Dr. Price, is it? He was present?"

"Yes, Belle told me that he was in the parlor, but he'd have no reason to kill Uncle Brian. She said Doc was drunk, anyway."

"I'll have a talk with him. He was there, never can tell what he may have witnessed. How about other men?"

"There were some customers, again according to Belle. You'll have to talk to her about them, but I can't feature a customer killing him."

"Debra," he said severely, "somebody killed Brian. Now, there are two choices. Either you killed him, or somebody else did. We've eliminated you, I hope, so if we can find that somebody else, we'll beat this charge. Otherwise, it's going to be tough, you might as well face that." He began to pace again. "Now, go through it once more."

"Again?" she said in dismay. "Why? I just told you everything I can remember."

"Maybe you did, maybe you didn't. You'll have to go through it several times, Debra. You'd be surprised how people in stress situations tend to forget things that happened, yet the unconscious mind dredges up the memory with retelling."

When she had finished telling it again, Stony sighed. "There are only slight differences, which is not too good, in one respect."

"Why is that?"

"Often, not always, you understand, it means that a witness is lying, his or her story being rehearsed so many times it's letter perfect."

Debra stiffened. "I am not lying!"

"I didn't say you were, Debra. It can also mean that a witness has a retentive memory. It doesn't really matter in your case, for I doubt very much that I will put you on the witness stand."

"And why not?" She made it a challenge. "I *want* everybody to know what happened!"

"Do you?" he said quietly. "Don't forget, you'll be swearing to tell the whole truth and nothing but. What if you're asked about the threat you made to your uncle? Think how that would sound to a jury. There is an old axiom in law, never put a client in the witness chair if there is *anything* said client might testify to that would be detrimental."

Debra, suddenly remembering that Brian Moraghan had been her father, not her uncle, remained silent. If that revelation reached a jury's ears, it would be disastrous for her.

Nora said, "Do you really think it will go that far, Stonewall? To the point where you will have to decide whether or not to put Debra Lee on the witness stand?"

"If you mean will we have to go into court, I would say that in all likelihood we will. It's something we have to prepare for certainly." To Debra he said, "You say nobody from the police or prosecutor's office has been in to see you?"

"Not a soul since I was thrown in here."

"Monday then, I'll see what I can do about a preliminary hearing. They may have hopes of simply bypassing that, but if that is true, I'll have to disabuse them." He glanced at Nora. "Nora, I'd like a few minutes alone with Debra, if you don't mind. It won't take me long, then we'll see about finding a place to stay."

"You can always stay at Rose's Emporium." A giggle bubbled up in Debra's throat, escaping like a hiccup.

He rebuked her with a glance. "This is hardly the time or place for levity, Debra."

After Browne had escorted Nora from the jail room, Stony faced Debra, hands on hips. "Now, I want to know why you took off from Nacogdoches like that. No word to me, not a thing. Why?"

She looked down at the floor. "I'd rather not discuss it."

"I think I'm entitled to know the reason."

"Maybe you won't like the reason." She looked up at him defiantly. "If you don't like it, does that mean you won't take my case?"

He colored. "Of course not! This is personal, between us, and has nothing to do with my taking or not taking your case. I thought I had made it clear that I was defending you, Debra."

"All right then, I'll tell you, since you insist. Do you remember our last conversation in Nacogdoches, when you said that a man wanted the woman he married to be a virgin?" She stared directly into his eyes.

He said warily, "I remember that I said something like that, yes."

"I'm not a virgin, Stony. Or perhaps I should say, I wasn't then, so it'll be clear to you."

His look turned incredulous. "You mean that's the reason you left without even saying goodbye? You can't be serious!"

"I'm quite serious. You said you'd never marry a woman who wasn't a virgin."

"I never said such a damned thing! As I recall, I said something to the effect that a man *prefers* to marry a virgin, but that doesn't mean it absolutely has to be. Debra, I find this hard to believe. You could have at least told me, waited until you saw how I reacted."

"I guess I was . . ." For the first time her voice faltered. "I suppose I was afraid of how you'd react."

"I must say I'm not very flattered that you would think that of me."

"Why shouldn't I think that?" she flared. "You gave me every reason to think it!"

"Debra, Debra, you silly girl. To have run from me over something as foolish as that." He reached down for her hands and drew her up. His voice gentle now, he said, "Don't you know that I love you?"

Her heart began to beat like a trapped bird in her breast. "How could I, you didn't tell me!"

"I didn't know then." His smile was rueful. "What was it somebody said? You never know how much you care for someone until they're gone?"

"Oh, Stony! Darling Stony!" Standing on tiptoe, she rained moist kisses on his mouth, cheeks, and nose.

He wrapped his arms around her and pulled her close, his embrace almost painful. His lips were tender, so incredibly soft. Her senses swam, and she reveled in the kiss, her blood flowing hot and sweet. The kiss lasted for an interminable time, and Stony was the first to step back. His color was high, and he wore a baffled look, as if frightened by the intensity of their embrace.

Breathing hard, Debra crossed to the barred window to stare blindly out at the blank wall across the way. Should she tell him about Tod Danker? At least then he might not think her so silly. But the very thought of relating that unsavory episode was repugnant to her. And what if Stony was revolted by it?

No, girl, she told herself, let well enough alone; you've got him back now, don't take the chance of bruising his love.

He said, "Debra?"

As she turned, sudden tears blurred her vision. "Yes, darling?"

He took a step toward her. "Why are you crying?"

"I'm happy. Didn't you know that a woman is supposed to cry when she's happy?"

He placed his hands on each side of her face and wiped the tears with his thumbs. He said gravely, "I suppose I have a great deal to learn about women, Debra."

"Oh, Stony! What's going to happen? To us, I mean?"

"Before we worry about that, we have to worry about you. I'm going to do everything in my power to get you out of this, my sweet Debra."

Stony's initial encounter with Judge Jonathon Ross was not encouraging. He soon realized that Ross was one of those judges with little schooling in the law, and with even less understanding of it. Texas, still in the backwash of the frontier years, abounded in just such men. To all too many of them, Judge Roy Bean represented the ideal judge.

That first meeting with Judge Ross took place in the courtroom. Stony had tried, without success, to meet the man first in private chambers, but Judge Ross would not grant him an audience. He did, after three days of unrelenting pressure and demand from Stony, grant a preliminary hearing. Since the hearing did not receive public notice, the small courtroom was empty of spectators, for which Stony was thankful. Aside from Judge Ross, a bailiff, a court clerk, and the prosecutor, Stony, Debra, and Nora were the only ones present.

The prosecutor, Clifford Haskins, was a small, intense man, with black, darting eyes and quick, nervous gestures, and he walked with the cocky strut so typical of many small men. Stony was later to learn that he was a special prosecutor sent down from Austin; the state of Texas wanted Debra Moraghan convicted—the outcry in the press throughout Texas had been strong—and the Corpus Christi officials had scant experience in prosecuting murder trials.

Haskins was at least six inches shorter than Stony, which boded no good. It had been Stony's experience that juries tended to lean toward lawyers of small physical stature when opposed by men towering over them.

On the bench Judge Ross stirred, his robes rustling ominously. "Well, Mr. Lieberman? You've been panting for this hearing. Now, what is it all about?"

Stony rose. "I have several motions to place before the bench, Your Honor."

"Motions?" Judge Ross scowled. "What motions?"

"First, I would like to move for a change of venue."

"What's that? Change of venue?"

"A motion to have the accused tried in another city removed from Corpus—"

Judge Ross said irritably, "I know what a change of venue is, Counselor!"

Oh, shit, Stony thought in dismay; that's probably the most stupid remark I've ever made in court! He realized for the first time just how nervous he was. Often he was nervous during trial preparation, but the moment the actual trial began, any nervousness vanished. Of course, he had never before defended a client with whom he was emotionally involved.

He hastily tried to make amends. "My apologies, Your Honor. I did not intend to lecture the court."

"I certainly hope not," Judge Ross said sternly.

"But I do move for a change of venue, Your Honor, because I do not believe that my client can receive a fair and impartial trial in Corpus Christi."

The judge leaned forward. "Are you saying that the good people of Corpus Christi are not a fair-minded people?"

"The accused has received a great deal of publicity, and I believe it would be difficult, if not impossible, to select a panel of jurors here who have not already made up their minds as to her guilt or innocence."

"From what I understand, this publicity has spread all over the state, and beyond."

"That is true, Your Honor, but the jurors in other cities would, hopefully, not feel as directly involved."

"Counselor, I resent the implication that the people of our fair city are less impartial than others," Judge Ross rapped the gavel. "Motion denied!"

Stony had not been optimistic about his chances for a change of venue, so he was not surprised.

Judge Ross said, "What are these other motions?"

"I only arrived in the scene a few days ago, Your Honor, and have had not time to prepare a defense. I do not even know if my client has been officially charged as yet."

Judge Ross said, "Mr. Haskins?"

Haskins bobbed to his feet, said respectfully, "The charge has been prepared, Your Honor." He looked directly at Stony. "First-degree murder," he announced smugly.

"I move for a dismissal of the charge," Stony said promptly.

Judge Ross scowled. "On what grounds?"

"On the grounds that there is not sufficient evidence to support a charge of murder in the first degree."

Haskins gave a bark of laughter. "Oh, we have the evidence, Mr. Lieberman. We do indeed!"

"Mr. Haskins is correct, Counselor. I have reviewed the evidence personally. Motion denied."

"But I have not had that opportunity, Your Honor. For that reason I ask for a trial postponement."

"How can you do that? I have yet to set a trial date."

"I would think that is one purpose of this preliminary hearing, sir."

"That is quite correct. Any remarks, as to a postponement, Mr. Haskins?"

"I am prepared to try my case as quickly as possible. I would certainly oppose any motion to delay. I have a busy schedule, as I'm sure you do, Judge Ross."

"True, true." Judge Ross opened his court calendar and quickly scanned it. He looked up. "I can schedule the trial to begin two weeks from today. I see that I have court time that entire week. Is that agreeable to you, Counselor?"

"Two weeks is very little time, Your Honor," Stony said in dismay. "I should like at least a month."

"What you like and what you will get, Counselor, are two different things," the judge said acidly. "The trial will commence two weeks from today."

Stony was silent for a moment, thinking hard. So far he had lost every motion, but the most important one of all he had held back until last.

"Well, Counselor? Any more motions?" Judge Ross said, his voice edged with sarcasm.

"Yes, Your Honor." Stony took a deep breath. "I wish to petition the court to set reasonable bail for the defendant."

"Bail!" The judge stared down incredulously. "First-degree murder is not a bailable offense, you well know that, Counselor."

Haskins said sharply, "The prosecution will certainly be opposed, Your Honor."

Stony said, "I well realize that bail is usually not granted in such cases, but the plight of the defendant differs in one important aspect. She is a woman. Being confined to jail is degrading, Your Honor—"

"More degrading than a whorehouse, Mr. Lieberman?" Haskins interjected.

Stony wheeled on him. "That remark is uncalled for!"

The gavel rapped lightly. "I agree. Such remarks have no place in my courtroom, Mr. Haskins." He directed his attention again to Stony. "A murder charge is a murder charge, Counselor."

"There are precedents, sir. I can quote—"

Judge Ross glowered, waved his hand. "Don't trouble yourself. Spare me."

"The point is, Your Honor, a judge has discretion in the matter of bail, he has the final word. If you could find it in your heart to feel sympathy for the defendant's plight, I feel confident that people would respect you for it." Stony was attempting, as subtly as possible, to plant into the judge's mind the thought that Debra's continued incarceration would eventually swing public sympathy to her side. As he ceased talking, he saw the judge's gaze come to rest on Debra in speculation, and Stony held his breath.

Abruptly Judge Ross rapped his gavel. "Very well, Counselor, I will set bail, but I shall hold you, sir, personally responsible for her appearance in court."

Haskins was up, his voice rising. "I object most strenuously, Your Honor! This woman has committed a most heinous crime! She must not be permitted to walk the streets, like any law-abiding citizen!"

Judge Ross batted a hand at him, said, "Bail is set at one hundred thousand dollars."

Stony's heart sank. How could they possibly post that much bail? A certain craftiness about the judge's eyes told him that the man had purposely set such high bail in the belief that it could not be raised.

Judge Ross went on. "You understand, of course, that the defendant will remain in jail until such a time as the required amount is posted?"

It was a completely unnecessary reminder. Stony choked back an angry retort, said glumly, "Yes, Your Honor, I understand."

Nora stood up beside him. "Your Honor, I will see to it that bail is posted for Debra Lee."

Judge Ross got a stunned look. He snapped, "And who are you, madam?"

"I am Nora Moraghan," Nora said steadily. She pulled Debra up beside her and put an arm around her waist. "Debra Lee is my granddaughter."

Judge Ross gaped in consternation. "You will post bail for this woman, the woman who killed your . . . the person who is accused of murdering your son?"

"Accused, I do believe, is the proper word, sir," Nora said dryly. "I happen to believe that Debra Lee is innocent. I haven't the slightest doubt."

Glowering, Judge Ross rapped the gavel. "This hearing is concluded." He stood up, nodded coldly. "I shall see both you gentlemen in court. Court is adjourned." He left the room, robes rustling.

Stony, slightly dazed, stood for a moment without moving. He turned at a gasp from Debra and followed the direction of her glance. Just inside the courtroom door stood Kevin and Kate Moraghan, looking around uncertainly.

Debra hurried toward them. "Mother!" As they made no response, nor moved toward her, she halted halfway up the aisle and said in a small voice, "Daddy?"

Seventeen

This second shock, coming as it did almost on the heels of the shoot-out at Rose's Emporium, left them stunned.

After they had read the newspaper piece, Kevin was the first to speak. "Do you suppose she found out?"

"About Brian?" Kate said slowly. "It's highly possible, knowing how rash-tongued he could be."

"Then if she did find out, she *could* have killed him, Kate, in a fit of rage. You know I've always been afraid of how she would react if she ever learned the truth."

Kate was shaking her head. "I refuse to believe that Debra Lee could kill anyone or anything. It's just not possible."

"I've always thought so, but she may have changed," he said tonelessly.

"No, not that much." She touched his hand. "You forget, darling, I've seen her, just a short time ago. She hasn't changed, grown hard and cold, if that's what you mean. There's a wide gap between being a whorehouse madam and being capable of killing."

"You're forgetting one thing, Kate. Anyone can kill in a fit of rage, especially someone as high-strung as Debra Lee is."

"What is it you're saying, Kevin? That we shouldn't go to her?"

"Of course not!" He stared at her in astonishment. "Of course we'll go to her. In fact, I'll ride back into Brownsville this afternoon and send her a telegram."

Yet they sat without moving for a little while, each occupied with private thoughts.

Finally Kevin stirred, said gloomily, "Did it ever occur to you, Kate, that the Moraghans may have a curse on them? Every since Daddy left the priesthood back in Tennessee to marry Momma, things have happened. First, the Moraghan-Danker feud and Daddy killing the two Danker boys. Then Daddy was shot dead by Sonny Danker, and I was left with a lame leg. In a fit of spite, I left Moraghan forever, dragging all of you with me. Now this, Brian dead and Debra Lee accused of killing him."

"Nonsense, darling, there is no such thing as a curse," said Kate, the eternal optimist. "Don't you think other families have their troubles?"

Kevin refused to be consoled. "Not as much as this, down through two generations. God knows what'll happen to the next generation. And if you stop and think about it, this would never have happened if I had remained on Moraghan."

"If you're blaming yourself for what's happened, Kevin, just stop it right now!" she said sharply. "You're more intelligent than that. If anyone's to be blamed for this, it's me. I'm to blame for allowing Brian to get me pregnant with Debra Lee. *That* is where this whole chain of circumstances began." Tears filled Kate's eyes.

"Aw-w, Kate, don't. Don't!" He got up and went around the table to her. "You know I can't stand to see you cry. All that is past history. You know I don't blame you for that, I never did." Pulling her up, he put his arms around her.

Voice muffled against his chest, she said, "I know, my darling, I know, and that's what makes it so hard. But I reckon what I'm crying about is Debra Lee, mostly anyway. I keep thinking about how she must feel, if she knows Brian was her real father."

189

"But Kate, what if—" He stepped back so that he could look down into her face. "What if she doesn't know? Then what do we do?"

"You mean, do we tell her?"

He nodded mutely.

She shook her head. "No, no, we can't, don't you see? Think what it would do to her, on top of everything else."

He said grimly, "It's not going to be easy, keeping mum about it."

"We must, Kevin." She touched his face. "We have to help her, not make it worse."

"Well . . ." He became brisk. "We'd better get busy. I'll ride in and get the telegram off right away."

"And I'll talk to the neighbors, see if they can take care of the children while we're gone."

In the end they had to hire someone, a local Mexican woman, a widow with two children of her own, to come and stay at the house. Since they had no idea as to how long they would be gone, they felt it wouldn't be fair to burden a neighbor with the chore. Consequently, it was over a week before they could board a stage for Corpus Christi.

Weary, dirty, and rumpled from the long journey, they sought out Rose's Emporium immediately. The woman who answered the door told them that Debra Lee was appearing in court that very morning.

When they entered the courtroom, both Kate and Kevin gazed around in bewilderment; neither had been inside a courtroom before, and they were uncertain as to the proper protocol.

Then Debra saw them and ran toward them. "Mother! Daddy!" When neither responded at once, she skidded to a halt, her face mirroring uncertainty.

Kate took a step forward, held out her arms. "Debra Lee."

Debra's face came alive, and she ran at them. Kate folded her into her arms, murmuring into her hair, "It's all right, Debra Lee. It's all right now."

Finally Debra stood back, slanting an uncertain

glance at Kevin. He stepped up and took her into his arms. "I'm sorry for your troubles, Debra Lee. For whatever good it will do, we're here to stand with you."

"Oh, Daddy! You can't know what it means to me, your being here. I thought—" She looked from one to the other. "Well, I didn't think you were coming. I thought you had washed your hands of your erring daughter."

Kate looked at her in astonishment. "Whyever would you think that? Didn't you get our telegram?"

"Telegram?"

Kevin said, "I got it off the same day we heard, over a week ago. The reason we couldn't come sooner, we had to find someone to stay with Michael and Lena."

"I never got any telegram. Where did you send it?"

"To that—that house," Kevin said. "Where else would we send it?"

Debra was frowning. "Belle never once mentioned it. I wonder why? That's not like her."

She was interrupted by Nora. "Don't you have a kiss for your mother, Son? After all these years?"

"Momma." Kevin swept her into his arms. "It's grand to see you, after all this time."

"And whose fault is that?" Nora said dryly. "It's too bad it took something like this to bring us together again." She glanced at Kate. "Neither of you have changed much that I can see."

"Hello, Nora." Kate was smiling fondly. She hugged her mother-in-law. "It is nice to see you." She looked at Stony. "And you, too, Stonewall. I'm glad you're here, defending Debra Lee."

"I'll do my best, Mrs. Moraghan."

"I'm also glad you're her lawyer, Stony," Kevin said warmly. Then, his face grave, he looked at Nora. "I am sorry about Brian, Momma. We didn't get along, but for something like this to happen. . . ."

The bailiff stepped in to take Debra's arm. "I have to take you back to jail now."

"Stony?" Stricken, she looked at him. "Can't I have a little time with my folks?"

"Bailiff, it can't do any great harm to wait a little,"

191

Stony said. "If you'll just stand outside the door, she can't escape, since that's the only way out of this courtroom."

The bailiff hesitated, then nodded reluctantly. "Well, all right. But don't forget, I'll be right outside, watching the door."

Stony said dryly, "I don't think it's likely we will forget."

After the bailiff had left, Kevin said, "Momma, about Brian . . . his body, I mean."

"He was shipped back to Moraghan. Anna didn't want me to have anything to do with it, but I saw to it as soon as I arrived here. He'll be buried on Moraghan, she at least agreed to that. He's probably in the ground by now. I reckon I should have been there. . . ." For just a moment her face worked with grief, then smoothed out. "I figure that the living are more important. Seeing to it that Debra Lee gets out of this mess is the most important thing right now."

"I agree," Kevin said soberly. "We arrived just in time to hear you agree to post bail for Debra Lee. Thank you for that, Momma." He looked past Nora. "Mr. Lieberman—Stony, just what are her chances?"

"I won't lie to you, Kevin. Everything is going their way right now, and we've got a judge who is not. . . . Well, I won't go into that. But as someone once said, we've just begun to fight."

The talk fell into generalities for the next few minutes, and Debra stood quietly, with Kate's arm around her. Finally she stirred. "Stony, Grandmother, could I have a few minutes alone with my folks?"

"Certainly," Stony said. He took Nora's arm. "Come along, Nora. We'll be right outside the door, Debra. Don't take too long, or you'll try that fellow's patience out there. There'll be time to talk later, when you're out of that jail, which, hopefully, will be tomorrow."

When the door had closed behind them, Debra said, "There is something I must ask, about something *he* said that night. He claimed that he was my real father. Is that true?"

Kevin winced, scrubbing a hand down across his face, his glance jumping away. Kate took her hand, said simply, "Yes, Debra Lee, it's true."

"You could have told me," Debra said coolly.

"We could have, yes. In fact, we should have," Kate said. "First, we thought we'd wait until you were old enough to understand. Unfortunately, we kept putting it off and putting it off, until we were afraid that it was too late, afraid the truth would hurt you."

"I am the one to blame, Debra Lee," Kevin said wretchedly. "I was afraid you'd hate us. . . . No, I was selfish, I was afraid you'd hate *me*."

"I did, when he first told me. I hated you so much I thought I'd never want to see you, ever again." Debra sighed. "But the more I thought about it, the more I knew that I could never do that."

"Then you don't hate me?" Kevin asked.

"Of course not, Daddy."

She threw her arms around him, hugged him fiercely. "I love you, I always will. To me, you'll always be my father."

"I'm glad, you can't know how happy that makes me," Kevin said fervently. "And I want you to know that I could not have loved you any more than I do, if you had been my real daughter. What am I saying? To me, you are my real daughter."

Debra stepped back. "You know the one I truly hated. . . . No, change that. I still hate him. Brian, I mean. Does that make me awful?"

"No, Debra Lee," Kevin said. "I can understand how you feel. But you must understand something. Brian was Brian. He had his ways. Brian always came first with Brian, no matter what."

Looking from one to the other, Debra felt a rush of love. She knew that the support they were giving her was a rare thing; few parents would rush to the side of a daughter as wayward as she had been. She was trying to think of a way to put this into words when the door opened and Stony stuck his head in.

"About finished in here? The bailiff is getting itchy."

"We're finished, darling." Debra stepped between her parents and took their hands. She said gaily, "Let's go face the world!"

"Together," Kevin said.

"No matter what," Kate said.

T.J. Dillon was livid with rage. "You did *what*? You let that harlot out on bail?"

"I was backed into a corner, T.J.," Judge Ross said. "I had turned down all his other motions. It would have looked bad if I had denied that one."

"I don't give a rat's ass how it would have looked!" Dillon pounded the arm of the divan. "We agreed that she should get what's coming to her."

"She will, T.J., she will." Judge Ross was reassuring. "I'll see to that, I promise you."

"You'd damned well better," Dillon snarled, "if you know what's good for you! If she gets off, you have no future in the state of Texas, Jonathon, depend on it!"

"And I was flabbergasted when her grandmother agreed to go her bail," Judge Ross continued. "I set it so high I was positive they could not produce it."

"I have to say that I don't understand it either, that bitch's grandmother coming to her defense, after she killed her son. And hiring that slick Jew lawyer to boot. That must be costing her. Goddamned women, who can understand them?" Dillon said blackly. "And the harlot's folks, I understand they're here?"

"That's what I was told, T.J."

"Well, I'm going to pass the word around. People in Corpus Christi will treat them like lepers. See how they like that."

"And that's another thing, T.J., about letting the woman out on bail. Some people, knowing she was locked away in jail, might build up a little sympathy for her. This way, they see her walking around like any decent person, it will likely offend them. You can be sure it won't create any good will toward her."

"I hope you're right, Jonathon." Dillon struck his meaty thigh with his fist. "I won't rest easy until that harlot is hung for her sins, and I'm depending on you to see to it. You're in the best position to see justice done here."

"Justice will be served, T.J.," Judge Ross said piously. "You have my word on it."

Eighteen

Debra wanted to return to the Emporium to stay when she was released on bail. Her parents and Nora were horrified, and Stony wouldn't hear of it.

"I'm not objecting on personal or moral grounds, Debra," he said. "But think logically. It's bad enough, you being a brothel madam, but imagine what people will think. Here you're out on bail, and you head like a homing pigeon for the Emporium. I know, don't say it. You don't care a whit for what people think. That's fine for you, but I have to defend you, and by God, for once you're going to do what I say. If you don't," he added grimly, "I'll have the bail rescinded, and you can return to that cozy jail and your jailer friend."

Debra stared at him. "You'd really do that?"

"You damned well better believe it, my sweet."

She laughed suddenly. "So masterful, my sweet, gentle Stony. You're right, of course. But I do have to return to check on the girls, and for some personal things. If I'm to appear in court every day, I have to look nice, don't I? And it's foolish to buy new clothes, when I have plenty there."

He nodded. "I can't argue with that, but I'm going with you."

"Stonewall Lieberman, in a whorehouse?" she said teasingly. "What next?" She touched his cheek.

He caught her hand and pressed it to his lips. "I'm no angel, my sweet. I've been in worse places."

They were seated in the lobby of the hotel where they all had rooms, and it was a gauge of her total absorption in him that she didn't once look around to see if they were being observed. "You'll have to tell me about them sometime, darling. I want to know the best and the worst about you. God knows," she fell solemn, "you already know the worst about me!"

"Come along, let's get it over with." He got up and helped her to her feet. "And stop feeling sorry for yourself."

With the back of her hand, she pushed the hair out of her eyes. "I'm not being sorry for myself, Stony, just realistic."

It was mid-afternoon, and since it was into summer now, it was hot outside, the sun beating down. There wasn't even a breeze off the Gulf to provide relief. Consequently, there weren't many people on the streets. But those who were, Debra noted, gave them sidelong, curious glances. And a few, mostly women, saw them coming a block away and crossed over to the other side of the street.

"You'll have to get used to it, until the trial is over and done, Debra," Stony murmured. "Just ignore them."

"I should already be used to it, since I've been getting the cold treatment from most Corpus Christians since I took over the Emporium. But I suppose it'll be worse now."

The Emporium had a shuttered look, all the curtains tightly closed. As they turned up the walk, Debra noticed a clot of youngsters across the street.

A clamor of voices rose at the sight of her: "There she is, there's the hoor!"

"She's a murderer, is the hoor!"

"Her ol' uncle came to play/ She took him to her bed./ When her uncle wouldn't pay/ She killed the old man dead!"

"Dear God, even the children! How can it get any worse?" Debra shrank into herself, shivering.

Stony put an arm around her protectively and hurried her up the steps. Just as they reached the door, a rock whizzed past Debra's head and thumped against the door.

Swearing under his breath, Stony wheeled about and started down the steps. The youngsters scattered like frightened quail, scampering off in different directions.

The front door opened a crack, and Belle peered out with frightened eyes. "My God, honey, it's you!" She opened the door wide and looked both ways along the street.

"They're gone, Belle," Debra said dully.

Stony, still breathing hard in his anger, stomped back up the steps, and they went inside. The moment they were inside, Belle slammed and bolted the door. In the dimness of the hallway, Debra saw pale, wide-eyed faces peering out at them through the beaded curtains of the parlor entryway. When the girls realized that she had seen them, they ducked back out of sight.

Now Debra recalled that she had not seen Belle since that last visit, the day Stony and Nora came. She had relayed a message to Belle, through Stony, that it wouldn't be necessary to find a lawyer, but she had expected the girls to be gone.

"Why are the girls still here, Belle? I thought most of them would be gone by now. I asked you to draw money out of my account and send them on their way."

"They can't leave corpus, honey. The day after I saw you last, a man came around with some papers and served them on each and every one of us. He said that if we left town, we'd be breaking the law."

Debra frowned. "Papers? What kind of papers?"

Stony said, "Subpoenas, I'm sure. To testify in court. Right, Belle?"

Belle nodded. "That's what the man said. Debra . . ." Her voice rose to a wail. "I don't want to get on the stand and testify against you. The others don't, either. What am I going to do?"

Debra looked at Stony in dismay. "Stony?"

"You have no choice, Belle. If you've been subpoenaed, you must take the stand."

"Then I'll keep my lip buttoned, I won't say a word!"

Stony was shaking his head. "No, Belle. You do that, and they can cite you for contempt of court."

"But what will I say?" Belle was close to tears.

"Just answer the prosecutor's questions." Stony's glance sharpened. "You don't know anything you haven't told me?"

Belle seemed to hesitate for an instant, then said quickly, "No, no, of course not."

"Then all you have to do is tell the truth, Belle." He smiled.

Debra said, "Are they all still here, the girls?"

Belle nodded. "Some were all ready to leave, but now they have to stay until they testify."

"Was a telegram from my folks delivered here?"

"No, honey. If one had been, you know I would have told you."

"The others, did they mention any telegram?"

"Nobody told me of one."

"Well, I'm going up to my room to gather up a few personal things. Ask the other girls about a telegram, will you? I don't understand what happened to it."

"Sure, honey." Belle frowned. "You're not staying here?"

"My attorney advises against it." Debra laughed. "I guess he's afraid it would ruin my reputation."

As Debra started for the foot of the stairs, June Blount came sailing out of the parlor and almost collided with her.

June widened her pale blue eyes in feigned surprise. "I'm glad to see you out and free, Miss Moraghan."

"I'm sure you are, June." She surveyed the girl with unconcealed disdain. "I see you're still wearing that sleazy blouse."

"Since you weren't here, I saw nothing wrong with my wearing it. It cost good money, I can't help it if you don't like it," June said sullenly. "Besides, I don't see what difference it makes. We're closed, no customers to see me in it."

"June," Debra said evenly, "I know you can't leave right now, but the minute you've finished testifying, I want you out of this house, out of Corpus. Is that quite clear?"

"Quite clear," June said, tossing her head defiantly. "And you needn't worry. I'll only be too glad to be out of this shithole!"

It was on the tip of Debra's tongue to reprimand her for the language, but she refrained, saying merely, "The minute you're free, you go." She went on up the stairs.

Stony came up behind her, catching up with her in the hall. In a low voice he said, "Debra, that wasn't a good idea, taking her over the coals like that."

"Why not? She's a tart, Stony," she said. "A working girl doesn't have to be a tart." She turned a cold look on him. "Or maybe you think we're all tarts?"

"Debra, that has nothing to do with it. But you've just made an enemy of the woman, and right now you need friends, not more enemies."

"She was already my enemy. Besides, what harm can she do me?"

"She's going to be on the witness stand. She can make up a few lies that would not do your cause any good at all."

Ordinarily, at the beginning of a criminal trial, Stony was meticulous about the selection of the jurors. In this one he figured that it didn't really matter. Any Corpus Christian selected for the jury would long since have made up his mind as to Debra's innocence or guilt—most, he feared, on the side of guilt. He would have liked to have had one or two men on the panel who had patronized Rose's Emporium, men who had at least a slight acquaintance with Debra in her own establishment. But he knew Haskins would have none of it, and in that he was correct. One of the first questions Haskins asked was if they had ever been a customer of Debra's "sporting house," and he dismissed the few prospective jurors who admitted to it.

Of course, Stony reflected, with inner amusement, it was quite possible that one or two might make the panel anyway, refusing to admit to such behavior in a public forum.

So Stony leaned back and pretty much let Haskins have his way, asking a question of a juror now and then just to let them know that he was still awake.

His only hope, he knew, was to change a few minds during the course of the trial, throwing more than a shadow of doubt on Debra's guilt. There was also a faint hope in the back of his mind that the real murderer might be discovered before the trial was concluded, but the odds against that happening were astronomically high.

Not only were the jurors in the prosecutor's pocket, but the majority of the witnesses would be as well. The only witnesses for the defense would be character witnesses; most of those were family, and Haskins could destroy their credibility by simply pointing out to the jury their close relationship to the defendant. His best hope there, Stony knew, lay in Nora, as mother of the dead man.

Stony arose only once to register an objection during the prosecutor's examination of prospective jurors. "Your Honor, I must object to the prosecutor's constant labeling of the Emporium as Debra Moraghan's 'sporting house.'"

"To whom does it belong then, if not to Debra Moraghan?" Haskins asked in a jeering voice. "To some person or persons unknown to this court? To the gunfighter, Bill Longley, perhaps?"

"That remark, Mr. Haskins, is uncalled for!" Stony snapped. "The accused is not even the legal owner of the house in question. It belongs to an individual by the name of Rose Sharon."

"That's a quibble," Haskins said with a shrug, "and defense counsel knows it."

The gavel rapped. "All right, gentlemen, cease and desist your squabbling in my courtroom. You might be a little more careful of your questions, Mr. Haskins."

"I will endeavor to do so, Your Honor," Haskins said suavely, hiding a smile behind his hand.

To the remainder of the prospective jurors, the prosecutor couched his key question differently: "Have you, sir, ever paid a visit to the house in question?"

Stony did not object again, knowing that he would only succeed in antagonizing the jurors.

The selection of the twelve jurors was completed well before the noon hour, with ample time remaining for the opening address to the jury panel.

Haskins was a walker, in constant motion, strutting back and forth before the jury box, with much waving of his arms, his voice rising and falling. The eyes of the twelve men followed him back and forth with the rhythm of a metronome.

"A dastardly crime has been committed, gentlemen of the jury, and the prosecution will so prove beyond a shadow of a doubt. The accused was discovered with the murder weapon in her hand and the blood of the victim on her person. The blood, if you please, of her own uncle!"

The prosecutor's voice rose to a shout. At Stony's side Debra gasped, and he groped for her hand under the table and squeezed it. In a whisper he said, "This doesn't mean a damned thing, Debra. It's typical attorney histrionics. Haskins has center stage and is making the most of it. Grit your teeth and endure. It'll probably get worse before he's finished."

And it did get worse, considerably worse, before Haskins turned away from the jury box. He gave Stony a triumphant look as he crossed before the defense table. Stony noticed he had sweated heavily, dark patches of perspiration on his shirt; even his black string tie had a wilted look.

In contrast, Stony spoke in a quiet voice designed to reach only the jurors' ears, and he stood in one place without moving, leaning on the railing, his glance moving slowly across the intent faces.

"Mr. Haskins gave quite a performance, didn't he, gentlemen?" he said in a dry voice. "I hope that I do not bore you after that. I certainly will not tire you, because I promise to keep my remarks short and to the point." He took a breath. "The key phrase, among all the ones the prosecutor flung at you, is 'beyond a shadow of a

doubt.' In his instructions His Honor will define for you
'reasonable doubt,' and it will be up to the prosecution
to have proven beyond reasonable doubt that the defendant is guilty as charged. If any doubt whatsoever
lingers in your mind, you should, in all conscience, find
her not guilty.

"The prosecution cannot prove the defendant's guilt.
The evidence they will present to you is purely circum-
stantial. The defendant was discovered with the death
weapon in her hand, true, and the victim's blood was on
her hands. We will not attempt to deny that. She came
into the room and discovered her uncle murdered. She
then reacted as any of us would have done under the
circumstances. In a state of shock, she withdrew the
knife before she realized that he was dead. Thus, she
was discovered by witnesses."

A strangled sound of derisive laughter came from the
prosecution's table. Stony swung around, glaring. "Your
Honor, I allowed the prosecutor to deliver his remarks
without interruption. I believe I should be accorded the
same courtesy."

Judge Ross had a hand over his mouth, and Stony
knew that he was smiling. The gavel tapped lightly.
"Yes, Mr. Haskins, please observe proper decorum."

Stony turned back to the jury. "The prosecutor,
gentlemen, will make much of the fact that the defendant is a brothel operator, you can be sure of that.
The defense will not attempt to deny her profession. But
I ask you to please keep something in mind at all times,
especially during your deliberations. The defendant's
profession has no bearing whatsoever on the crime with
which she is charged. I am sure that you gentlemen will
give her a fair and impartial hearing. Thank you for
your kind attention."

Following the noon recess, the parade of the prosecution's witnesses began. Stony admired the way that
Haskins went about it. He was well grounded in trial
procedure and constructed a sound foundation for his
case, beginning with the two lawmen first on the scene
of the crime and then the doctor who had examined the

body as to cause of death. Stony had very few questions of these first three witnesses, since their stories were factual and straightforward.

Then Haskins began putting those on the stand who had been in Rose's Emporium that night. He started with Doc Price, then the four customers present, and the girls last. In shrewd anticipation of what Stony's line of defense would be, Haskins ended his examination of each witness with the same question: "At any time during the evening, did you see a stranger on the premises, someone you had not seen before?"

Every witness answered in the negative.

When Haskins was finished with Doc Price, Stony strolled over to the witness stand. "Dr. Price, in response to the prosecutor's question, you stated that you did not observe any strange faces on the evening in question. That is correct, is it not?"

Doc Price, painfully sober, his hands trembling slightly, shot a troubled glance at Debra. "I'm afraid that is correct, Mr. Lieberman."

"Now, would you tell the members of the jury where you spent the evening in question, what part of the house, I mean?"

"From the time I arrived until we heard . . . the scream upstairs, I was in the parlor." He cleared his throat. "I was drinking."

"You did not go upstairs during that time?"

"No, sir, I did not. Not until we all rushed up to Miss Moraghan's room."

"Now Doctor, from the parlor, do you have a clear view of the stairs going up to the second floor?"

"Not unless you stand in the doorway. There's a beaded curtain over the doorway, you see, and the staircase is set back at an angle."

"Then, it *is* possible that someone could have gone up or down those stairs, without your knowing it?"

Doc Price said eagerly, "Oh, yes, entirely possible. In fact, that's what must have happened."

Haskins said wearily, "Objection, Your Honor. Purely conjectural on the part of the witness."

Judge Ross nodded. "Sustained. The witness is instructed to refrain from such conjecture."

"Dr. Price," Stony said, "you have come to know the defendant, Debra Moraghan, quite well, have you not?"

"I have, yes."

"Then, in your considered opinion, is she capable of committing the crime with which she is charged?"

Doc Price answered quickly, "No. It is simply not in her to kill."

The prosecutor was a shade slow. Now he jumped up, bellowing his indignation. "Objection, Your Honor! The witness is in no way qualified to answer that question! That was not a proper question, and defense counsel well knows it!"

"Objection sustained." The gavel rapped. "The response of the witness is stricken from the record, and the members of the jury are instructed to ignore it."

Doc Price smiled slightly, while Stony managed to keep a straight face. He had known in advance that the response would be stricken, but it was planted firmly in the jury's mind, and he was grateful to the doctor for being so quick to answer.

"Now Dr. Price, how familiar are you with the layout of the house?"

"Quite familiar. I have been physician to the 'house in question' for several years."

His answer drew laughter from the spectators, and Stony waited until the judge had gaveled them into silence before continuing with his cross-examination. "How many entrances to the house, doctor?"

"Three. The front door, of course, one off the kitchen, and one off the hall in back, to the outhouses behind the main house."

"Are those doors usually locked?"

"Not during business hours. Oh, sometimes the front door may be bolted, but the kitchen side door and the back door are left unlocked."

Stony said musingly, "Then someone could easily have slipped in and out of either back door. . . ." His gaze had been on Haskins as he spoke, and as the prosecutor started to rise, he said quickly, "Strike that. No more questions of this witness, Your Honor."

Haskins spoke without getting to his feet. "Sir, do you know of your own personal knowledge that those rear doors were unlocked on the night of the murder?"

"I sure do," Doc Price drawled.

"Oh?" Haskins wore a sneer. "And just how did you know that, sir?"

"I knew because I made several trips to the outhouse and the door was always unlocked. Man drinks as much liquor as I do during an evening, frequent trips to the privy are necessary."

Laughter once again swept the audience, and Haskins waved a hand, dismissing the witness.

You missed a lesson in trial practice, Mr. Haskins, Stony thought gleefully; always know the answer before you ask a question.

In general, the questioning of the girls followed a set pattern. The prosecutor asked all of them if they had noticed any strange men in Rose's Emporium that evening, and Stony countered with queries as to whether or not they knew if the back doors were unlocked.

Only with one girl did Stony vary his questioning. That was when Sally, the piano player, was testifying. Debra had told him that, aside from Belle, Sally was her best friend among the girls.

"Sally, you know the defendant quite well, I believe?"

"I do, yes, sir."

"In your opinion, do you consider Miss Moraghan capable of murder?"

Haskins popped up. "Your Honor, I thought we had settled this matter. It is an improper question, as defense counsel well knows. The witness is not qualified to answer such a question."

Stony assumed a put-upon expression. "Your Honor, I made it clear that I was asking for an opinion only. The prosecutor inquired of the medical examiner as to the time of death of the victim, and he was permitted to respond."

"Counselor, the medical examiner is an expert in that field and as such is qualified to answer. This witness"—Judge Ross made a small gesture of contempt—"is scarcely qualified to give an opinion as to your client's criminal capabilities." The gavel banged. "Objection sustained."

"No further questions of this witness." Wearing a look of dejection, Stony turned away to resume his seat at the defense table. Actually he was quite pleased. He had known, again, that Sally would not be allowed to answer the question, but this was the second time he had tried the same question on a witness. The jurors, unschooled in the nuances of trial procedure, should, by now, be wondering why the prosecutor and the judge did not want to hear the question answered.

The next witness was Lupe Vazquez, cook and housekeeper for Rose's Emporium. Stony was a bit surprised that Haskins would put Lupe on instead of Belle and June Blount, the last two of Debra's girls, but as the prosecutor began to question Lupe, Stony grasped the reason.

"Mrs. Vazquez, you have been employed in the house in question for a number of years, have you not?"

Lupe frowned. "House in question, señor?"

A titter went through the courtroom, and Haskins flushed a bright red. "At Rose's Emporium, I mean."

Lupe bobbed her head. "Sí, señor. I cook and housekeep for Rose for long time. Now do the same for Señorita Debra."

"During the evening, you spend most of your time in the kitchen, do you not?"

"Sí. Sometimes the men want food. They get hungry, after."

This time the laughter was a roar. Judge Ross banged the gavel repeatedly. When the room had finally quieted, he snarled, "Another such demonstration and I will clear the courtroom! And you, Madam," he glowered down at Lupe, "just answer the questions as asked."

Lupe looked baffled. "But I did, Señor Judge."

Haskins said quickly, "On the night the murder took place, were you in the kitchen as usual?"

"Sí."

"Until what time?"

"Until house was closed, after man found dead."

"Now think carefully before you answer, Mrs. Vazquez. Did you, at any time, see a strange man in your kitchen?"

Lupe frowned severely. "Nobody come into my kitchen. I do not permit. Only Señorita Debra."

Haskins took on an eager look. "Did Debra Moraghan come into your kitchen on this particular evening?"

Lupe shook her head firmly. "No, señor."

"You are positive of that? Remember, you have sworn to tell the truth here."

Lupe said indignantly, "I do not lie!"

"Of course the accused *is* your employer, and you feel a certain amount of loyalty toward her, do you not?"

"Your Honor, is the prosecutor asking a question or making a speech?" Stony said. "Is he trying to impeach his own witness?"

Haskins shrugged and turned away to the evidence table to his left, picked up a tagged butcher knife, rust-brown with dried blood. He held it up before Lupe. "Mrs. Vazquez, I show you this knife, the state's Exhibit A. Do you recognize it?"

Lupe recoiled slightly. "Si. Is my knife, from my kitchen."

"Are you positive?"

"Si."

"Did Debra Moraghan know of this knife and where it was kept?"

"Si. Sometimes she help me, in kitchen."

"This, gentlemen of the jury," Haskins turned and held the knife out to the jury, "is the knife that was used to slay Brian Moraghan!"

"Your Honor, this is the third time that the prosecutor has shown this exhibit to the jury," Stony said in a dry voice. "Does Mr. Haskins credit them with faulty memories?"

Haskins smirked, returned the knife to the table. "Your witness, Mr. Lieberman."

Stony strolled over to the witness stand. "Lupe, about this knife the prosecution is so proud of—"

The gavel tapped. "Counselor, I suggest you rephrase the question."

"My apologies, Your Honor. The butcher knife, Lupe. Is it kept in the same place all the time in your kitchen?"

"Si. In the knife rack."

"In plain sight of anyone coming or going through your kitchen? Not hidden away in a drawer somewhere?"

"Si, anybody can see." She added belligerently, "But nobody come and go in my kitchen."

"Yes, about that. Lupe, I will not suggest that you in any way neglected your duties. But I ask you to think back to that night. Think very carefully. You never left your kitchen *once*, all evening?"

Her mouth set stubbornly. "I did not leave my kitchen."

"Not even . . . pardon me for being indelicate, Lupe, but you didn't visit the outhouse all evening?"

"Si, but I did not think that was what the other man meant."

"But did you go to the outhouse?" he prodded gently.

"Si. I am not a young woman."

"How many times?"

"Two . . ." Her brow furrowed, then she smiled and held up three fingers. "Three."

"Three times. And how long did you stay each time? Five minutes, as much as ten minutes perhaps?"

"No watch, señor."

"But you can estimate, I'm sure. Would ten minutes be a good guess?"

"Si. But no more."

"Now, the first time you returned from the outhouse, did you happen to notice if the butcher knife was missing?"

"No, señor."

"The second time?"

"No, señor. The knife, she is always there." She made a helpless gesture.

"I understand, Lupe. The knife is one of those things we don't really miss until we reach for it and it isn't
209

there. Did you have an occasion to use it during the evening?"

"No, señor."

"One more question, Lupe. Did you notice the knife missing at *any* time during that evening, up to and including the time you heard Miss Moraghan scream and rushed upstairs with the others?"

Again the helpless shrug. "No, señor."

"Yet it *was* missing by then, we know that now, don't we?" he said. As Judge Ross stirred with a rustle of robes, Stony said quickly, "That will be all, Lupe. Thank you."

Haskins bounced up, and with a rapid-fire barrage of questions, he tried to shake Lupe's story of her trips to the outhouse. The more he questioned her, the more obstinate she became—she had gone to the outhouse three times.

Evidently realizing that he was only implanting it more firmly in the minds of the jury, Haskins abruptly terminated his questioning.

The next prosecution witness was June Blount.

Beside Stony Debra stirred, murmuring behind her hand, "Godalmighty, she's wearing that tacky blouse!"

In amusement Stony noted that the men in the jury box sat forward, intently studying June.

All the time she was being sworn in June's venomous gaze was on Debra. "Now you see what I mean, Debra?" Stony whispered. "She really has it in for you. I hope she knows nothing damaging, she's aching to testify against you."

June had nothing really damaging to say—she was perhaps a little more vehement in her negative responses to the prosecutor's questions as to whether or not she had seen any strangers in the house.

Haskins's questioning was brief, and when he turned the witness over to Stony, Stony waved a hand. "No questions of this witness."

June didn't move from the stand, and Judge Ross, occupied with reading something before him, didn't note this at once. Abruptly June leaned forward, her burning gaze on Stony. In a low voice she said, "Why don't you ask me if I think that woman is capable of murder?"

Stony was too astonished to react immediately, and Judge Ross, apparently equally astounded, raised his head to frown down at the witness.

Stony said, "I have no questions for you, Miss Blount. You may step down."

"Well, I have an answer for you!" she said in a shrill, carrying voice, her face ugly with spite. "I not only think she could kill someone, I know she could!"

For a moment Stony toyed with the thought of questioning her, digging for the reason behind her animosity, but he discarded the idea—it could easily open a Pandora's box.

Judge Ross had recovered from his surprise. He banged the gavel and said in a thunderous voice, "Young woman, you will stand down at once, do you hear? At once, or I shall fine you for contempt of court! I will not tolerate such behavior in my courtroom!" He slammed the gavel down again, with a sound like a gunshot.

June's belligerence collapsed like a pin-punctured balloon. She shot a terrified glance up at the judge, began to shake, and then bolted from the witness stand, almost falling in her haste.

When quiet descended following her exit, Judge Ross said, "Call your next witness, Mr. Haskins."

The prosecutor's next, and final witness, was Belle.

Belle was clearly terrified. After sending one timid glance Debra's way, she never looked at the defense table, her gaze fastened instead on the strutting prosecutor. She sat with her legs held together as tightly as possible, and she held a small handkerchief, which she kept twisting back and forth.

Haskins was as abrasive as usual as he examined her, and Belle became increasingly distraught, close to tears more than once. Stony thought of objecting but decided it wouldn't hurt their cause if Haskins did drive her to tears.

After firmly establishing the fact that Belle had not seen a stranger, aside from Brian Moraghan, that evening, Haskins switched his line of questioning. "I believe

211

it was you who admitted the victim, Brian Moraghan, into Rose's Emporium. Is that correct?"

"Yes, sir, I answered the door. There was this man, demanding to see Debra. He wouldn't give his name, just said he had to see her."

"He didn't identify himself then? But your employer instructed you to send him up anyway, without first learning who he was?"

"Yes, sir."

Haskins aimed a sneer at the jury box. "But of course that's easily understandable. Her visitor was a man, after all!"

Stony rose. "Your Honor, I move that the prosecutor's remark be stricken."

"So ordered, Counselor. Please try to refrain from asides to the jury, Mr. Haskins."

"You escorted Brian Moraghan up to your employer's bedroom and left him there, is that correct?"

Belle hesitated a moment before answering. "Yes, I did."

An alarm pinged back in Stony's mind. There was something in Belle's demeanor that bothered him, as it had at the house the other day, but he couldn't quite pin it down.

Haskins said, "Now, did you see the victim alive again?"

Belle nodded reluctantly. "Yes, sir, I did."

"Would you tell the court how that came about, please?"

"Well, after Debra went out for a while, I became curious. I hadn't seen him leave, so I went up to check."

"And what did you find?"

"I knocked, but there was no answer, so I finally eased the door open and saw Mr. Moraghan lying across the bed."

"He was alive then?"

"So far as I could tell, yes."

"How was he lying?"

"On his back."

"There was no light in the room?"

212

"No, it was dark."

"But there were lamps on the walls of the corridor?"

"Yes, sir."

"And did some of this light fall across the bed when the door was opened?"

"It did, yes, sir."

"Enough to tell you that he was still alive?"

"Well—" The handkerchief twisted, twisted. "I was sure I saw him breathing." Then, in a rush: "I saw no blood!"

"No blood." Haskins gave the jury a meaningful look. "But when you heard the scream and rushed upstairs, there was a great deal of blood, was there not?"

"Yes." Belle shuddered. "Dear God, yes!"

"Now, Belle, let's go back a little. You testified that the accused went out for a while. Would you tell the members of the jury how this came about? What the defendant said and what you said?"

Belle hesitated, and again the warning pinged in Stony's mind. He leaned forward, his whole attention concentrated on the woman in the witness stand.

"Well, nothing was *said*." Belle spoke slowly, looking down at her hands twisted together in her lap. "I was downstairs, seeing to the customers. I happened to be standing by the beaded curtains to the hallway and happened to look out in time to see Debra rush down the stairs and out the front door."

"Was it usual for the accused to leave the house like that, during a busy evening?"

"No, sir, but I thought. . . . Well, it wasn't my place to run after her."

Now Belle had a touch of righteousness about her, and Stony knew what had been nagging at him—she was lying! And that had to mean that she knew something damaging to Debra. He cursed himself for not interrogating her more closely. Apprehension coiled in him like a watch spring too tightly wound, but he knew there wasn't a damned thing he could do.

"All right," Haskins said. "How long was the defendant absent?"

"Until late. I didn't check a clock for the exact time, but it was near midnight or after."

"You did see her when she returned?"

"Yes, sir, I did."

"Did you have a conversation with the defendant at that time?"

"I did."

"Then would you please tell the court the substance of that conversation? Relate what you said and what the defendant said, to the best of your recollection."

"Well—" She swallowed, looked up at Judge Ross in appeal. "Do I have to, sir?"

"You do. Answer the question, witness. And remember that you swore to tell the truth here."

Stony stirred, framing a protest, then subsided.

"Well," Belle said slowly, "I remember telling her that I had been worried sick and asked where she'd been. Debra said that she had just been out walking. She said that she and her—her uncle had had a spat, that he was drunk and passed out in her room—"

"They had a spat," Haskins interjected. "Did the defendant tell you why they quarreled?"

Belle said quickly, "No, sir, she didn't."

"Continue, please."

"Well, then Debra asked if I'd seen him leave and I said no, but that I had peeked into the room and saw him still passed out on the bed. Then she said—" She stopped short.

"Then she said what?" Haskins said impatiently.

"She—well, she damned him and said that she thought he'd be gone. She said she'd, uh, fix him, I could be sure of that."

" 'Fix him'? Is that the word she used?"

"Yes, sir."

"What happened next?"

"She started up the stairs, and I asked her if she wanted me to go with her, or maybe one of the men. She said no, that she—she didn't need any help handling him."

"What else was said?"

214

"Nothing, nothing else." Belle gave an audible sigh of relief. "She went on up the stairs."

"And you saw nothing more of her until you heard the scream?"

Belle bobbed her head. "That's right, yes."

"All right, Belle, now tell the court what happened when you heard the scream."

Belle spoke slowly, fumbling for words. "I was in the parlor, making the night's count of the receipts. It was about closing time. I was at the small table near the door, and I knew it was Debra the minute I heard the scream. It froze my blood, I can tell you. I ran out, knocking over the table in my hurry, and up the stairs. The door was open to Debra's room, and I went in."

"Tell the court exactly what you observed."

"Debra was—" Belle closed her eyes, swayed from side to side, her hands twisted together in an impossible knot. "Debra was on her knees beside the bed, that bloody butcher knife in her hand, and her daddy was— oh, sweet Jesus!" Her eyes flew open, and she clamped both hands over her mouth.

A deathly silence fell. Stony wasn't sure he had heard correctly, and then Debra clamped a hand on his thigh, her fingers digging in painfully. She whispered, "Godalmighty! How could she know?"

The prosecutor was the first to recover. He took a step forward, said in a voice as soft as silk, "What did you say?"

"It was a slip of the tongue!" Belle said frantically. "I meant to say her uncle!"

Stony had turned his head to place his mouth close to Debra's ear, and his gaze moved to the first spectator row immediately behind the defense table, where Kevin and Kate Moraghan sat. One look at their faces told him the answer before he voiced the question in Debra's ear, "Is it true?"

Her lips barely moved. "Yes."

"I should walk out of here right now. Didn't I plead with you to tell me everything?"

"I didn't think it mattered. Honest to God, I didn't!"

215

She groped for his hand under the table. "Darling, please don't desert me now."

Haskins was speaking, "I don't believe it *was* a slip of the tongue."

"It was, I swear!"

Haskins bored in relentlessly, "I think what you just said was the unspeakable truth. The accused murdered her own father!" The prosecutor's voice soared. "Tell us what you know, Belle. Tell the court the truth or be cited for perjury. Was Brian Moraghan the father of the accused?"

Belle stared down at her knotted hands.

"Your Honor, I ask the court to instruct the witness to answer the question."

Stony rose. "Your Honor, may I remind the prosecutor that this is the state's witness? He is heckling his own witness."

Haskins said angrily, "Your Honor, it should be obvious that this woman is a hostile witness. The prosecution has the right, nay, the duty, to vigorously examine her."

"I tend to agree, Mr. Haskins," Judge Ross said. "Objection overruled. Continue your questioning, Mr. Haskins. And witness, you are instructed to answer without further delay."

As Stony dropped back down into his seat, Belle finally raised her eyes and looked at Debra. She whispered, "I'm sorry, honey. I would have died before I—"

Judge Ross glowered. "Madam, you are not to converse with the accused."

Haskins was openly gloating. "Now, Belle, shall we continue? Tell the court how you knew that Brian Moraghan was the father of the accused."

Belle sighed softly and began to speak. "I was curious about this man, a complete stranger, and did something I know ain't right. I listened at Debra's door." She paused, looking down at her hands.

"You eavesdropped on their conversation, is that correct? Tell the court what you overheard, Belle, to the best of your recollection."

"Well, he had come down from East Texas to demand

that Debra leave the Emporium. When she refused, they began quarreling. Debra said that he had no right to tell her what to do, and he claimed that he did, since he was her real father. First, she didn't want to believe him, accusing him of lying. But he finally convinced her, I reckon. Then he said again that's why he had the right to tell her what to do. That's when Debra blew up. She said that all that did was make her his bastard daughter, make her hate and despise him. Then he said something like, listen to me, Daughter. . . ."

She swallowed and fell silent. Tears appeared in her eyes.

Haskins said, "Then it would appear that Debra Moraghan did have a strong motive to kill him, would it not?"

"Your Honor," Stony said, "this is improper questioning, and the prosecutor well knows it."

The gavel tapped lightly. "Yes, Mr. Haskins. Please confine your questions to facts, not conjecture. Objection sustained."

Haskins said, "Continue, Belle. Then what was said?"

"Then she, Debra, said, 'Don't call me that! Don't ever call me that! I'll—I'll—'" Her voice became little more than a whisper.

"Speak up, Belle," Haskins said harshly. "Speak up so we can hear you."

" 'I'll kill you, you bastard!' " Belle shouted, her eyes squeezed shut. "She screamed, 'I'll kill you, you bastard, before I let you tell anyone I'm your daughter!' "

Pandemonium broke out in the courtroom, voices rising like a storm roar. The gavel rapped repeatedly, without success.

Nineteen

The telegram was waiting for Debra when she got back to the hotel after court had adjourned for the day. She took it from the desk clerk without too much interest—she was still numb from the shock of Belle's testimony. She crossed to one of the lobby divans and sank down wearily, dimly noting that the man on the other end of the couch hastily departed.

She opened the telegram and read: "Rose Sharon dead Stop Her will bequeaths all Corpus Christi assets to you Stop Please advise Stop Dwight Blaine attorney representing deceased Stop."

Stony said, "What is it, Debra?"

"Here, you take care of it." She gave a short, bitter laugh as she handed the telegram up to him. "You're my lawyer."

"Debra . . ." Without reading the telegram, he sat beside her, took her hand. "You can't give up now, sweet. We're not that much worse off than before."

"Please, Stony! I may be stupid in many ways, but even a halfwit would know that any chance I had of a not-guilty verdict went up the flue the moment that jury learned that Brian was my father. Imagine what Corpus Christians are thinking right now. Godalmighty, murder is bad enough, but killing your own father is beyond the pale. That little rooster of a man put his finger on it . . . 'the unspeakable crime!' " She looked into his face and was contrite at his stricken expression. "Ah, Stony, I am sorry. I should have warned you, but I had no idea it would come out, and I wanted to spare Mother and Daddy any more pain and grief. And Grandmother Nora, she didn't know. Now she does!"

"Nora is a strong woman, she'll bear up. No, I blame myself, Debra." His face was grim. "I had a feeling that Belle knew more than she was telling me. I should have interrogated her harder. It probably still would have come out, but at least I would have been prepared. And you did tell me that you had threatened to kill Brian, and rather loudly."

"So now what do we do?"

He shrugged. "This won't change my trial plan much, it will just make it more difficult, that's all." He looked off, across the lobby. "And if we lose, I'm going to appeal, you can be sure of that."

She seized on the hope. "Can we do that?"

"Hell, yes. The trial record will show error after error. And Judge Ross is prejudiced against you, that would be obvious to the deaf, dumb, and blind."

"But what are the chances of winning in a higher court?" Her eyes searched his face, and her shoulders slumped at what she saw there. "Not all that good, are they? Darling, I want to say this now. . . ." She touched his lips with a finger. "No matter what happens, no matter how it all turns out in the end, I won't blame you. I know you're doing all you can."

He said glumly, "You never feel that you've done enough, when you—" He broke off, looking away.

"When you lose?" she said. "I'm sorry, sweetheart, I shouldn't have said that." She leaned over to kiss his cheek, then became brisk. "I want to go over to the house, Stony, check to see if it's locked up. After all, it's mine now. Most of all, I want to talk to Belle, tell her I'm not angry. Poor Belle, she must be feeling terrible."

"It's supper time, shouldn't we eat first?"

She shook her head. "Later, maybe. I'm not very hungry right now."

As they walked across town to the Emporium, Debra thought of the telegram in her pocket, and Rose Sharon. A spasm of grief gripped her. She would miss Rose. Although she had known that the woman was dying, it was still a wrench. Rose was one of the few people outside of her own family whom Debra had ever felt affection for.

The house was dark, no crack of light showing, and the front door was locked. She used her key on the door, holding it open until Stony could light the wall lamp in the entryway.

Debra cocked her head, listening. The house was very still. It was the first time she could remember when a murmur of voices, the tinkle of female laughter, couldn't be heard. It was as she had suspected—the girls had all fled the house, as from a place of pestilence. But Belle, Belle should still be here.

She raised her voice. "Belle, are you here?" There was no answer. "Do you suppose she's gone already?"

"I shouldn't think so," Stony replied. "She's not through testifying yet. I haven't had my turn."

"She may have fled rather than have to take the witness stand again. Anyway, what does it matter? The damage is done. Stony, there's a small bar in the parlor. Would you pour me a brandy? I'm not much of a drinker, but I could use one about now. I'm going back to the kitchen to see if Lupe is still here."

The kitchen was empty, the great iron cookstove ice-cold to the touch. Debra stood for a moment, listening to the house again. The silence was a little eerie.

For a bawdy house, she thought sardonically, it's certainly quiet!

She shivered suddenly, left the kitchen, hurried along the hall, and pushed her way through the beaded curtains.

At the bar Stony glanced around at the clatter of beads. "What's wrong?"

She hurried across the room to clutch his hand. "Nothing, not really." She laughed shakily. "It's just that with the house empty, it gives me a strange feeling, almost as if it's haunted. And a violent death here. Two, in fact.

When we were here the other day for my things, it didn't bother me too much, going up to my room, because the house was full of people. Now, I wouldn't go up there for anything!"

"Here, you do need a drink." He handed her a glass of brandy. "Maybe this will help. Or we can leave now, if you wish."

"No, I want to stay awhile. At least we're alone in here, and the bad things are outside the house at the moment." She took a drink of the brandy.

They crossed the room to the long sofa and sat down close together. Debra took another, smaller drink and leaned her head back, eyes closed. "I never did tell you about that other death, did I, Stony? About the famous shoot-out at Rose's Emporium between Bill Longley and Blackie Piper?"

"No, but you don't have to talk about it if you don't care to."

"I think I should. I'm sure that Haskins will bring it out during the trial. I'm surprised he hasn't already."

In a monotone she told him about Bill Longley and the circumstances of Piper's death. The brandy glass was empty when she had finished. Twisting it between her hands, she said, "I'd never witnessed death by violence before." She shuddered. "It was awful, Stony, just awful. I'll never forget it, you can be sure of that. And then for Brian to have been killed only a short time later. I'll never forget either as long as I live!"

"Here, you need another brandy, sweet." He went to fetch her another drink. As he came back across the room, he said, "You probably haven't heard, but Bill Longley resides in a Texas jail right now, about to go on trial for the murder of his own cousin. It's likely he'll hang for it, they say." Stony flinched as the import of his words sank in.

"I can just hear what people are saying. Two of a kind!" Her short laugh was a humorless bark. "Only they'll think I'm the worse of the two. Longley only killed his cousin, I killed my father!"

Abruptly, and unexpectedly, she began to cry, great sobs wracking her body. Stony sat down beside her. He took her into his arms and cradled her head on his shoulder. "I am sorry, sweetheart. I seem to be damned tactless today. Go ahead and cry, it'll be good for you."

He held her tightly, rocking gently, one hand stroking her hair. It took a few minutes for Debra to get herself under control. It was not so much the fact that Bill Longley's circumstances were like hers, but the use of the word *hang*. For the first time it really struck deep into her heart and mind that she might easily be hanged before this was over. Debra had never really thought about her own death before.

As her sobs slowly eased off, she became acutely aware of the man next to her, aware of the strength and sinew of him, of his maleness. She had read somewhere that awareness of impending death was a powerful aphrodisiac, and she knew now that this was all too true. She had been convinced that the horrible experience with Tod Danker had ended for all time any carnal yearning she might feel toward a man. That was not so. She was fully aroused, and she wanted this man, yearning toward him with a feeling so powerful that it dizzied her senses.

Tears still stood in her eyes as she turned a blind face up, urgently seeking his mouth.

Stony gave a start at the touch of her lips on his. Then his arms tightened around her, and she felt the tentative probe of his tongue in her mouth. The salt taste of her own tears, the brandy flavor, and the taste of *male*—all were overwhelming.

She murmured something, she knew not what, and tried to fuse with him. She opened her lips wider to accommodate his invading tongue, and the sudden jolt was almost as thrilling as though he had penetrated her body with his organ.

In her writhings against him, buttons had popped from her blouse. Feeling cool air on her breasts, Debra groped for his hand, then guided it to her exposed breast, the nipple already tumescent.

Stony sucked in his breath, cradled her breast in his hand for a breathtaking moment, then pulled away from her and moved all the way to the opposite end of the sofa.

She felt bereft. She gazed at him forlornly. "My darling, why do you move so far away?"

He was breathing heavily, his face flushed. Without looking at her, he said unevenly, "Debra, I don't think this is wise."

"Why not, pray? We love each other, and I want you, desperately."

He raised and lowered a hand. "It's just . . . well, the circumstances are not right."

"Is it because I'm not a virgin, Stony?"

His head whipped around. "Goddamnit, Debra, don't talk foolishness! I thought we'd settled that."

She edged along the sofa toward him. "Darling, I want you. I want to love you." She was close enough now to place a hand on his thigh. "If the trial goes wrong for me, this may be our only chance."

"That's unfair, Debra."

"Right now, I don't care about being fair. Do I have to beg, darling?"

With a groan he turned and took her into his arms, embracing her so fiercely that it drove the breath from her. As he kissed her, a faint stubble of beard rasped her chin. Now his hands were on her, under the loosened blouse. He cupped her breasts, rolling his thumbs across her nipples, and Debra felt her passion spiral out of control.

He took his mouth away to mutter, "I've wanted you forever, it seems. But shouldn't we at least go upstairs?"

"No, not in my bedroom where Brian died. And not in the other rooms, where men paid for love. Here, on the sofa. It's large enough. If it isn't, there's always the floor."

The sofa was large enough, just barely, to accommodate their rage of passion. For such it soon became, as their need, so long denied, threatened to race out of control.

Few preliminaries were necessary. They made frantic love with most of their clothes on. While Stony sat back to unbutton his trousers, Debra hiked her skirts high and hastily removed her undergarments.

It had been in Debra's mind that since she had never had normal intercourse with a man, she would be hopelessly inept, at a loss as to what to do. But it took place easily; a primal instinct as old as time took over, and as naturally as breathing, she opened to him, and he went into her with a lunge. She cried out at the unbelievable rapture of his entry into her. Her thighs rose and clamped around him, a silken corral for his wildness.

A sunburst of ecstasy began almost at once. Debra's head went back, bumping hard against the rigid arm of the sofa, and she cried out again, not from pain but from the overpowering pleasure of her orgasm. Her pelvis drummed against him as she spasmed in a wrenching seizure of sensation.

She sank back onto the sofa, her hips still, but she did not relax the clasp of her thighs, and Stony drove into her repeatedly.

Afloat in after-sensation, she stroked his back and shoulders. His rhythm began to quicken, then quickened still again.

"Yes, my darling, yes!" she said hoarsely. "Now, now!"

And then to her vast astonishment, as she felt the first mighty throb of his penis inside her, Debra's second orgasm was upon her, an explosion of ecstasy so intense that she was sure she would faint. Her hips came off the sofa in a great arch, a bridge holding him high, as she shuddered again and again. Stony was still now, except for the pulsing of his organ inside her.

She reached up and took his head in her hands and brought his mouth down to hers, glorying in the labored rasp of his breath. She cradled his face in the crook of her shoulder, whispered in his ear, "I seduced you, didn't I? I've heard of women doing that, but I never thought I'd have the brass! Oh, I *am* wicked!"

"My sweet, sweet Debra," he murmured, "if there was any seducing going on, we share equal guilt, as we lawyers are prone to say. . . ."

Debra went tense as the beads rattled, but before either of them could move, a sneering voice said, "Well, if this ain't a pretty sight!"

Stony moved quickly, swinging around to a sitting position, somehow managing to pull his trousers up at the same time.

Debra, recognizing June Blount's voice, did not bother to arrange her clothing—she would not give the woman that satisfaction. She sat up slowly, finally looking at June, who stood just inside the curtain, hands on her hips.

June grinned unpleasantly. "Paying your lawyer's fee, are you, honey?" When Debra didn't answer immediately, June said, "Too good to work on your back like the rest of us, are you? I always knew that if I stuck around long enough, I'd catch you at it. And what do you know, I did!"

Debra said calmly, "I thought I told you to leave this house and not come back, once you'd finished testifying?"

"Oh, I'm leaving all right, I can't wait to get out of this place. I've just been down to buy a ticket on the steamer leaving in the morning. I've come back here to pick up my things. And don't worry, I won't be staying tonight. I'd sleep on a park bench first."

Stony, his trousers on and buttoned, his dignity restored, was frowning at the woman in the doorway. "Tell me, Miss Blount, why did you say what you did in court? Do you hate Debra that much?"

"You're damned right I do!"

"But for what reason?"

"Because she thinks she's better than the rest of us. But this proves that she ain't, I was right all along." She laughed harshly. "One thing I'm sorry for about leaving. I'd like to stay around and see her hung. But then I'm sure it'll be in all the papers, no matter where I am when it happens."

Debra had a sudden thought. "You accepted that telegram from my parents, didn't you, June? You accepted it and then destroyed it."

"That's right, honey, I did."

Anger began to blaze in Debra. "You're a slut, June, a spiteful slut, and I should have—"

"Should have what? Killed me? Like you did your own daddy?"

"I never killed anyone."

"Oh, I know that—" June stopped short, dismay registering in her face.

Debra could only stare, but Stony was off the sofa in an instant and seemed to reach June at a single bound. He was just in time, for she had turned to flee when he caught her arm in a firm grip.

He demanded, "What did you mean by that?"

"Nothing! I meant that I knew she did kill her daddy."

"Oh, no, I won't swallow that. You know something, and you're going to tell me. *Now!*"

She whimpered, face screwed up in a grimace. "Ouch, you're hurting me!"

"I'm going to hurt you worse, young lady, much worse," he said grimly, "if you don't tell me what you know. If you think I won't get rough with you because you're a woman, disabuse yourself. This is too important to observe the niceties."

He twisted cruelly, and June went to her knees. Debra had never seen Stony so coldly furious.

"Please, please don't hurt me!" From her knees June stared up at him, tears flowing freely.

"Then talk, damnit! What do you know?"

"That night . . . I saw a man, a stranger." She gulped back tears. "I had taken a customer upstairs, and he went to sleep on me. I had just opened the door to my room to go back downstairs when I saw this man going into Debra's room. He—he was carrying a butcher knife."

"Did you recognize him? Had you ever seen him before?"

"I didn't get a good look at him, his face was turned the other way."

"There was nothing about this man to identify him?"

"All I know is he was wearing a slicker."

"Godalmighty!" Debra exclaimed. She exchanged a look of sudden understanding with Stony.

"June, this slicker," Stony said. "Could it have been a duster?"

"I suppose, I don't know! Ain't they the same thing?"

"Pretty much."

"Please," June said. "Let go of my arm now, please, and let me up. I've told you all I know."

He eased his grip, then helped her to her feet. "All right, June. You may go now, but I have a word of advice for you. Do not leave Corpus Christi. I'm calling you as a witness for the defense."

"You think I'm going to tell in open court what I just told you?" Some of her defiance had crept back. "And help save *her* hide? I'll deny I ever said anything, and when I'm on the witness stand, you can't twist my arm like this."

"You can be thrown in jail for contempt of court. You're liable to a charge of perjury as it is."

"So, have me thrown in jail. I'd rather do that than help Miss Goody-goody over there."

"Have it your way, June," he said tiredly. "But if you leave town, I'll have a warrant out for your arrest before you're out of sight. Now go, just go."

As June left the room hurriedly, Debra said in a dull voice, "Tod Danker. I should have guessed as much. The old feud, it's still going on."

"I've never understood how a feud could linger on through generation after generation, but if Danker did kill Brian, that must be the reason. I can't think of any other."

"Oh, it can pass from father to son." She gave a short laugh. "Who should know better than me?"

He stepped to the sofa, frowning. "What do you mean?"

Not really aware that she had spoken aloud, Debra glanced up at him with a start. "Oh." She sighed. "I suppose I'd better tell you, now that we know he killed Brian. I swore to myself that I would never tell you. Sit down, Stony, and I'll tell you why I left Nacogdoches so hurriedly. Don't sit too close, you may not want to touch me, ever again, after you know."

"Know what, Debra? And nothing would ever keep

me from wanting to touch you." He sat down close to her. "Now, what is it?"

"Tod Danker raped me," she said almost inaudibly. "On the way home that last night after I saw you."

"He what!" He reared back. "For God's sake, Debra!"

"Apparently he saw us together in town and followed me. . . ." Without looking at him even once, she told him what had happened that night. She relived it as she talked, and it was like relating a recurring nightmare, the details stark and clear and terrifying.

When she was finished, Stony pulled her against him. "Ah, you poor baby. What a dreadful goddamned thing! But wait. . . ." He moved back, tipped her face up to his. "Was that the reason you left without a word to me?"

She nodded mutely.

"But that was stupid! I'm sorry, I'm sorry. But it *was* a silly thing to do. How could you ever think that I would possibly blame you?"

"Maybe it was silly of me, I've thought so many times since," she said in a small voice. "But it was such a humiliating, degrading experience. I felt soiled, and I couldn't bear to have you know."

"You still should have told me, told somebody!" In his agitation Stony got up to pace. "That bastard should not have been allowed to get away with it." He punched a fist into his palm. "I would have killed him myself!"

"You see? That's the very reason I didn't tell anyone. I knew it would stir up a mess of trouble. The main reason I didn't tell Grandmother Nora, Brian, or my folks, was that I was afraid it would start up the old feud again. But it looks like the feud didn't need that to start it up again. It has never died, at least not for Tod Danker." Her mouth had a bitter twist.

"At least now we know who killed Brian."

"*We* may know, but who is going to believe us? You heard what June said, she refuses to tell her story in court. And even if she did, just because she saw a man in a duster in the house doesn't mean that it was Tod Danker."

"I know." Stony nodded in an absent manner. "Knowing it and proving it are two different things. I doubt that we could even prove that Danker came to Corpus Christi. He wouldn't have come by stage, he's not that stupid. He must have ridden horseback. And as sheriff, he doesn't have to disclose his whereabouts to anybody. He can be out of town for days, saying he was somewhere in the county investigating a crime, and who could say otherwise?"

He paced silently for a few minutes, then stopped to face her. "There is only one thing to do. I have to face him with what I know, try to convince him that I know more than I do."

"But you said it yourself, Stony, he's the sheriff."

"Sheriff or not, he's not above the law. And as an attorney, I am an officer of the court."

"How about the trial? It's several days journey to Nacogdoches and back. What are you going to do about the trial?"

"I have to talk Judge Ross into adjourning court for several days. Tomorrow's Friday. If I can finagle him into an adjournment and leave for Nacogdoches tomorrow, I could be back up there by Sunday or sooner." He smiled, his face intent. "And I've thought of a way that might work toward getting a postponement. It's a risk, for both of us, but. . . ." He sat down to take her hand. "Debra, do you trust me?"

"You know I do, darling, with my life," she said without hesitation.

He told her then, succinctly, what he had in mind.

The moment court convened the next morning, Stony was on his feet. "Your Honor, I wish to petition the court for one week's recess."

Haskins shouted, "I object, Your Honor, I object most strenuously."

Judge Ross scowled down at Stony. "For what earthly reason should I grant your petition, Counselor?"

"There *is* a good reason, Your Honor."

Judge Ross said forbiddingly, "There had better be, Mr. Lieberman, there had better be." He sighed, leaning back. "State your reason, Counselor. Do you wish to approach the bench?"

Ordinarily, to make such a motion, Stony would have, but on this occasion he wanted everyone in the courtroom to hear that reason. He took a deep breath. "The defense asks for a week's recess at this time because my client is pregnant, Your Honor."

The courtroom broke into an uproar, and it took Judge Ross several minutes to gavel the spectators into silence.

When all was quiet, the judge glared at Stony in a cold fury. "Mr. Lieberman, you have violated court procedure, and you well know it! Such a motion should not have been voiced within the hearing of the members of the jury."

"Your Honor, it is blatantly obvious what defense counsel is attempting here," Haskins said angrily. "It is a ploy to solicit sympathy for the defendant!"

"Pregnancy is a fact of nature, Your Honor," Stony said blandly. "I saw no reason to conceal it. My client is a woman, after all."

"If this is some sly trick, Counselor," Judge Ross said dangerously, "you will sorely regret it, both you and your client. You know this will have to be verified by a medical examination."

"Of course, Your Honor, that is to be expected," Stony said. "The defendant will be available. The defense has nothing to hide."

"Very well, Counselor, you leave me no alternative. But harken to my words, sir." Judge Ross leaned forward. "If your client is found not to be pregnant, I will see to it that you never again practice law in the state of Texas. Is that understood?"

Stony managed to keep an impassive face, his bridges burned irrevocably. "I understand, Your Honor."

"Very well. But you do not get a week, sir." The gavel rapped. "This court stands adjourned until ten o'clock Tuesday morning of next week. And I further order that the defendant stand ready for a medical examination for pregnancy on Monday morning."

Twenty

Tod Danker was not illiterate, but reading for him was a laborious chore. Usually he didn't bother, except for the few documents that his office required him to read, but Danker painstakingly had read every line of every newspaper account that had appeared about the death of Brian Moraghan, the subsequent arrest of his niece for his murder, and her trial.

He would have loved nothing more than to have a front row seat at the girl's trial, listening to every word, each one a strand woven into the noose that would eventually end her life, yet he knew that would not be wise. He had to be content with the newspaper coverage; fortunately, that was quite thorough, since the trial of Debra Moraghan was the most sensational event that had occurred in the state of Texas for many, many years.

On this Monday morning the newspaper account of the previous Thursday's court proceedings left him stunned, weak from an onslaught of feeling akin to the sexual—Brian Moraghan had been the girl's father!

Danker could scarcely believe what he was reading. In his office, booted feet propped upon his desk, the duster folded back out of the way, he read the article again, chuckling to himself from time to time. Without taking his gaze from the newspaper, he opened the desk drawer and groped for the whiskey bottle. The bottle was halfway to his mouth when the door to his office opened without warning and three men came in. They aligned themselves before his desk.

Danker froze, the bottle almost to his lips. He blinked at them, his thoughts circling frantically. Fear clenched his guts when he recognized the Jew lawyer. Then he relaxed a little when his gaze moved to the second man—Garth, the cigar-smoking banker. It couldn't be anything really bad. Garth was his friend, a prime mover in his election to the office of sheriff. The third man he didn't recognize. This one wore a long coat, and he had his hands out of sight under it, as though cold. Danker had noticed that he limped slightly coming across the office.

His movements studied, Danker lowered his feet to the floor and was reassured by the drag of the Colt holstered on his hip. "Mr. Garth, I wasn't expecting you to drop in. To what do I owe the pleasure of this visit, gents? Not that you're not always welcome." He glanced at Stony Lieberman. "I'm surprised to see you here, Lieberman. I thought I heard that you were in Corpus Christi, defending the Moraghan girl." He could not suppress a sudden smile. "Don't tell me that the trial is over already and they've nailed her to the wall?"

Stony said dryly, "No, it's not over, Danker, not officially. But it's all over for you."

Danker frowned. "What's that supposed to mean?"

"It means that *you* killed Brian Moraghan. We have an eyewitness who can identify you."

Again, fear clawed at Danker's insides, but he managed to keep his face empty of expression. "You must be out of your head, fellow." He appealed to Garth. "You don't believe any of this crap, do you, Mr. Garth?"

Garth took the half-smoked cigar from his mouth. "I'm not saying I believe or disbelieve anything. These fellows asked me to come along. All I can tell you, Danker, is that I'm taking nothing on just their say-so."

Danker tried a scornful laugh. "Then I can tell you, Mr. Garth, that they're blowing smoke past you. Hellfire,

I ain't been out of town in months. What's more, I can prove it." It had been the wrong thing to say, and he knew it before the words were even out of his mouth. He *had* been out of town, on three separate occasions, and not just the quick trip to Corpus Christi and back. He tried to cover up. "Course, I am sheriff of this county, and I do have business to tend to. . . ."

Now Stony was smiling. "Well, Danker, you'd better name those witnesses—and right now. If you were out of town long enough to ride to Corpus Christi and back, we've got you by the short hairs."

Danker blustered, "I'm the by God sheriff of this county, and I don't have to prove nothing to you birds!" Casually he dropped his right hand below the level of the desk.

"That's true, Danker, but if you're arrested, you'll have to prove your innocence in court."

"Arrested?" Danker stared. "You can't arrest me!"

"Oh, but I can," Stony said calmly. "As a duly licensed lawyer in the state of Texas, I am an officer of the court. And didn't anyone ever tell you? Just because you're an elected sheriff, that doesn't make you immune to prosecution for a criminal offense."

Panic was nibbling at the edges of Danker's mind. He felt cornered, with everyone against him—as the whole world had always been against the Dankers, starting with his grandmother. "You're talking crazy. What reason would I have to kill Brian Moraghan? I hardly knew the man. Hell, I don't think I talked to him a half-dozen times in my whole life."

"Because he was a Moraghan."

"You mean, that old feud?" Danker snorted. "That's dead and buried long since."

Stony said silkily, "Not according to Debra. She says you told her it's still alive."

"What are you talking about? I never talked to her, not ever!"

The third man, the stranger, took a step forward, hands still under his coat. "You raped my little girl, you Danker sonofabitch!"

Danker blinked at him. "Who're you?"

233

"I'm Kevin Moraghan."

A red rage washed over Danker, and he forgot his fears, forget everything but the man before him, the man who had killed his daddy, a murdering goddamned Moraghan! Was there never an end to the Moraghans?

He sneered. "Shit, I didn't have to rape her. How can a man be accused of raping a whore?" His hand clamped around the butt of the Colt.

Kevin Moraghan went pale. In a trembling voice he said, "You can't talk about Debra Lee that way. I won't let you!"

"*You* won't let? I'm not the only one that says it, everybody knows what she is. And your goddamned brother, he thought he was too good for the likes of me." He glared at the hated face across the desk and shouted, "Yes, I killed him! Just like I'm going to kill you. I won't be satisfied until there are no more Moraghans left on this earth!"

He shoved the chair back with a crash, springing to his feet, the Colt drawn and coming up. His eyes widened in astonishment as he saw Kevin's hand emerge from under the coat, a pistol in it. Danker felt a coldness in him as he realized that he could never bring the Colt up in time. He, Tod Danker, was being beaten by this skinny, limping man!

And then the gun in Kevin's hand roared, and the bullet smashed into Danker's chest. In a reflex action he fired the Colt, but it hadn't even cleared the desktop, and the bullet gouged splinters from the floor.

The impact of the bullet sent him reeling back against the wall. As the life-force drained out of him, Danker's last thought was one of utter disbelief—once again a Moraghan had bested a Danker.

The three men stood as frozen as figures in a tableau as the sound of the gunshots died away.

Kevin was the first to move. He gave a start, looked around dazedly, then shuddered mightily, and let the pistol fall from his suddenly lax hand.

"It's happened again," he said. "Twice in my life I've held a pistol in my hand, and twice men have died by my hand." His voice became agonized. "Dear God, will this bloody feud never end?"

Stony touched him on the arm, said gently, "This should see the end of it, Kevin. But I do wish you had told me you were carrying a gun."

Since the moment when Stony had told him of Danker's sexual assault on Debra and the near certainty that he had killed Brian, Kevin had been acting strangely. He had reacted a few seconds slow to any remark directed to him and had seemed scarcely aware of the world around him.

Now Kevin looked at Stony with burning eyes. "You know, Stony, I hardly remember sticking it in my belt. I dimly recall buying it in a gunsmith's shop in Corpus Christi, but I don't think I could find the shop again if my life depended on it. I must have had in mind to kill him all along, for what he did to Debra Lee, more than anything else."

Kevin ran his fingers through his rumpled hair. "You know what Momma told me when she heard what had happened to Debra Lee? She said that was how it all began, the feud, all those years back. I'd never heard the real story before. While Daddy was off to war, the Danker boys raped Momma, staked her out on the ground like the Indians used to do, and raped her. That's why Daddy tracked them down and shot them. God, what a vile family! Generation after generation. It must be passed down like some disease."

"Thank God he admitted to killing Brian before you shot him." Remembering, Stony turned to the man on his left. "Mr. Garth? You heard, heard him admit to killing Brian Moraghan?"

"Huh?" Garth turned a dazed look on Stony. In his fright the cigar had fallen from his mouth, and he looked tense enough to bolt from the room at a wrong word.

"You heard Tod Danker admit to killing Brian?"

"Oh, yes, I heard. I heard every word. What was wrong with Danker? Was the fellow crazy?"

"In a way, I suppose that's a fair assessment. The thing is, Mr. Garth, will you testify to his confession, should it be necessary? You're well thought of in East Texas, they'll believe you."

Garth took a few minutes to collect himself. He got what Stony tended to think of as his "banker look"—the expression he wore when supplicants came to him for loans.

"I'll make a bargain with you, Lieberman," the banker finally said. "I'll back you all the way, if you and Moraghan there will keep quiet about my part in making Danker sheriff of this county."

"I can agree to that," Stony said. "Kevin?"

Kevin shrugged. "I certainly won't be telling anyone. In fact, I knew nothing about it until now. The less I have to say about Tod Danker in the future, the better."

"You have our word on it, Mr. Garth," Stony said. "Now I have a telegram to send to a judge in Corpus Christi."

As he started to turn away, Garth took his arm. "One other thing, Lieberman. About the election coming up. . . ."

"What about it?" Stony said. "I thought that was all settled."

"Well, uh, we may have been a little hasty there." Garth cleared his throat. "Anyway, the whole picture has changed now. The voters are going to be mighty impressed by your part in uncovering Danker as a murderer."

Stony said dryly, "It's a bit late, I'd say. I've done almost no campaigning, and I'm not starting at this late date."

"That may not matter, there's nobody opposing you, not really."

Stony smiled slightly. "How about the fellow whose name you proposed as a write-in?"

Garth shrugged. "He doesn't amount to a hill of beans. That's the reason I brought it up. With this new development I'm sure I can bring Barton and Peters around to backing you again."

Remembering his thoughts that day the three men came to his office, Stony was tempted to tell Garth to go to hell, but he remained silent. He had some leverage now, leverage he could use to get them off his back later, if it became necessary.

Besides, the likelihood of his being elected was small, very small indeed.

T.J. Dillon was in his study, perusing the newspaper account of Bill Longley's hanging. Standing on the gallows, looking out at the upturned faces of some four thousand witnesses to his execution, Longley had observed, "I see a good many enemies around, and mighty few friends.'

Dillon exhaled a breathy sigh of relief. He no longer had to fear Longley's threat.

Now all he had to do was wait for Debra Moraghan's trip to the gallows. What remark would *she* make as she stood with the noose around her neck? As unpopular as she was in Corpus Christi, she'd be lucky if she had any friends at all in attendance.

His head came up as he heard a knock on the front door, then Consuela's voice and the deeper voice of a man.

Footsteps sounded down the hall, followed by Consuela's knock on the study door.

"Yes, what is it?"

"You have a visitor, Señor—Señor Bradford Carpenter."

"Come on in, Bradford."

Dillon's eyes narrowed at the sight of Bradford Carpenter's smiling face. The smile set his teeth on edge—it was unbearably smug and had a hint of triumph in it.

"What is it, Bradford? I thought the way you stormed out of here the last time that I'd never see you in my house again."

"But this is a special occasion, T.J." Carpenter hooked his thumbs in his belt and rocked back and forth on his heels. "I come as a bearer of glad tidings."

A nerve began to tick under Dillon's right eye. "What glad tidings? I know that the harlot claims she's pregnant and she was to be examined this morning. That idiot Jonathon swallowed her lie and granted a recess until tomorrow. You've come to tell me she's not pregnant, that's your glad tidings? No need for that, I already knew she was lying."

"Oh, I don't know anything about that, T.J. The news I have concerns a telegram that Jonathon just received." He stopped, his smile spreading.

Dillon grunted. "Well, get on with it, Bradford!"

"The telegram was from Stonewall Lieberman. The real killer of Brian Moraghan has been found, in Nacogdoches. A man by the name of Tod Danker, the sheriff of Nacogdoches County, of all things. He's dead, but he confessed before he died, in front of witnesses. How about them apples, T.J?"

Dillon reared back as though struck. "I don't believe you, you're lying!"

"Nope. Sorry to disappoint you. Jonathon has the telegram, you can see it any time you want."

"Then Lieberman is lying. It's some kind of a trick, to delay things. He's a Jew, you know how they are."

"No, T.J., I don't know how they are. But you'd like to believe that, wouldn't you?"

"Get out!" Dillon shouted in a burst of frustration and rage. "Get out of my house!"

"Oh, I'm going. But not just yet. I have a message of my own to deliver. The way I see it, you have two choices. You can leave Corpus Christi—"

"Corpus Christi is my home. Nobody drives me away from here!"

Carpenter shrugged. "Suit yourself. It's true I can't make you leave. But that brings us to the second choice." He cocked his head, the smile still in place. "You know what you've always reminded me of? A spider, a fat spider, squatting in here, weaving your devious webs. Well, no more, T.J. If you insist on remaining here, it'll be hands off. No more meddling into things that are none of your business."

Dillon puffed up. "You can't stop me, Bradford."

"There, you're wrong. I'm getting on, I know that, but I'm far from dead yet, and I still have some influence. Jonathon has already seen the light. You think I don't know that you put a bug in his ear to railroad that girl? I sat in that courtroom and watched him behave outrageously. He's a disgrace to the bench. He promised me he'd instruct the jury to return a not-guilty verdict. He also promised he'd resign from the bench. If he doesn't, I'll see to it he's defeated when he comes up for reelection."

"I'm not Jonathon, you can't frighten me."

"I have no intention of frightening you," Carpenter said quietly. "But if you meddle into affairs outside this house again, if you try any of your usual shenanigans, I'll see that everybody knows about this one and how sorely you failed. It'll make you the laughingstock of Corpus. There's no one more vulnerable to laughter than a man of power who's come a cropper. People delight in it. You've always operated pretty much in secret. I'll let the light of day down your rathole. You're finished, T.J. You know me well enough to realize that I don't make idle threats. From this day forward, you're a spider without a web."

Twenty-One

Winter came early to East Texas that year. The first week of November a blue norther whistled across Moraghan, sending the temperature plummeting thirty degrees within two hours.

When Debra awoke on Thursday morning in her old room upstairs, the air was frigid. She had left the window cracked the night before. Slipping out of bed in her bare feet, flannel nightgown billowing around her, she ran to the window and slammed it shut, then stood transfixed, staring outside. The norther had deposited a layer of snow over everything.

Otherwise, the day was brilliantly clear, and the rising sun reflected off the snow, almost blinding her. She stood blinking against the glare, hugging herself, hopping from one foot to another on the bare wooden floor.

It was the first time she had seen any snow to speak of in ten years. She had missed it, she thought, Godalmighty, she had missed it! If she had any choice in the matter, she would not return again to the Rio Grande Valley, that place of scalding sun, dust, and drought.

She gave a start as she heard Nora's querulous voice in the room next door. "Maria! Damn and blast that woman! Maria, if you don't get up here, you're fired!"

Debra, already moving toward her clothing hanging

on hooks beside the bed, called out, "Grandmother, I'll be right there."

Nora grumbled something inaudible in reply. Debra had returned to Moraghan with her grandmother after the not-guilty verdict was handed down, and had been staying with her since. Despite Nora's inner strength and fortitude, she had not been well; Brian's death and Debra's ordeal seemed to have drained her. And strangely, the revelation that Tod Danker had killed Brian seemed to have an even more adverse effect on her. When Debra had questioned her about this, Nora said, "It all started with me, girl, all those years ago. Now it looks like it'll never end. I somehow feel responsible. I know, Debra Lee, I know. It's probably foolish of me, but I can't help feeling that way."

Then, a little over a week ago, Nora had come down with a severe case of influenza and had been bedridden since. For a time it had seemed that she would succumb; the will to live appeared to have gone from her. Thank God, she had been getting better the past few days.

Debra smiled to herself. Grandmother Nora's recovery was a mixed blessing—she was grumpy as a bear just out of hibernation.

Dressed, Debra hurried next door and found Nora out of bed and getting into her clothes.

"Grandmother!" she scolded. "You shouldn't be up and around."

"Why not? I can't loll in bed forever. I'm feeling much better today." Nora shrugged her dress down over her head. "I'm hungry. Looks like my appetite is back. And yelling for Maria is like spitting into the wind. She's deaf as a post, or at least claims to be."

Debra knew that is was useless to argue when Nora was this set on something. Besides, she was secretly pleased that the woman was ready to leave the bed. She picked up a shawl from the nearby rocking chair. "Put this around you, the house is freezing this morning. Maybe Maria has made a fire downstairs."

Nora was a little wobbly on her feet and reluctantly leaned on Debra's arm going down the stairs. Debra helped her into the sunroom. Maria had built a fire in the fireplace, and the small breakfast table was set. As Debra eased her grandmother into a chair at the table, Maria came in with a tray.

"Well, there you are," Nora said dourly. "Didn't you hear me calling you?"

"I hear. You, old woman."

"Then why didn't you come up? I may have wanted my breakfast in bed, for all you knew."

"I knew you would be down this morning. See, I already made your breakfast, you and Miss Debra."

Nora made a small sound of laughter. "Because your grandmother was a witch, right?"

"For years I have told you this," Maria said with simple dignity, "but you would not listen." She added darkly, "I know many things other people do not know."

"Well, I don't want to hear them," Nora said crossly. "Just put the food on the table before it collects icicles."

Debra, accustomed to these acrimonious exchanges between the two women, listened and smiled. She knew that either woman would be devastated if anything happened to the other. Maria set a platter of eggs and sausage patties on the table, along with a platter of golden-brown pancakes, a pitcher of heated syrup, and a pot of coffee.

Debra quickly filled their plates, and Nora began eating with gusto. Debra's appetite had also been heightened by the brisk weather. They ate for a time in companionable silence.

Finally Nora sat back and gave a contented sigh as she poured herself a fresh cup of coffee. "One appetite the aged keep is that for food. Don't ever get old, Debra Lee. When you've gotten as old as I am, you've seen too much, you're prey to every ache and pain and disease known to man, and Death is licking his chops in the next room. And don't bother giving me that hog manure about me not being old. I'm older than God. Or almost." Her earlier mood had returned, and she said petulantly, "Where is that man? Where is Stonewall?"

"He'll be out here sometime today, I'm sure, Grandmother. You know he wanted to wait in Nacogdoches until he knew how the election came out. Myself, I don't know why he bothers." She made a face. "How can he win with me like a dead weight around his neck? I'm still not sure I've done the right thing, coming back here. He'd be better off if I just went away somewhere."

"Don't talk foolishness, girl!" Nora rapped the table with her knuckles. "The man loves you, you know that, and you love him. Hellfire and spit, that's more important than any election. Debra Lee"—Nora reached over for Debra's hand—"what's past is dead and gone. You have to forget it."

"That's easy enough to say, but many people will never forget. I'm sure that many of them are still convinced that I'm the whore who killed her own father, and they'll always think that."

Maria had come into the room quietly. Now she spoke. "If you are talking about the lawyer man, he just rode into the yard."

"Stony!"

Her reservations forgotten, Debra was on her feet and running for the front door. She reached it just as Stony came in, stamping his boots on the sill to rid them of snow. She skidded to a halt, remembering the election. Would he ever forgive her for causing him to lose the judgeship he so coveted?

He looked up at her. His expression was grave and told her nothing. He looked pale and tired, his face had at least a day's stubble of beard, and his eyes were bloodshot.

"You look dreadful, darling."

He scrubbed a hand across his face. "It's understandable, I haven't been to bed yet."

"The election," she asked. "What happened? You lost, didn't you?"

He was coming toward her. Without answering her directly, he said, "Where's Nora?"

"In the sunroom. We just finished breakfast."

"Come along." He put an arm around her shoulders, squeezed lightly, and guided her into the sunroom.

Nora's face lit up at the sight of him. "Stonewall Lieberman, it's about time you were showing up."

Debra twisted around to look into his face. "You didn't answer my question, Stony."

His face remained sober for just an instant, then that slow, sweet smile spread. He threw his arms wide. "I'll have you know that congratulations are in order. And some respect, as well. You are looking at Judge Stonewall Lieberman."

"Oh, darling! You won!" Debra threw her arms around his neck and rained kisses on his face. "But I would have sworn that you would lose." She added accusingly, "And you thought so, too."

He nodded. "True, I did. But I reckon I was wrong. Oh, all the precincts haven't reported in yet. But I won by a comfortable margin in Nacogdoches, and the reports from the other towns pretty much follow along."

"I'm glad for you, darling, you know I am." She kissed him again, then shook her head in bewilderment. "But I don't understand it, I surely don't."

"Could be you underestimate the good sense of people," Nora said in her dry voice. "A judge should be elected because he knows the law and is good at it, not because of his personal life."

"The fact that I had little opposition, only a write-in candidate most people never even heard of, had a great deal to do with it, I'm sure. Anyway, who the hell cares how it came about? I'm a judge, goddamnit!" Stony said exuberantly, and pulled Debra into his arms for a quick hug. "Oh, that reminds me, sweet, I picked up the mail in town. There was a letter for you. It was mailed some time ago and has been following you around."

He took a slim packet of letters from his pocket and gave Debra the top one. There was no return address, and the postmark was smudged, so she couldn't make out where it was mailed from.

As Stony crossed the room to give the other letters to Nora, Debra ripped open the envelope. Inside was a single sheet of lined paper, torn from a schoolchild's writing tablet. Her gaze dropped to the bottom of the

244

page and a chill passed over her when she saw the signature—William Longley. A message from beyond the grave!

She read the brief letter.

Dear Miss Moraghan:

I have just heard about your trouble. I am certain that you will come out all right. You did not kill anyone. If I know anything in this sorry world, I know that. I am only sad that I am not free to help you, as I did once before.

I count you among my friends, Dear Miss Moraghan. I have only a few in this world.

I am sure that you have heard about my trouble. Unlike you, I am guilty, and they will hang me soon. Please do not mourn for me. Hanging is my favorite way of dying.

Your friend,
William Longley

Debra felt a welling of sorrow as she finished the letter. She let it dangle from her hand and stared sightlessly out the window. Bill Longley had been a bad man, there was no doubt of that, yet he had been nice to her. She shivered, thinking how fortunate she was to have escaped his fate.

"Debra?" Stony touched her arm. "What is it?"

"It's a letter from Bill Longley. It must have been written only a day or so before they hanged him." She gave him the letter, and he quickly scanned it.

At the table Nora looked up from the opened letters in her lap. She cleared her throat. "Well, Debra Lee? Are you going to tell him? You said you would when you knew the election results."

Stony looked from one to the other in bewilderment. "Tell me what? What are you two up to?"

"You're going to have to marry me, Stonewall Lieberman," Debra said.

"For God's sake," he said in disgust. "Is that all you two are plotting? I wanted to marry you in Corpus, be-

245

fore we came up here, remember? But you wouldn't have it, you wanted to wait until after the election."

"No, you don't quite understand. You remember the reason you used with Judge Ross to get him to declare a recess?"

"Of course I remember. . . ." He stopped, his eyes beginning to widen. "You don't mean?"

"Yup." She nodded. "You weren't lying after all. If you don't marry me soon, people are going to wonder about the short-term baby of their newly elected judge's wife."

He began to smile. "How long have you known?"

"Weeks. It must have happened that night in the house."

"Goddamn." He whooped and swept her up in a crushing hug. "I'm going to be a daddy!"

Nora said, "And I'm happy for myself as well as for you two. It's high time I was having a great-grandchild."

Debra looked up into his face. "So, are you going to marry me, Judge Lieberman?"

"I'll marry you today, tomorrow, any time you say." He took her in his arms again.

As they kissed, Nora said dreamily, "It'll be nice to have a wedding on Moraghan again. It's been far too long. And maybe that will get Kevin and his up here."

ABOUT THE AUTHOR

FOR CLAYTON MATTHEWS, author of more than 100 books, 50 short stories and innumerable magazine articles, writing is not only his profession but his hobby. Born in Waurika, Oklahoma in 1918, Matt (as he is known to his friends) worked as a surveyor, overland truck driver, gandy dancer, and taxi driver. In 1960 he became a full-time author with the publication of *Rage of Desire*. More recent books by Clayton Matthews include his highly successful book *The Power Seekers* (winner of the WEST COAST REVIEW OF BOOKS Bronze Medal for Best Novel in 1978), *The Harvesters* and *The Birthright.*

PATRICIA MATTHEWS

Now You Can Read
All These Books
By One Of America's
Queens Of Historical Romance

A magnificent new novel by the author of
TIDES OF LOVE

FLAMES
OF
GLORY

by Patricia Matthews

Here is a sweeping, romantic saga set against the backdrop
of the Spanish-American War. It is the story of Jessica Manning,
a beautiful young woman torn from the arms of dashing
Rough Rider Lieutenant Neil Dancer by the hot-blooded
passions of ruthless Brill Kroger. And it is the story of
Neil's relentless desire to win Jessica back—a desire that
drove him to pledge his very life to rekindle the flames of
their glorious love.

*Read FLAMES OF GLORY, a large-format paperback, on sale December
15, 1982, wherever Bantam paperbacks are sold or use this handy coupon
for ordering:*